Shifting Sands

PAMELA ST ABBS

DEDICATION

For Suzan, Lynn and Jo

CONTENTS

ACKNOWLEDGMENTS

With thanks to Alison, Jackie and Rosie for reading through the book and for your comments. With thanks as always to Bill for his support.

CHAPTER ONE

Watcher viewed the pale sanded beach and awaited the victim. The time was barely nine in the morning and the day was Friday. As the school holidays had started in North Norfolk families were already pottering about finding a patch of sand to call their own for the day with seats, towels and brightly striped wind-breaks. At the back of the beach was a crescent of beach huts painted in every hue and a tea kiosk. Its small generator was breaking the air with its distant hum. Beyond, a wood of pine trees with the intense blue of the sky above created a backdrop to the scene. On the eastern edge of the beach a bank channelled the tidal river estuary. The bank formed a walk-way to the town of Banksea. The Watcher was stationed at the end of the bank. To the left ranged the beach and to the right the river idled through the man-made banks becoming shallow with the ebbing tide. The smell of salt and seaweed filled the nostrils. The sun did not warm Watcher's back. Plenty of time, no need to rush. Deep breaths. Calm.

Georgia Lomond was cooling her pale twenty-year-old body in the shallows of the North Sea as it lapped Banksea Beach. She watched her grandfather put up his blue and white striped deck-chair on the leeward side of the multi-coloured wind-break, which she'd hammered into the sand with a stone to offer a little privacy and shelter from the breeze coming from the direction of the river bank. She got up, splashed out of the sea and walked over the damp sand, recently evacuated by the tide, to her Grandpa Will.

She delved into her beach bag and checked the time on her phone. 'It's eleven o'clock,' she told him very aware of her Scottish accent with the rolling 'r's in this eastern part of England where the vowel sounds were lingering, and some syllables were lost completely. She loved the slow rhythm of the Norfolk accent as she connected it with her grandfather.

'Off you go then, pet,' he said with affection.

'I ought to go,' she said apologetically. 'Mum would want me to.'

'I want you to go, little one,' he replied. 'But beware of strangers bearing gifts. There is no such thing as a free lunch.'

'It's lunch and afternoon tea, and I had to pay for it, Grandpa Will,' Georgia returned.

'That sounds like Strath-Kind School. Anyway, what's a school in East Anglia doing having a Scottish name?'

Georgia ignored him. He knew the answer. 'Will you be all right?' She frowned with concern. 'I'll take the car to the school. I'll be quicker getting back.'

'Of course, pet. I won't need the car for anything.' Grandpa Will settled himself down and planted his hat over his bright blue eyes, large bony nose and weathered face. 'Enjoy yourself,' he said.

'I'll be back by about six this afternoon.' Georgia glanced up at the pale blue and white beach hut situated just about in the center of the group. Very few of them were occupied today and none of those were near theirs.

'Okay, pet.' Her grandfather looked cosy on his matching deck-chair.

'If you get too hot…'

'I will sit in,' he confirmed gently waving in the general direction of their hired beach hut. 'See you later.'

Georgia picked up her large plastic woven bag and walked through the woods behind the beach huts. There was shade here and the air was completely still. The smell of pine filled her nostrils. Her chest felt tight with nerves. She couldn't really see why that should be. She shook her mane of wet red hair as if to shake off these feelings. On reaching the caravan park she found the caravan she'd hired for herself and her grandfather for their holiday at Banksea Beach. Inside she turned the shower on to get rid of the sand, which seemed to have infested every part of her, before her return to her old school and, again, she reached into her bag to check the time.

Elizabeth Rattagan sat on the train watching the scenery go by and listening to the soothing rhythm of the wheels going over the rails underneath her. She wore flat neat sandals and a dark blue linen skirt suit. This she felt was suitable for the occasion and the six am train from her East Sussex home to London.

Electric wires alongside the track raised and fell to different levels beside her with brief glimpses of their supporting poles as the train rushed by them. Snapping out of her reverie briefly she considered them to be a little like her thoughts which had been relentlessly tearing at her brain until it ached.

Now the green water of the North Sea appeared to form over the train window glass. Just the thought of swimming made her muscles tingle. Her body remembered the activity of swimming and the strange mingling of herself with the sea as if the water in the very cells of her body fought against at the same time as becoming one with the sea. A new image came to her of her fellow sea swimmers competing against her to be the first to reach the slipway at Banksea Quay. They would have to get past her to do that and, she would not be letting them do that.

Why she had chosen to make this journey north from her home was beyond her.

The train pulled into Platform One at Guildham Station. 'London train on Platform One,' shouted the loud speaker, but, already, people were crushing into the carriages.

Elizabeth looked up. Baggage had to be moved to make room for these city workers. She returned to her national newspaper. She'd read the main articles before Guildham now she was drawn to those strange adverts placed by various people for various reasons.

Scanning through Elizabeth picked out Gwendolyn's name, her closest school friend, among a block of solicitors' will notifications. She read it again. Gwendolyn Blythe couldn't be dead. Elizabeth had lost contact with her. Despite social media Gwen had disappeared from her life. This person must simply have the same name, she told herself.

To find Gwendolyn was really the point of her journey after all. Seeing her name in the paper, Elizabeth realised she needed this old friend and fellow member of the swimming team. This trip had all been arranged only this morning when she'd received an email about the old girls' day. It was timed at five am. The email address didn't make clear who it was from, but she guessed it was probably one of the old girls who'd got married. It worried her that they had managed to find her, but also part of her was pleased.

She sighed. Gwen had been the perfect school friend. She'd listened to Elizabeth's untruths and taken her out on Sundays. Yes, that was the reason she was heading north today: to find Gwen. It was, after all, she who had talked her into open water swimming which had given her the gift of being able to feel freedom from the world, immersed in moving, living water.

Outer London was whipping by in a mass of back yards and warehouses until darkness swamped the passengers as the train entered a tunnel. The window mirrored her face clearly now. She startled at the sudden sight of her blond curly hair reflected back at her.

Out from the train and into Waterloo Station, she made her way below ground. She could hear the rumble of the tube trains weaving away below her. She reached her platform. The air from the moving trains buffeted her. She held on tightly to her bag as she got on the train for King's Cross.

She caught the sound of clipped public school voiced children chatting and giggling.

Her own accent was nearly gone. It had been acquired through the years she'd spent at Strath-Kind School trying to be one of the pupils, donning the voice along with the school uniform. She'd found the accent useless back in the real world, antagonising non-public school folk and giving expectations of wealth to men who thought of themselves as her suiters. And so, she'd happily returned to the softer sing-song annunciations of her home region of Sussex. But now as she approached this place so full of difficult memories she found she had no ear for the soft musical sounds of the south coast and she shifted physically and mentally towards her old boarding school.

King's Cross Station was a hollow sounding space, modern clean and bright. She joined the queue at the gate to the platform for her train and tried to see if she could recognise any of her fellow travellers. But before she could have a good look the gate opened, and the queue made its way through to the platform.

She found the only un-booked seat out of a set of four arranged round a table on a carriage close to the front of the train. Only the first four carriages went through to Banksea Halt. When the other passengers arrived for their seats she placed her bag on the luggage rack at the end of the carriage.

The train moved off. Elizabeth settled down for the last train leg of her journey. She would have to get a taxi from the station. There never had been a regular bus service out to the school. She shut her eyes. She was alerted by a tall, soft bodied woman with long, rich auburn hair tied back. She had a child on her hip and was pushing through the narrow aisle apologising as she went. A similarly tall but thin young man with a mass of straight black hair followed her. A moment later a penetrating scream came from the direction of the table opposite.

A mature, neatly dressed woman stood up in the aisle between the two rows of seats on either side of the carriage. Her ash-blond head was shaking while her manicured hands were brushing at her white pencil-shaped skirt. It was covered in a red liquid. The garment was loose fitting, possibly for comfort or perhaps because she'd lost some weight recently. Elizabeth couldn't decide.

Another trickle of red liquid was spreading over the woman fine blue and white-striped jacket. Her tailored square shoulders trembled with temper. Her chin was tilted in what looked like disgust. Her lean body seemed to tower over the tables.

Elizabeth looked down at the suited woman's tapping feet and observed her patent blue sling back shoes with an inch and a half heal. This woman was glaring at the yellow haired young woman with the toddler on her lap.

'My daughter is just a baby,' said the yellow-haired young mother taking the beaker of juice from the child and replacing the lid.

'The lid came off,' complained the woman in the aisle dabbing ineffectively at the red juice. 'You couldn't have put it on properly. My suit will need dry cleaning.'

'I can't afford that,' said the mother. She looked upset.

The child swung her arm back knocking the lidded cup of juice on the table over and towards the man sitting opposite the mother.

For Elizabeth, the whole thing happened in slow motion. She watched the cup roll across the table. Elizabeth hoped that the lid would stay on the beaker this time. All she could see, with the woman standing in the corridor, was the arm from the man stretch out, catch the cup and stand it up. The lid had remained in place and the valve in the spout had prevented any leakage.

'The child shouldn't have juice. It's bad for her,' said the lady in the suit.

'It's her medicine. Not that it is any of your business.'

'Excuse me,' said Elizabeth to the woman still standing in the aisle and tapping her blue patent sling backed shoe. 'Let me pay for the suit to be cleaned. I think the baby got excited when that other woman walked by with her baby.'

Both the suited women and the woman with the toddler looked blankly at her. The mother recovered first. 'I couldn't let you do that,' she said.

'It wasn't your fault,' said the suited woman to Elizabeth. Her voice was cold and flat.

'Perhaps you can afford to have the suit cleaned yourself,' retorted Elizabeth.

'Please, don't fuss,' said the mother. 'You're upsetting my daughter.'

The toddler grizzled and wriggled.

'If I give you my address you can pay me back when you can afford it,' insisted Elizabeth to the young mother. She opened her purse and parted with her taxi money. She would be walking from the station to her old school. She failed to give the mother her address. It wasn't something she wanted to give out.

Cambridge station came and the woman with the marked suit got off the train as did many others. The fen landscape of golden wheat stretching to the horizon was soon flashing by her beyond the carriage window as the train travelled north. More stations came and went. Elizabeth turned away from her fellow passengers. Banksea Halt was rapidly approaching. She braced herself. Going back to her old school was never going to be easy.

Gwen blipped the throttle of her dark blue sports car at the traffic lights and weaved her way onto the dual carriageway. The morning sunlight flickered through the railings of the bridge over the road. She guessed, so many of her school contemporaries must already be in influential positions. This day could be worth four of her usual days scrabbling her way through life.

She slipped into the gears and nudged her car along the road. When a man gestured at her for overtaking in what she thought was a particularly neat manoeuvre, she told the bloke through the window, 'No prisoners today, sorry!' He didn't hear. He wasn't meant to.

Closer to the school on the approach road to Banksea a public swimming pool had been built since her time at Strath-Kind School. The school pool she remembered as being small and smelling strongly of chlorine. But it had been somewhere to practice, she preferred the sea. She'd swam miles in that pool. She'd achieved her life saving certificate there too, using Lizzy as the body she had to tow around the pool.

Three hours from the time that she set out Gwen reached the bottom of Strath-Kind School's drive. She looked at her clock, twelve forty-five am. Glancing up, she saw Lizzy Rattagan in a shabby blue suit and even shabbier sandals. She rolled down the window and called, 'Elizabeth Rattagan,' followed by, 'Lizzy, darling, do you want a lift?'

Lizzy accepted with a smile. She must be so impressed, Gwen thought. She knew she looked gorgeous in her designer dress. She prided herself in her ability to get an individual, sophisticated look and today she thought she'd achieved the effect perfectly.

'Jump in, jump in. Let me move this stuff. She pushed her single delicate handbag to one side in the passenger foot-well.

'So, you didn't become a missionary, then?' asked Lizzy.

Gwen laughed, Lizzy was always so funny. She loved having her around. It was like having your own entertainment channel all to yourself. 'How's my saviour?'

Lizzy didn't answer. They rolled up to the top of the drive along the large sweep of fine gravel to the front of the red stone, Victorian gothic building which was their old school.

Lizzy looked out of her passenger side window. 'Do you see anyone you know?' she asked.

Gwen looked at the collection of different aged women elegantly dressed massing in front of the large timber double doors which stood open welcoming the sunshine as well as the visitors inside. Some were familiar. There was a very slim girl with long red hair. She was chatting to a full-figured woman with a bonneted baby on her hip.

'Isn't that Shana Peterson?' asked Gwen pointing to the woman with the baby on her hip.

'Is it? She was on the train. She walked by. I didn't think she looked anything like the girl I remember.'

'We've all changed, Lizzy. That looks like a wedding ring. So, she might not even be Peterson anymore.'

'She looks quite young and she was with a man a bit younger than herself on the train. He isn't here.' Lizzy frowned. Gwen thought she looked worried.

'Perhaps he's gone out for the afternoon,' said Gwen.

'Let's go', said Lizzy with a nervous tremor in her voice looking in the opposite direction to the school.

'Where?' asked Gwen, slightly taken aback by her friend's behaviour. The women ranged in age from their early twenties to their fifties. Few of her own age group of early thirties were there. There would be problems developing a rapport with these people in the time she had available.

Perhaps it was just as well Lizzy wanted to leave. To get anything from these people would mean she might have to exchange information with them that she was not willing to part with. She would not engage with these old-girls, she would just talk to Lizzy for a while and make a retreat into her other being – or someone else, who knows? No-one would know that for a short while she was her own self. Perhaps it was too ambitious to try to escape her present circumstances even briefly.

'Did you pay for lunch or tea for this shindig?' asked Gwen gesturing towards the queue of past students.

'Neither,' said Lizzy frowning.

'I only paid for tea,' lied Gwen. 'We're too early. This lot are here for their lunch. The sun was inviting. 'How about the beach? ' she asked Lizzy. Her school-time friend nodded her head. Lizzy seemed to be taking deep breaths.

'It'll be all right, Lizzy,' said Gwendolyn, looking at her watch: one in the afternoon. It was already lunch time; again, she modified her view. These rich influential women were worth a go. There might be some escape after all from her present existence. 'I'll pay for your school tea. We'll go to the sea-side for an hour and come back later. How about Banksea?'

Lizzy nodded at last focusing on Gwen and not into the far distance. Lizzy, at last, looked relieved.

.

CHAPTER TWO

At Horseton Police Station Inspector Campbell's phone buzzed in an amiable tone on the desk in front of him. He leaned forward, distracted by the process of updating his work log on the computer with his right hand, and reached his long thin left arm towards the device, past his pile of papers and his screen. The office was open plan and even more cramped than his previous work accommodation. He briefly regretted no longer having an office to himself as he stretched out his sun-browned fingers to pick up the device. It seemed to try and slide away. He scrabbled his mobile phone into his hand and clicked the screen with his index finger. Outside the window, which occupied one complete wall of the building, was a walk-way which took fellow workers to the car park. He watched those who were leaving for a lunch break.

The work mobile phone indicated that it had received a message. He gathered himself together as he turned to look at it. He preferred messages to phone calls; they allowed him to consider his response without the inevitable and very apparent pause. He wondered if he could leave responding to the message until he had remedied the hollow feeling in his stomach with his lunch. He knew he shouldn't, but his brain worked much better when it was fed.

The message read: 'No need to panic, Inspector. You are already too late. On a beach not too far away you will find a dead body. Watcher' He felt every sinew tighten and his focus sharpen.

Campbell didn't recognise the sender's number. He frowned. 'Where?' tapped out Campbell with his left hand on the portable device while lifting the office land line phone and pressing a quick-dial number with his right hand. He pressed the land line handset to his ear; there was no reply on the extension. He could not do everything himself so he called across the office, 'Sergeant Jenner!' He wasn't sure if she was there.

'Yes,' she said. She was only two desks away. Her neatly bobbed blond haired head popped up above one of the screens that divided the open plan office into areas obscuring Campbell's view.

'Get this position traced,' he said, his Edinburgh accent adding to the urgency of the direction.

'Right away,' she said looking at her own phone to get his number. He was always unpredictable but this explosion of sound from her superior was unexpected. She looked at him. A strange fire was burning within him, an aggravation, an energy. This overt expression of activity was not like him. Usually he gave the appearance of being languid, cool but, like a swan, all the activity was happening out of sight in his mind.

'How far do you think "not far away" is?' he asked.

Jenner shrugged. 'About twenty-five miles,' she suggested. 'What's this about?'

He passed her his portable phone and she read the message. 'That's a lot of beaches to look at,' observed Jenner. 'We are right in the middle of a stretch of very popular beaches in this area of the North Anglian coast.'

'To find the body, if there is one, is going to be difficult, let alone finding this messenger, this "Watcher" character.' Campbell unwound his long legs and rose from his seat. 'I'll have to go and see Tarnish. We will need more of our people on the ground to make a search.'

'We won't get them at this short notice. They'll all be in the cities keeping an eye on the pubs and clubs on a Friday,' said Jenner.

'It's early yet,' he said. 'The pubs and clubs won't get going for hours.'

The phone rang. Jenner answered it, listened and said to Campbell, 'The Watcher calls have been traced to Cambridge. Police are in the vicinity and are going to investigate.'

'Good,' said Campbell and then he walked away among the forest of open plan desking towards Superintendent Tarnish's office.

Inspector Campbell felt the sun on the back of his neck. He'd taken the precaution of putting on protective cream. He leaned languidly on the promenade railings overlooking Daneton Howe beach. It seemed unwise to disturb every sleeping sunbather and ask them if any of their party was dead. The whole thing could so easily be a hoax and could produce panic without cause. And that is what Superintendent Tarnish had said so he had diverted only a few of the officers from the towns and cities to search the beaches for a body. "A needle in a hay stack," he'd said.

But since that discussion there'd been another message. This time the message had come from a different phone and had come via the operations desk not from the messenger directly. They had timed the call at five pm. It was signed Watcher and told Campbell to be here at Daneton Howe Beach at six pm. No reason was given. But he had to assume it was the same 'Watcher' that had contacted his work mobile. The message had given him very little time to get here. It was now six pm.

Campbell disengaged emotionally with the environment as he analysed the beach with the two-toned orange and white sand stone cliff rising towards the town of Daneton and disappearing into the sand dunes at Daneton Howe. Many people would have come and gone during the day.

Children were still playing on the soft pale-yellow sand which they had used to construct castles with turrets, boats, and dolphins appearing to skim across the beach between the straddled deckchairs. Two ladies in their seventies were knitting. He wondered how they avoided getting sand in the wool. A boy of about five years old approached a heavily built man in a deck chair who wore a green-striped shirt and, over his head, a baseball cap. It was pulled down over his closed eyes. The boy's mother made a game of chasing her son and managed to divert him from disturbing the resting man in the deckchair.

Since the Anglian police forces had been amalgamated he had found himself working in different areas. He'd not been to this beach for work before, but he'd visited it with his family many times and enjoyed the sand and sun the same as the people were doing here today. Somehow it took on a different dimension as a place of work. He noted the beach kiosk / tea shop at the top of the beach with the small town of Daneton behind it and the constant flow of people walking along the short promenade from their parked cars to the beach.

He phoned Jenner from his mobile. 'Hello, Jenner,' he hailed in his broadest Edinburgh accent. The familiar shapes his mouth formed as it made the sounds was comforting. 'Any news of the trace on Watcher's new mobile?'

'No, there's no sign of it or its user. The police down in Cambridge have taken a look-around. The Cambridge police got to the area just after your first call came in.'

'Where was the phone?'

'They think both of Watcher's phones might be in the river now. They think the person sending the messages was on the path next to the river. The first phone was traced to a location towards the city centre when it stopped being traceable. The second phone is also now untraceable – last location for that one was under a bridge at an open part of the river, parkland.'

'Did they see any sign of Watcher?' asked Campbell.

'They got there too late. What cameras there are in that area were not working. It was busy. Could have been anyone, Sir.'

Campbell said, 'Aye' and 'thank you,' and put his phone away. He had observed the whole scene in front of him at Daneton Howe for half an hour now. It was already six-thirty. He wondered whether he should clear the beach. There were no indications that this was a terrorist threat, the experts had informed Superintendent Tarnish. Campbell had been surprised at their expert lack of interest.

Just a couple of dozen volunteer policemen, Special Constables, had been found to walk the beaches within twenty-five miles of the Horseton office during the afternoon; just two to each beach. But this beach was well beyond that limit. However, since Watcher's second message, a couple of them had been drafted over here. They'd been checking and rechecking even before Campbell had arrived.

One of the Special Constables was being called over to a pair of ladies he'd observed knitting. One was waving a black umbrella at them, the other was still knitting. Campbell was impressed briefly by their colourful behaviour.

At least, he considered briefly, this exercise was allowing him to avoid the chaos at home with his wife and children departing for Scotland to see relatives. A discomfort he easily avoided with work. That message from the operations desk had been an ideal reason to extend his working day.

Campbell's phone rang: standard ring tone. He answered it.

A steady but cheerful female voice said, 'Hello, Inspector Campbell. Lindy here. I've received a call from a Harriet Epsy. She requested an ambulance for her uncle, Robert Epsy, as she can't wake him. As we knew you were down there I thought I ought to let you know. There'll be an ambulance arriving soon with a paramedic.'

Campbell recognised her voice. 'Thanks, Lindy.'

He scanned the busy beach again looking for the pair of volunteer police constables. He spotted them walking towards him. One was ambling along casually looking about the beach, clearly taking in everything without appearing to be searching. The other looked towards Campbell and then away. Neither of them wished to betray his presence. Campbell reached for the radio and asked them if they'd seen anything untoward. The one that had looked at him replied that they hadn't.

'What did the ladies want?' Campbell asked them.

'They were complaining about children playing on the beach.'

A movement caught Campbell's attention. On the periphery of his vision he was aware of an ambulance approaching the promenade close to the kiosk-tea shop, and, in front of him, he was aware of an athletically built woman sitting on the sand. The anxious twist of her head was what had caught his attention with her black curly hair tumbling out of the top of a deep bandeau. He estimated that she was in her mid-to-late-twenties. She directed an anxious look at Campbell. Her face was tanned in a way that told of an outdoor lifestyle.

She looked at the man beside her. Campbell thought he looked thin and frail in his deck chair. His Panama hat must have fallen beside him as the sun was still fierce enough for his shiny hairless head to need it.

Campbell ducked under the promenade railing, dropped down onto the beach and set out towards her and her companion without waiting for

11

the ambulance crew.

He saw her beckon to the ambulance driver and the paramedic and driver were already out of their vehicle behind Campbell and heading towards the woman, who must be Lindy's Harriet Epsy. Campbell scanned the beach. Harriet and the frail man seemed to be by themselves. He could not detect any other members of her party. He nodded reassuringly at Harriet and continued heading towards them, wondering if this could be the dead body from Watcher's message.

By the time he reached them the Special Constables had also arrived and were already forming a discrete barrier with their presence a few feet away from Campbell and Harriet Epsy by facing out towards the other beach visitors.

When Campbell reached Robert Epsy, he put out his hand and touched the man seated loosely in the deckchair by his shoulder. The stricken man had sallow cheeks with bony features. He felt lifeless. Campbell saw that there was nothing he could do for him. Robert Epsy looked clean and tidy with a fresh long-sleeved t-shirt, beige slacks, socks and sandals. Campbell stood back to allow the ambulance crew access to the stricken man. After examining him the blond pony-tailed green clad paramedic reported that he'd probably had a heart attack a little while ago and passed away.

'He's been asleep for a while', said the young woman with the bandeau. Her dark eyes flashed searchingly at Campbell. He did not display his reaction instead he introduced himself and checked her name against that given by the call centre. She curled a lock of her hair that had fallen from the mass poking out the top of the bandeau with her finger and returned it to its previous containment. 'Harriet Epsy. This is – was – my uncle, Robert Epsy.'

'Are you both local?' enquired Campbell.

'My uncle is, but I'm not these days. I've come back for an old girls' reunion at Strath-Kind School.'

'That's some distance away,' said Campbell. 'There are closer beaches, like Banksea.'

'My uncle is a Daneton man. My parents used to live here. I was closer than most of the girls at Strath-Kind. It was mostly a boarding school then. My family took me daily to school.'

As the ambulance crew had finished with the uncle the paramedic decided to check Harriet for shock. She moved Harriet further away from the dead man. Once the paramedic had completed her examination, the ambulance driver took Harriet up the beach to the kiosk-tea shop to make sure she sipped her way through a hot sweet cup of tea while the paramedic returned to the body.

Campbell was already checking Robert Epsy over as discretely as he could. The dead man's arm flopped from his lap.

The paramedic put it back. 'The poor man is quite cold. Blood has not been pumping around his body for a while,' whispered the paramedic to him. 'It looks like his heart has stopped. He wouldn't be the first person to go that way on the beach.'

Campbell and the paramedic could find no sign of unlawful activity on the body of Robert Epsy within the limitations offered by the exposed beach.

'He'll get an autopsy anyway as a sudden death,' observed Campbell.

'I could do with my ambulance driver back, so we can make the body ready for removal,' said the paramedic.

'I'll go as I need to speak to Harriet Epsy.' Campbell went up the beach to relieve the paramedic of Harriet at the tea kiosk, which he found was more like a tiny tea shop with a few tables squeezed inside for taking refreshments out of the weather than just a kiosk dispensing food and drink through a window.

The driver nodded his relief and Campbell steered Harriet to a bench away from the holiday makers. Campbell took down her address and asked if she'd seen anything unusual prior to her uncle's passing. She looked at him as if he was mad.

'Sort of like a fright?' she asked. She carried on talking without waiting for an answer. 'I walked up to the tea hut here. I just left him here dosing. When I came back he was sound asleep, so I didn't want to disturb him. It was only at tea time I thought I ought to wake him. And...' Her voice faded away as she saw Robert Epsy being brought up the beach. 'Uncle Robert,' she said as she stared at the loaded stretcher being placed in the ambulance. Campbell watched her closely. He tried to assess her reaction to Robert Epsy's passing.

'What happens now?' she asked.

He repeated his earlier statement made to the paramedic. 'It's a sudden death so the coroner will be involved and there'll be an autopsy, I'm afraid.'

Harriet nodded and wrapped herself in a beach robe, picked up her bags and went towards a blue car parked along the side of the road nearby.

'You should phone someone. You might be too wobbly to drive.' Campbell folded away his notebook with the details of this event duly logged.

'Oh yes, you're quite right,' she said. 'I'll phone my friend.'

Campbell's phone rang. 'Excuse me,' he said, and he turned away. It was well past six pm and there was no apparent sign of Watcher's promised murder on this beach.

Kara Leonard walked across the sandy promenade from the tiny tea shop in her worn out flat ballet style pumps towards the spidery man in a suit standing on the promenade. Squirrel-like he was talking with his head tilted towards his phone which he held to his left ear.

She'd served tea and cakes and sandwiches and washed up at her little sink just by the window of the shop. From there she could see across the beach. She enjoyed watching the stories of the people on the beach unfold before her during the day. She had a story to tell and she was sure that man was a policeman, not that he looked like any policeman she'd ever seen before.

The gangly policeman nodded at her distractedly and raised his hand in a cross between a greeting and a request for her to halt.

'Excuse me,' she said to him. He looked up from his phone. His beady nut-brown eyes examined her. 'I saw that girl a while back – the one with the dead man. I heard her say to that ambulance driver that she was with her uncle when they came up for a cup of tea earlier in the afternoon.'

Kara felt aggravated. She ran her fingers through her short cropped sandy-pink hair with frustration. 'He's not her uncle.'

'Inspector Campbell.' The tall man extended his hand and shook hers. 'Why do you say that?' he asked.

'Because they were kissing and not like uncle and niece.'

Inspector Campbell turned to where the girl with the black hair and the bandeau had got into the car. He saw the vehicle retreating rapidly down the road. It was already out of range for him to take its registration number.

'Now may I take your details...?' he asked the woman in front of him. Kara felt herself bouncing with indignation even though she was just standing still.

The policeman seemed agitated and a little distracted, which annoyed Kara intensely but he still carried out the duty politely.

Once he'd thanked her, she was surprised to see him wander off unhurriedly to his car.

'Aren't you going to do anything?' she called after him.

CHAPTER THREE

Watcher paused to look back. The pine woods formed a concealing blanket from the eyes of the bathers on Banksea beach. Watcher briefly snatched a view of the scene: there was the lithe girl with long red hair; there was the victim in the blue and white striped deck chair.

The wait for the girl's return had seemed so long for Watcher but had only been a matter of minutes. And here she was. It was always a shame to miss the startling outpouring of misery from the victim's loved ones, but there was more work to do and the police would have to wait. Capture was not an option.

Georgia Lomond was at last back at the beach hut relieved to be away from her old school. It had seemed more duty than anything else. She had expected it to be fun. There were quite a few from her year group there. She couldn't believe the variety of skilled women that had been formed from the motley collection of students that she remembered. She turned on a little camping stove and placed the kettle on top.

Georgia poked her head out of the hut door and called, 'Grandpa Will, do you want a cup of tea?' There was no reply, so she went onto the veranda to look at him. The deck chair was on the beach where she'd left him. It was facing away from the hut towards the sea, so she could hardly see him snuggled down asleep.

The children had gone from the beach. The sand was less busy than earlier in the day as at tea time the families had packed up and gone home. She was partly reassured by the fact that he was still sitting in the evening sunshine, but he was very still. She went to check on him. As she came around the side of the deck chair she became aware of something strangely wrong with him. He seemed too slumped in his slumber. Her stomach felt hollow, a tense emptiness. Her muscles in her upper arms wanted to twitch. Her eyes wanted to roll but she kept them still.

Grandpa Will's legs spread in front of him in a relaxed position. She fell to her knees beside him and put out her hand and touched his shoulder. She knew he was dead. It was as if a switch had been turned off inside of him. Tears spiked her eyes. She bit her lip stifling a scream. Grandpa Will's head rolled to the side showing a puncture wound at the base of his head. She clasped her hands to her mouth.

Watcher moved away, satisfied.

Campbell drove along the side of the caravan site and drew up behind the pine wood at the back of Banksea Beach in response to the telephone call he'd received at Daneton from the Horseton office.

Could Watcher have sent the police to the wrong beach, Campbell wondered. The murder was at Banksea not Daneton. And Watcher could not have been at either beach at that time if Watcher sent those messages from Cambridge. It took at least two and a half hours to get to Banksea from Cambridge by train and that was quicker by far than driving a car on the tiny winding roads that headed out to the coast. Campbell had been at Daneton Howe for over an hour looking for Watcher's dead person and dealing with Robert Epsy. If this was all arranged by Watcher, he either had to be able to hack phones or he had to have an accomplice.

The policeman co-ordinating the police entry point stepped back to let Campbell through the pathway marked out through the pine wood. 'It's that way,' he said

Campbell recognised him. 'Thank you, Officer Howard,'

The moment his feet touched the ground under the trees deep with pine needles he felt a sadness knowing that he was about to see a murdered man. He braced himself. He took a deep breath of the pine scented air and breathed out slowly.

This beach was just outside the twenty-five-mile limit from the office they'd set after the first message from Watcher which had gone to Campbell's phone. Extra uniformed police had been drafted in since the report and they had already cleared the beach and set up a cordon. Beyond this, those that had stayed were busy giving statements. Surely someone would have seen something, wondered Campbell. He spotted Sergeant Jenner and Detective Constable Garden and went over to them.

'Anyone said that they've seen anything yet?' he asked.

'I'm afraid not, Sir,' said Jenner.

'No chance the murderer is among the crowd?' asked Campbell, watching the people from the beach being herded to one end and being asked about anything they might have seen during the afternoon.

'It's mostly children with their grandparents, Sir,' said Jenner. 'Tide's just started to run out so not much in the way of swimmers or kite or wind-surfers.'

Campbell nodded. It had only been a chance. There would be security cameras in the car park that could be checked. They would not have caught everything. The access along the bank to the beach wouldn't be covered, let alone the beach itself. He ached to see the face of Watcher or his accomplice. He had to put them as main suspects for the murder at this point.

Campbell saw Garden talking to a red-haired woman in her early twenties with kind shoulders and a roll in the upper spine as she squatted on the beach hunched in a foetal shape beside the dead man slumped in the deck chair.

Campbell was startled at the similarity of the scene to that which he'd just left at Daneton Howe.

He made his way along the sand. More uniformed regular police had already been diverted from other duties and were screening off the immediate area around the dead man. DC Garden introduced the girl as Georgia Lomond and discretely manoeuvred Georgia away from the body.

'The pathologist, Colin Lincoln, is on his way, Inspector,' said Garden.

'There's blood,' said Georgia, now standing a couple of feet from the body.

Campbell said, 'Where?' He detected Georgia's Scottish accent but could not yet place which area it came from, too warm for Edinburgh.

'At the base of his neck,' said Georgia. 'Just a little.'

Campbell tilted his head as he took in this information. He hunkered down and looked at the victim without touching him. He noted the puncture wound at the base of the victim's skull.

'It's so unfair,' Georgia blurted out through her tears. 'My grand-father's only just recovered from the death of his wife. I brought him here for a break. I only left him for a few hours.' She took a deep shuddering breath and calmed herself.

'For how long exactly?' asked Campbell.

'I left about 11.30am and I was back by 5.30pm.'

'That's six hours?' confirmed Inspector Campbell in a quiet reasoning and non-confrontational voice.

'Yes,' she said with a small pucker of reflection forming on her brow.

'Where did you go?' asked Campbell.

'To my old school, Strath-Kind, about three miles from Banksea Halt,' she said, and then, looking directly at Campbell, she added, 'I should never have left him.' Her eyes were startlingly blue, almost like crystal in their tearful brightness.

Campbell walked her further up the beach. 'Tell me about him. For a start, what was his name?' he asked using his accent to lull the girl's shock.

'William Cecil Broadgate. We called him Grandpa Will.'

'As your family name is Lomond that makes him your maternal grandfather?'

'Yes, that's right.'

'Is he married?'

'No,' said Georgia.

'We will need to contact your mother. If you could give us her details? She would be his next of kin?'

'Yes, she would.' Georgia Lomond opened her beach bag and took out her phone. She fiddled with it for a moment and passed Campbell the device. He took down the details and passed it back to her.

'Tell me about his life,' he asked. 'We are most interested in anything that might link to what has happened to him.'

'He was not the sort to make enemies, Inspector. He was so kind. He would do anything for anybody. But his generosity can be his undoing.' She looked at her dead grandfather longingly. 'He had been a shattered man; he was just about on the mend. He was only seventy-six.'

'What do you mean?' asked Campbell.

'His personal life has been too complicated. He was not a man of business. He was retired, had been for as long as I can remember. He wouldn't have that sort of enemy.'

'Would you ...' Campbell expressed 'expand' with a sweeping gesture of his arm.

'He married a woman some twenty years his junior,' she started then she looked up towards the pine wood and then down at her painted toes disappearing in the sand. 'He knew she wasn't well. He thought the cause of her illness was the fact she'd been deserted by her husband and he'd swindled her out of all her money. He wanted to help her -- poor foolish man.'

'How do you mean?'

'There was no swindling husband. She was clinically ill,' Georgia explained. 'She had schizophrenia. She heard voices in her head. She ended up locking him in the bathroom for a week – the neighbours had to break in to rescue him.'

'And she died recently?' asked Campbell looking for confirmation.

Georgia nodded. 'She didn't die then. She was hospitalised and medicated. She had a reaction to the medication. It took a few months to develop.'

'Did you know her?'

'I couldn't help,' insisted Georgia.

'It is almost impossible to help under those circumstances, ' said Campbell. He walked a few steps further up the beach. 'How old was his second wife?'

'She was in her fifties.'

'What was her name?'

'Fenella,' Georgia replied, reddening. 'What has she got to do with anything? She's dead,' she snapped. She shook her head apologetically, 'I'm sorry I'm not myself.'

'Can you tell me her surname before she married your grandfather?'

'Florris.' Tears appeared in the corners of Georgia's eyes.

Campbell changed the subject before her emotions stopped her talking to him. 'Where are you staying?'

Georgia sighed. 'I rented a caravan for us just on the site the other side of the wood there. Grandpa Will has a house just outside of the town but I thought it would be nice to be right on the beach. This is a fair walk from the town and it's a nuisance parking the car down here each day. You get parking here with the caravan. I thought it would make a bit of a holiday for us.'

'Could you show me the caravan where you and your grandfather were staying?' As Campbell could see the pathologist and a mass of crime scene examiners arriving from the direction of the pine wood, he wanted to move Georgia before she realised they were there.

'Yes, of course,' she said.

To one side Campbell observed a small tea kiosk with its small generator still humming away – not turned off when the police cleared the beach. Such places were always a good source of information, he thought, reminded briefly of the larger one at Daneton Howe. He put his hand up to Jenner who was walking towards him.

'Just a moment,' he said to Georgia. 'Can you excuse me?' He strolled over to Jenner and asked her to visit the kiosk herself. He muttered something about valuable information. 'And on another aspect to this we will need to get something out to the media as soon as possible. Can you draft something for them?'

'Absolutely,' said Jenner. She continued in an informative tone: 'Garden has been assigned as family officer to Georgia Lomond.'

Campbell nodded. 'See if you can get someone else. I want her on the investigation team. And have her replacement meet us at the caravan.' He turned to Georgia Lomond and raised his voice slightly, 'What number is your caravan?' The reply came and he repeated it to Jenner.

'The full team of crime scene examiners have arrived now,' said Jenner quietly swivelling a brief meaningful glance in the direction of Georgia Lomond.

'Yes, I saw them,' he said drawing out the affirmative with his Edinburgh accent. 'She won't want to see that. I'll ask the crime scene examiners if I can take her out by the bank.'

With a nod from their leader Campbell steered Georgia away from the pine wood. Georgia concentrated on her feet sinking into the soft sand as Campbell took her towards the bank at the far end of the beach. When they got to the path she slipped on her red canvas shoes.

He asked Georgia if she knew what happened to Fenella's previous husband.

'I don't really know much about Fenella,' replied Georgia. They reached the caravan and Georgia shook as she took out the key. 'I'm sorry,' she said.

'We will be needing a statement from you,' he replied.

'Yes,' she said quietly.

'May I have a look at his things?' asked Campbell.

'He hasn't much here, just a few clothes.'

'Still…'

'Yes, of course.'

'You're not from Edinburgh,' said Campbell.

'I was born in Perth. My family live between Edinburgh and Glasgow now.'

'Ah, Perth's a grand place. Norwich reminds me of it in some ways.' He caught her frowning at him. 'Just my opinion,' he said and turned to

Grandpa Will's clothes. 'I could do with a cup of tea and so could you,' he said. He could see she was still thinking about Norwich and Perth. It was a small distraction, but it had worked; she seemed to have lost a little of her shocked look as she filled the kettle and put it on.

Elizabeth Rattagan stood her bag beside the sofa-bed and opened the zip of the main compartment. She had a frock in there that would do for this evening. She hadn't intended to stay. She had bought a return ticket, but she knew she had nothing to go back to Sussex for and Gwen did invite her to stay. She was grateful that Gwen had booked a cabin at the bird sanctuary near Banksea. She hadn't wanted to share a room with her, but she had no money for anywhere herself so when Gwen said she'd booked this place and offered her the accommodation she'd felt a tremble of relief and given an instant, 'Yes.'

The sun was low in the sky and shone through the cabin window. What a relief to relax after an afternoon watching Gwen work her way through the old girls at the school. It wouldn't feel right to her to approach the past pupils and look for money making opportunities. Gwen was so different to her.

There was a sofa bed in the living area which she was lounging on. It had a television in front of it. She grabbed the remote and turned on the tv and rolled onto her stomach. She luxuriated in her comfort and smiled languidly at her sandy shoes slipped off by the door. For a moment all her past worries left her. She flicked through the channels until she caught sight of the very road this bird sanctuary and cabin were on. She paused. She looked again. Yes, there was the gorse and hawthorn along the side of the road. And there were the wooden gates hooked back with the cattle grid at the front of the site. She could almost see the cabin she was sitting in. She caught the words 'found dead' and 'suspicious circumstances' from the commentary. 'Wow, Gwen,' she called out. 'You won't believe this.'

Gwen wandered in from the bathroom and stated flatly, 'There's a footpath from here down to Banksea beach. I expect that's why they used this location.' In answer to Elizabeth's enquiring look she said, 'I've stayed here quite often over the years.'

Gwen watched the television with her while she dried her hair. A pleasant looking woman described as Detective Sergeant Jenner was asking for anyone who saw anything suspicious on Banksea Beach today to come forward and speak to the police.

'We were there at lunch time,' said Elizabeth.

'Did you see anything?' asked Gwen.

'No,' said Elizabeth.

'Well then,' said Gwen.

Elizabeth took that to mean that as far as Gwen was concerned that was the end of the matter.

Just as a picture of the beach with the arc of beach huts backed by the pinewood came on the screen Gwen turned to Elizabeth and said, 'We're going to be late. You've not even started to get ready yet.'

'Sorry Gwen. Do you really think these people will help you?'

'And you Lizzy: how have you got into your muddle? A good young lawyer like you should be rolling in cash and look at you. Not a bean.'

'I'd rather not talk about it.'

'Okay. Well let's go see if I can get some work through these women. You didn't used to be like this. No-one was braver than you, and here you are some fearful mouse.'

Elizabeth said, 'Just leave it,' more sharply than she intended.

'Well, let's get on. I'm really looking forward to our outing to the Gull Inn.'

'I don't really know most of them, Gwen.'

'It's another chance to win round some of the girls. Persuade them to invest.'

'What exactly is this scheme you want to persuade them of?'

'Ah, well. You have no money, so you are safe?'

'Is it illegal?'

'Nothing you have to worry your little lawyerly-mind about. Are you having a shower. There are towels supplied with the cabin and I have plenty of soap and shampoo you can use.'

Elizabeth Rattagan stood outside the Gull Inn waiting for Gwen to leave the bar.

Gwen staggered out. 'Do you fancy a swim?' she asked.

'You're drunk,' said Elizabeth.

'We could walk down to Banksea Harbour, Lizzy,' wheedled Gwen.

'We can walk down but we haven't got costumes,' Elizabeth objected.

'This time of night no-one will know,' urged Gwen.

Elizabeth was almost persuaded. Some old spark from her past kindled a flame inside her that she hadn't felt burn for a long time. The urge to swim overcame her inhibitions.

'There's that spot by the harbour wall where we can leave our things.' Gwen waved her hand in the general direction.

Elizabeth recalled the harbour area which was only ever used by a few small sailing boats and for swimming races. It was tempting. 'Are you sure you can manage, Gwen?'

'You saved me once.'

'I've not swam in ages. I couldn't rescue a float now and you are a full-grown woman.'

'Just teasing, Lizzy. I swim all the time perhaps I can pay you back and rescue you?'

'I used to be your body for the life-saving certificates.' Elizabeth laughed. It was strange to hear a happy sound coming from her very own body.

'And I yours,' said Gwen. 'Chilly work even in a heated swimming pool.'

They walked down to the harbour. It was just as Elizabeth remembered it. At night the town lights reflected on the water. They made their way down the slipway, where the small boats were floated in to the water, ignoring the no swimming signs.

'Don't remember them being there,' remarked Gwen.

Elizabeth shrugged her shoulders and started to strip off as she thought they were suitably hidden from view.

They stepped into small cool waves which lapped calmly around them. They swam a couple of circuits of the harbour. Elizabeth found the technique came back to her readily enough, but her muscles were unused to it. Gwen surged ahead.

One of the smaller sailing boats fired up its engine used for getting the vessel in and out of the harbour.

Elizabeth shouted out to Gwen, 'Watch out,' fearing that the boat would move into her old friend.

But Gwen had heard the noise herself. She stopped, trod water and looked around. She located the boat and swam back to Elizabeth out of its way.

'Enough?' asked Gwen.

'Enough,' agreed Elizabeth. Perhaps the cold water had sobered Gwen up, but she wondered whether her friend had been quite as drunk as she'd made out.

CHAPTER FOUR

Elizabeth Rattigan was pleased to be back at the cabin on the edge of the bird sanctuary. She sunk down on the sofa which she and Gwen had made up into a bed before they left for the Gull Inn in Banksea town centre and the collection of numerous past students from Strath-Kind School.

Elizabeth smiled: she'd had more fun than she'd thought possible. She'd laughed until she'd cried at the familiar stories of shared childhood experiences. Gwen had carefully worked the room, handing out business cards with one of those anonymous but business-like email addresses on. Elizabeth was grateful Gwen had taken the remains of a bottle of vodka and a bottle of tonic water to her bedroom. She doubted she would see her until late tomorrow.

She decided that she would shower in the morning. She really didn't want to disturb Gwen. Her interfering, condescending sympathy was becoming irritating. She supposed that for Gwen that was what passed as friendliness. Had she been different at school? Or, had she not noticed Gwen's behaviour in her desire to have a friend? Had she really been that desperate? She thought she might have been. This whole trip had been to find Gwen. She'd hoped for so much from their old friendship and it wasn't there. She shook her head, perhaps this was tiredness talking.

Her holdall stood beside the sofa-bed slightly open as she'd left it. She unzipped the side pocket and reached inside for her toothbrush which she'd carefully wrapped in a plastic bag. As she did so her fingers touched something alien to the memory she held of her packing. Something paper was stuffed in beside the plastic wrapped toothbrush.

At first, she wondered if the mother on the train had simply returned the money she'd given her for the suited woman's dry cleaning. To be honest she would be quite pleased if she had. Pulling the paper out of the side pocket she could see that it was an envelope. On the envelope was a name. It wasn't her name and it wasn't Gwen's name. She stared at it. She'd heard the name before that day. She was sure it had been mentioned on the news bulletin about the murdered man on the beach. Yes, that was it: Inspector Campbell.

All thought of sleep slipped away from her. She retrieved her phone from her handbag and pressed in the number for the police. Her mind was reeling with the possibilities of how anything could have been placed in there without her realising. The only opportunity for someone to have interfered with her luggage could have been the train. From there she'd carried it herself to Strath-Kind school and after that it was in Gwen's car. Did Gwen know about this?

'Gwen,' she called deleting the phone call. She went up to Gwen's bedroom door directly off the living room and knocked. The reply was a grunt. 'Did you put this letter in my bag, Gwen?' she knocked again. 'Gwen, this is important.'

The door opened, and a very bleary eyed and dishevelled Gwen opened the door. 'What?' she demanded.

'I found this in my bag. Did you put it there?'

'Course not. Let me see it,' said Gwen shoving hair out of her eyes. 'Inspector Campbell?' she queried the name on the envelope.

'I think it must have got into my bag while I was on the train. It was not very far from me.'

'Well, we'd better give it to him.' Gwen leaned on the door jamb for support.

'I thought so too, but supposing it's about me.'

'Whatever do you mean?' Gwen wavered apparently unable to work out the question in her alcohol befuddled brain.

'My reduced circumstances are not of my making.'

'What has this letter to do with that?' Gwen seemed to sober slightly.

'I don't know but I'm thinking now that there must be a connection.'

'What have you done, Lizzy?' Gwen was frowning and wagging her finger at her in what she clearly thought was a humorous way.

Elizabeth persisted with, 'I thought the law would be about righting wrongs and it has nothing to do with that.'

'I could have told you that. Lawyers deal with criminals,' said Gwen bringing her bottle of vodka and glass and sitting next to Elizabeth on the sofa.

'I understand that. That is why I took work in the Crown Office making the case for the prosecution.'

'Hence the shoes,' said Gwen, her public-school voice sounded strident. 'Criminals probably pay better.'

Gwen tweaked the letter out of Elizabeth's hand and went to open it.

'No,' said Elizabeth, 'don't do that. It could be important evidence.' She snatched the letter back.

'My head is thumping, Lizzy. Call the police or don't call the police. I care not.' Gwen dragged herself up and carried her vodka and glass into her bedroom.

Elizabeth followed her, 'Sorry, Gwen, I just…'

Gwen slammed her bedroom door in Elizabeth's face.

Elizabeth sat back down on the sofa bed and looked at the envelope again. She wondered about opening it: supposing it accused her of something? Already means had been found to remove her from her job and therefore her income; why not something worse, something that could put her in prison?

She would think about it. Whether she would just give it to Inspector Campbell or whether she would open it first. There was a small voice at the back of her head suggesting she should destroy it, but that was against her lawyerly instincts. She could not destroy it and it was impossible to ignore. She could not pretend it was not there.

Raymond Campbell entered his cottage. He'd unlocked his front door. When Margaret was there he would go in through the back door because it would always be unlocked. The sun was low and bright in the late evening sky. Light streamed in through the windows, but the rooms seemed dull without the bright noise and activity his wife, Margaret, son, Edmund, and daughter, Victoria, gave to the rooms. Margaret for the first time had moved from hinting at him going with them to Scotland to asking him directly to accompany them on their visit to see family.

He hadn't been able to reply. He had walked away. He regretted it, but he couldn't change it and if asked again he would have tried to say no. But the events that kept him away still felt raw, and yet it must be more than twenty years since they happened.

He missed Margaret, Edmund and Victoria already.

He ran himself a bath. Stripped off unceremoniously and got in for a soak. He allowed the events of the case to settle in and examined his tiling. Yes, it was a good job: neat rows, even grouting. And Margaret had chosen the tiles herself, and despite her flamboyant artistic preferences she'd gone for something tasteful and simple.

Wedged himself into the bath, he closed his eyes.

Campbell knew he was tired. He only failed to block out the past when he was too tired to be busy. He felt himself slipping into slumber.

Raymond Campbell recalled that he had always been a solitary child, removed from the hurly burly of tenement life by his nature and his unwillingness to talk about himself or his family. By saying nothing he protected himself. Harry Binding -- the older lad from across the landing -- would give him a sly kick if he found Campbell sitting in the stairwell.

'What are you looking at?' Harry Binding would ask. Young Raymond was always looking at something. Observing was what he did, that and listening.

He woke with a jolt. The bath water was cold. He wrapped himself in towels and crawled into bed where his deep sleep held him in tormented dreams which he could not remember in the morning.

Campbell arrived at work, drank some strong coffee with hot milk and thought of Georgia Lomond and her Grandfather, William Cecil Broadgate. The victim must not slip out of focus, as inevitably attention would be drawn in so many different directions. He took time to read the pathologist's report. A lot of the laboratory test results would not yet be available, but it was a start. He closed the folder.

He wanted the morning meeting to be an effective start to the investigations. Campbell viewed the mixture of officers, uniformed and non-uniformed, before him: those on duty on Friday were taking the opportunity to physically relax after their strenuous efforts the day before. Leave had been cancelled and as many officers as possible were on shift for the morning meeting.

Campbell noted DS Adam Parnold returned from his holidays. Even sitting down, he was tall. His blond head nodded in the general area of Jenner and other members of Campbell's team. He heard Jenner ask, 'Good holiday?' and Parnold reply, 'Great thanks.'

Garden was with some of those that she used to work with when she was in uniform. She was sitting near the back with Lindy Greyling sitting beside her.

'Right,' said Campbell bringing the rabble to order. 'Glad to see you back,' he directed at Parnold. The mixture of personalities in his team worked well together. Parnold was a blood hound of a policeman. His energy at pursuing a criminal was essential. Jenner, as usual, had organised everybody and everything. The events on Banksea Beach were dealt with through displays of all the information they had. She must have been working on this from a very early start this morning. Crime scene photos were pinned on the board and maps of the area displayed. A time line of events was also shown giving the events of Daneton Howe Beach a mention due to the message from Watcher for Campbell to go there. Campbell couldn't decide if the death of Robert Epsy was a decoy or a coincidence.

'William Cecil Broadgate died yesterday at in the afternoon. He was seen alive by people on the beach until about four in the afternoon.

'There's a puncture wound in the neck. The pathologist has worked through the night to get us this preliminary report. A rod like implement entered the base of his jaw and penetrated his brain. An additional rod was placed in his diaphragm and plunged upwards into William Cecil's heart.'

Campbell paused: the puncture wound to the heart was new information. He allowed it to settle within him and with his colleagues. He breathed deeply and rose slightly onto the balls of his feet.

He applied his business as usual voice: 'Either wound our learned forensic pathology colleagues tell us would have killed him. This murderer wanted this man dead. This murder didn't happen by accident. The person who carried this out could be a professional, a medic or perhaps ex-military. Or just someone who has acquired this information. And why would anyone want to kill him? His granddaughter thinks him a gentle soul, but grandchildren often see their grandparents in a special light.'

Campbell thought about the knitters on Daneton Howe Beach.

'So, we'll want the location of anyone we interview for that time span. And we need to ask them about their profession and training, background and any connection to William Cecil Broadgate. He had difficulties with his wife who recently died -- Fenella. It might be worth tracing her family and seeing if they had a grievance. She might have had children from a previous marriage. She was in her early fifties while William Cecil was in his seventies. Her name before she married William Broadgate was Florris.'

Campbell was still thinking about the weapons used in his murder. He consulted the pathologist's report. The rods had been removed but would have had to have been thrust in with some force and, therefore, would have needed to have been strong. Probably not knitting needles then, he decided.

'William also has a house just on the edge of Banksea Halt,' Campbell continued. 'I collected the keys from the caravan that he was staying in with his grand-daughter. Parnold, would you check out William Cecil Broadgate's house, please?' asked Campbell.

'Yes,' said Parnold.

'Jenner could you liaise with any findings Parnold obtains and check out William Cecil's family?'

'Yes,' she agreed.

'And you did some work at the scene. Would you like to give us the highlights?'

'The beach was checked, and that process will continue today,' reported Jenner. 'The main event was a search looking particularly for the weapon or weapons. The scene of crime folks were complaining about the slightest wind shifting the sands, hiding and moving evidence. The tide would have pulled anything away from below high-water mark. While we were surveying the site, the pathologist was giving the body an initial examination and the tide was rolling out. The area was given a bit of a check but there's been another tide since.'

Jenner continued. 'I found the kiosk woman, Jess Barratt, she explained that she had to lock up the kiosk from time to time to visit the public toilets in the car park. She said she hadn't seen anything. They don't have a real security camera in the kiosk due to the lack of electricity. The generator only keeps the ice-cream cold, apparently. The camera used to run on a battery, but they couldn't afford to keep replacing it, so the camera's just a dummy.'

While Jenner spoke, there was some shuffling at the back. Lindy Greyling, whispered to Garden and retreated out the back door. A moment later she returned with a piece of paper which she handed to Garden. Garden stood up. 'This message has just arrived.' She passed Campbell the docket.

He read it and said, 'Sarah Radley has been on the phone and she was insistent that she wants to see me. She runs the tea kiosks along the beaches from Daneton through to Banksea beaches so she's Jess Barratt's boss; hence her connection with this investigation.' He sighed and continued, 'But Sarah Radley wants to talk about the wrong death: Robert Epsy. We believe he died of a failed heart about the same time as William Cecil was stabbed. We have it on the board,' he waved at the white board and its pictures, diagrams and coloured writing depicting the people and events involved, and continued, 'because of Watcher's message which took me to

Daneton Howe Beach in the first place. I think the message could well have been a straight decoy. The death is likely to be a side issue, but the information that Kara Leonard at the kiosk at Daneton gave me was strange. She said the couple were not related, though Harriet Epsy told me, the telephone centre and the paramedics Robert Epsy was her uncle.'

Campbell hunched himself squirrel-like in thought. 'I don't know, could there be a connection to our murder of William Cecil Broadgate at Banksea and the death of Robert Epsy?' Campbell shrugged. 'Both Harriet Epsy and Georgia Lomond went to Strath-Kind School.' Campbell paused, after a moment he said, 'DC Garden, can you visit Sarah Radley and see what she has to say? The pathologists haven't found any identification on Robert Epsy and I didn't find any either.'

'Yes, Inspector,' said Garden.

'Strath-Kind School needs looking at,' continued Campbell. 'Primarily Georgia Lomond's alibi needs checking. This link needs to be explored. A list of attendees at this old girls' day might be obtained from the school. Sergeant Jenner you're to investigate there.'

'Sir, do you think the perpetrators are professional hit men?' asked Jenner.

'They could be.' Campbell tossed the idea about in his head. 'There does seem to be some sophistication to the methodology. But don't be blinded by that. This type of school provides our secret services with their employees and our medical services with a selection of professionals.'

Once viewing from local security cameras had been arranged with other members of the team and the usual requests to the public for information sent out, Campbell closed the meeting. As he walked out of the room the clerk arrived to tell him there was a phone call. 'Thank you, Lindy.'

'It's from a member of the public and it sounded important. The call came from Banksea,' explained Linda. 'Elizabeth Rattagan.'

'Do you know what it's about?'

'She's got a letter addressed to you.'

DC Sally Garden parked at the end of the promenade where the orange-red cliff finished, and she walked towards the tiny tea kiosk at the other end of the short prom. Behind her the town ended and Daneton Howe's rolling sand dunes spread out with vast areas of flat sand between them and the sea.

As soon as Garden entered the kiosk she noted the security camera and, very quickly, she was listening to Sarah Radley: a slim energetic woman with eyes as dark as her own and curly hair dyed yellow with auburn flecks.

'Kara's not been in to the kiosk today. But I've been talking to her about that Harriet Epsy woman. I'm Kara's boss, Sarah Radley.' The woman sounded breathless and her wild loose curls trembled as she spoke. 'When I was picking up the money, she told me the story. She said she'd told Inspector Campbell about how she and that man, her supposed uncle, were carrying on.'

Garden acknowledged this with an encouraging nod. 'How did you recognise them? Have you got security camera images?'

'Kara'd taken a few pictures on her phone of the beach. There were some fantastic sand sculptures and castles the families had made. She had been taking photos of them. She didn't tell you because she thought she'd get into trouble. Invading people's privacy, that sought of thing.' Sarah paused. 'There'll be some security images of Harriet and the man that died as Kara said that they came up to the kiosk for a cup of tea not long after lunch time.'

'So, you have working security cameras here at Daneton?' asked Garden.

'Yes, we have,' snapped Sarah Radley.

'You haven't at Banksea Beach,' said Garden.

Sarah Radley grunted acceptance. 'On the prom, here at Daneton, we've got proper electric. The man Harriet called Uncle didn't come up to the kiosk according to Kara. I recognised Harriet instantly from the footage. I remember her. I used to have a cafe in town until I got the kiosk and she used to work in the lingerie shop opposite. I think it was her mum's business. I'd worked with her Uncle Robert previously at the post office. He went and worked in a betting shop and me and my friend took over the cafe opposite Harriet's mother's shop. Paula Green and her daughter, Louise, have that shop now.'

'Harriet's uncle Robert had taken early retirement in the fullest of health to relax and enjoy life. His working life had been stressful. Within weeks he'd developed heart trouble.'

'I see,' said DC Sally Garden trying to encourage Sarah Radley with thoughtful interest.

'The doctors stabilised his condition but the only way he could return to full fitness, he thought, was with a heart transplant. But everything went wrong inside him, and they could not give him the full dose of drugs, even so they thought he would pull through. Then my friend, who I used to work with at the post office, phoned up and said he'd died.'

'You are quite sure Robert Epsy is dead?' asked Garden.

'I'm sure. I went to the man's funeral. Whoever was here yesterday wasn't Harriet's uncle, Robert Epsy.'

'Can you sort me out some photos of Harriet and her real uncle?'

Sarah Radley nodded. 'I'll sort out the security recording of Harriet as well and I'll have to dig out some old photographs of Robert. That must have been a good fifteen years past since Harriet's mother had the shop.'

'Can you let me know when you've got them, and I'll pick them up. I could take the security footage away with me today, if that's okay?'

Sarah Radley's brow was sweating. 'Yes, that's fine. And, there's something else I want to talk to you about. Let me show you.' Sarah Radley turned around and marched out of the kiosk and down the slope onto the beach. She waded out onto the sand and DC Sally Garden followed.

After walking past probably twenty beach huts Sarah Radley stopped. 'Look.' She directed Garden with an open hand.

'These are burnt beach huts,' observed Garden. Just a few blackened timbers were spread around four distinctive areas where beach huts had once stood. She pursed her lips: this was, surely, what Sarah Radley had really been brought out to see. Perhaps Sarah Radley thought one of her tea-kiosks might be next. Garden advised, 'The fire brigade have already been out to this incident and have established that it was arson. It is being investigated.' Garden frowned. 'In what way are these associated with Robert Epsy's death?'

'This, Officer Garden, is related to the death at Banksea not that man who Harriet called Uncle Robert. I wouldn't have called you lot out if it wasn't important.'

'In what way is this burnt-out beach hut in Daneton connected to the murder at Banksea?' asked Garden.

'I own all the kiosks along this bit of coast as far as Banksea. I go around through the day topping up stock and collecting takings. Jess Barratt's at Banksea mostly.'

Garden watched Sarah Radley's dramatic pause for a moment and then asked, 'And?'

'A pair of beach huts at Banksea have been burnt too,' said Sarah Radley with triumphant raised eyebrows and questioning twist of her mouth.

'This sort of casual arson is usually a local crime. This type of arsonist doesn't travel far.' Garden pointed out.

'Fire destroys evidence,' Sarah Radley pointed out in a tone that indicated Garden was extremely stupid.

'They have not been burnt since the murder. These are stone cold. There would have been some heat left if they'd been burnt since,' said Garden.

'Yes, these are old ones. But the ones at Banksea have been burned recently.' Sarah Radley paused. 'It must be just plain vandalism here at Daneton. Still, you are investigating?'

'Yes,' DC Garden reassured her. She thought for a moment and sucked the end of her pen. 'Did you or your ladies see anyone hanging about before the beach huts were set on fire?'

'Oh, I hadn't thought about that,' said Sarah Radley. She followed this very quickly with, 'There's one boy I see here often – always hanging about the beach. He's a right waster so Jess Barratt tells me, anyhow. She says she's seen him at Banksea Beach too.'

'Do you know his name?'

'Bradley… Bradley Yorkman. Jess will tell you about him.'

'Thank you.' DC Sally Garden nodded in confirmation that she had noted down about Jess Barratt in the kiosk at Banksea and Bradley Yorkman. She'd talk to Jenner as she'd already spoken to Jess Barratt and see if she ought to have another word with her. 'Do you know where Harriet Epsy's working now?' asked Garden returning to the death on Daneton Howe's beach.

'No, I don't. I haven't seen her in a while. Jess Barratt used to be friends with her. They are more-or-less the same age.' Sarah Radley's eyebrows twitched in acknowledgement that she might just get some more urgent follow-up on the arson attacks out of this. 'Look, she said, giving Garden her business card. 'I'll give you a phone and let you know when I've found the photos. In the mean-time if you want me you can contact me on my phone.'

Sally Garden tucked the card away inside the front cover of her notebook and put her completed notes in her breast pocket. 'And the video recording,' she reminded Sarah Radley. 'Could you also get Kara to send through the pictures she took on her phone of the beach.'

Jenner drew up outside Strath-Kind School. The gravel on the drive crunched under her feet as she went to the front door. The heavy outer doors were open and a further set of half glazed doors beyond were closed. A woman in her fifties came in response to her press on the electronic bell. Her greying hair was bright, mixed with dark blond and cut into a short style which gave her the look of being sharp and up to date.

After Jenner made her introductions the woman introduced herself as, 'Headmistress, just call me Headmistress or ma'am.'

'May I have your full name?' asked Jenner. She smiled to herself as she observed the wood panelled interior intermittently decorated with gothic carvings of animals and leaves.

'Of course, you can,' came the rich voiced reply. Jenner had never heard anyone as posh as her. 'Arabella Macfine. My great-grandfather set up the school, hence the Scottish name. I have been headmistress for the past five years and a teacher here for five years before that.'

She was clearly used to answering the obvious questions with little prompting. 'We can talk in my office,' she continued, opening her hand towards the door on the left of the front hall.

Once seated in a deep leather chair she took a glance around the room at the cups and old uniforms and sport strips on display. When Arabella Macfine sat down in her equally luxurious leather chair opposite, Jenner explained, 'You understand that we have found a murdered man on Banksea beach.'

'Yes, can we help in any way.'

'There is a connection with the school we have to investigate,' explained Jenner. 'The grandfather of one of your ex-pupils was the victim. Initially I have to check whether she was here yesterday afternoon.'

'I heard about it on the news last night,' said Arabella Macfine reaching for a list on her coffee table which sat between the two chairs. 'William Cecil Broadgate, so that will be Georgia Lomond.' Without looking at her list and with concern in her voice Arabella said, 'She was here all afternoon as they all were. I was giving a talk on the history of the school. It was from three to four thirty and then we had tea which took about an hour.'

'Did you notice any of them leave during your talk or at tea?'

'No,' said Arabella, offended, 'why would they do that?'

'Do you know what professions the people have who came here yesterday?'

'I have some information, but it will not be up to date. They are not obliged to tell us.' Arabella looked down at her list. 'I've got a group photograph taken at the end of the day. Those that were there at the time took part. Most of the girls will have taken their own photographs.'

'Do you know where we can reach them?' asked Jenner.

'I've got some of their mobile numbers, though I believe a few of them are staying at the Gull Inn. I couldn't tell you which ones.' Arabella Macfine leaned forward. 'Georgia gained a scholarship to come here, Sergeant. Her parents were in Scotland. She never settled as a border, so she stayed with her grandfather.'

'Can you tell me anything about Georgia Lomond?,' asked Jenner, 'you seem to have knowledge of the school from before you came here as a teacher.'

'I have always been here. I grew up with my family in the farmhouse which was part of the school estate,' explained Arabella Macfine. 'I have only recently become headmistress here, about three years ago. Before that I was the swimming coach. I live at the gatehouse now. You can see some of our trophies, Sergeant, about the room. Georgia Lomond was in the school distance swimming team at the time. She was very good. Nice girl too. It's a shame about her grandfather.'

'You must have known him quite well?' Jenner queried.

'In as much as he always turned up to see her swim. That was all.'

'You will send me any more details about the reunion day and the attendees as well as the contact details?' asked Jenner.

'Of course,' said the head mistress. The phone rang and the headmistress answered it. 'I'll email you any information I have, Sergeant.'

'Thank you,' said Jenner, handing her a card with her contact details on.

CHAPTER FIVE

Campbell stood in the shade of the open doorway of the cabin which faced west. He glanced behind him. Tall grass waved on their sandy coloured stems bleached by the sun. Their ripe seeds rattled in their dry cases. The distant sound of a curlew broke the air. A slight breeze came up from the sea and reminded Campbell that it would be hot later. This letter Elizabeth Rattagan reported could be nothing more than a waste of police time. On the other hand, if this letter came from the murderer, he mused, this piece of evidence was vital and to be handled with care.

A slightly built female police officer came up behind him from her car. She introduced herself as, 'PC Grandler,' and added, 'Mary Brown's on her way.'

'Good,' said Campbell. On closer inspection, he observed her long thin features and her dark-cream coloured skin, a shade darker than his own. 'This could be a vital piece of evidence. I would appreciate Dr Brown's forensic steer on this one.' He knocked on the door.

At least, thought Campbell, the early morning meeting had kicked the investigations into action. That was always a relief. Other police officers were collecting Banksea's security camera footage for Friday. Watcher must have visited somewhere where there was a camera.

Elizabeth Rattagan opened the door to Campbell. He confirmed her name and in turn she checked his offered identity. On stepping over the thresh-hold he could see that there was no-one else in the room. PC Grandler turned away with a respectful dip of the head. She headed back to the car to await Mary Brown.

'Have you rented this cabin yourself?' he asked conversationally.

'It's my friend Gwen. She rented it. We're here for the old girl's reunion at Strath-Kind School.' Elizabeth seemed about as calm as he'd expect anyone to be who'd found a strange document apparently planted in their bag. There was an almost imperceptible tremor to her whole body which she was containing quite well. He had, however, to consider the fact that she might be the author of the letter or possibly even Watcher. Forensics might help decide if she was the author of the letter. He looked at her carefully, noting not only her blond curly hair, medium height and a hint of scrawniness about her broad frame, but also a slight stoop in her bearing with defensive folding of her arms across her body. Her feet were slightly pigeon toed as she stood before him, and yet her bearing was curiously pleasant.

He considered whether the most urgent item was to open the letter or whether to find out more about its provenance. Under the circumstances of the recent murder and the receipt of telephone messages of death by Watcher, he thought that opening it should be an urgent option. But the letter had already languished in her bag for twenty-four hours, so in what way could it describe anything imminent? The sender could not possibly know in what time scale it would have been discovered. He opted to find out as much about the letter as he could before he was distracted by its contents.

Elizabeth Rattagan looked tired. Her hair looked bedraggled, but she managed an 'Ah good. I'll get the letter.' She fetched the letter and Campbell opened the bag he'd brought with him and she put it straight inside.

He asked, 'Now, Miss Rattagan, how did you come by this letter? Is it Miss?'

'Yes, Miss is fine. It must have been placed in my bag while I was on the train up here. I took the London train to Banksea Halt on Friday morning, the nine fifteen.'

'What about your friend, Gwen, is it? She's had access to your bag.'

'I spoke to her last night.' Elizabeth looked down and gently shook her head clearly taken back to the previous night. 'She reacted like she'd never seen it in her life before.'

'Did she say she hadn't seen it?'

'Well, no,' replied Elizabeth Rattagan. 'She was a little drunk. We'd been for a night out with some of the girls from the Strath-Kind School. We drove down to the Gull Inn. We walked back,' she added.

'And your bag remained here?'

'Yes.'

'And you were both there all evening?'

'Yes, we were.'

'And the cabin here?'

'Yes. It was all locked up, Inspector. The letter must have been put in on the train on Friday morning when it was on the luggage rack. That was the only time it was beyond my reach.'

'Can you describe who was sitting about you and where you'd placed your bag, Miss Rattagan?'

Elizabeth Rattagan sat on the sofa and reflected a moment rubbing her forehead as if trying to squeeze the information out of her head. 'I found the only seat that wasn't booked: an aisle seat on a table. The window seat opposite was soon taken by a grey-haired man in his fifties. He was wearing a dark trousers and coat and sturdy middle weight black shoes. He flicked a packet of crisps for his journey on the table. He wore a ring set with a diamond: the band wasn't gold, silvery. I remember a small diamond stud glinted in his left ear. Ah no, one in each ear.'

Campbell found Elizabeth Rattagan's recall remarkable.

She closed her eyes. 'When he took off his coat he was wearing a dark plum jumper and a shirt with a red and white collar,' she continued. 'I'm not good at ages but I guess that he might be in his middle fifties, a little younger than my parents would have been. It was already too warm for jumpers, so the diamond studded man removed that as well. He went and put it in his bag, which was next to mine in the luggage rack at the end of the carriage.' She looked up, her gaze searching Campbell for a response.

He obliged with a nod and an interested, 'Continue.'

'The two tables, the one I was at and the one the opposite side of the aisle were the nearest to the luggage rack. And, there wasn't any further seats between the table and the rack.'

'That was very observant. Can you remember the other people around you?'

She nodded. 'An oriental woman sat next to the man with diamond studs. She was opposite me, Inspector,' continued Elizabeth without hesitation. 'She was in her middle forties, I would guess.' Again, Elizabeth closed her eyes as if to bring the picture in her mind and project it on her eyelids.

Campbell had started to draw a diagram noting the seating arrangements. 'Which way were you facing: towards direction of travel or with your back to the direction of travel?'

'Facing direction of travel,' she said.

'And do you remember which carriage you were in?'

'Oh, I don't know. I wasn't in the carriage set aside for quiet, that was for sure, and I wasn't close to the catering car. I was quite near the front of the train because I was going to Banksea Halt and the train divides up before then, so I needed to be in the front four carriages. I think I was in the second carriage. Yes, I noticed that as I got out at Banksea Halt.'

'That will be a real help. You say most of the seats were booked?'

'Yes.' Unprompted, Elizabeth continued with her descriptions as if she couldn't help herself from downloading this burdensome knowledge. 'The Oriental woman: she was very lean with dark shoulder length hair scraped back into a workmanlike pony-tail. She wore a pin-tucked dress, suitable for cocktails or a meal out and well-worn flat comfy shoes all in a business-like black. In her bag, she also carried a tablet device. She asked the man with diamond studded ears if he could move his 'jacket etcetera' from the seat so she might sit down. She spoke without an accent like someone who's always been a UK resident. She had an academic air, studious but confident, business-like. Her legs bowed outwards slightly as she rolled onto the outer edge of her shoes. This was particularly noticeable because of her thinness.'

Elizabeth paused. 'I remember the diamond-studded man moved his coat and she sat down. The Oriental Academic carried a good quality dogs-tooth fabric bag with leather trims and immediately settled to using the email function on her phone swiftly, with both thumbs. She got out at Cambridge. She passed the rack as she got out.' Elizabeth looked up at Campbell. She seemed mildly surprised not to be still on the train.

Campbell thought that she must have visualised herself back into the train and have an almost photographic memory. Despite her unkempt hair and weary face there was a core of intelligent professionalism that was beginning to show in her attitudes and movements.

Elizabeth Rattagan continued. 'The man next to me was a man in his late fifties with a pronounced belly wearing the cotton uniform of a technician. He hummed quietly and took out a newspaper to occupy himself. He sat by the window next to me. Well, the truth is I'd taken his seat to start with and I had to move to the aisle seat. That's when I put my bag on the rack and sat opposite the oriental academic.'

'Were there any movements through the carriage, people walking by the luggage, that sort of thing?' asked Campbell.

Elizabeth nodded. 'We'd been travelling half an hour when a woman came by carrying a baby with a man about the same age as herself. I think they were walking through as they'd been in the catering car or were looking for their booked seats, something like that anyway. She had long hair -- really straight. That silky hair does that. She had it held back in a pony-tail. Oddly enough, later-on, I found out I knew of her. Her sister had been at school with me, Shana Peterson. It was odd because I didn't recognise the girl on the train at all, but Gwen said it was Shana as soon as she saw her at the reunion. Then last night we found out she was her sister. I remember the child coming to school occasionally with her parents to see Shana. She must have been ten years younger than Shana.'

'And her name?' asked Campbell.

'Abigail Pilmer. She's grown up into a very beautiful woman. Italian extract, I believe; auburn hair.'

'And the people on the table opposite?'

'I can't forget them,' It was almost a groan. 'There was this lady with a slightly older baby than Abigail Pilmer's and she had a falling out with a lady in an immaculate suit who was sitting opposite the baby. It looked like a girl. She spilt drink on the Suited Lady. The Suited Lady got off at Cambridge as well. I think there was a man next to the suited lady, but I didn't really see him properly.'

'When they got off did anyone else get on?'

'I don't remember. The carriage was quite quiet after that. I think the man opposite the mother baby with the spilling cup had brown hair. I think he stayed on the train until Banksea Halt. The train split down at Cambridge, that's it: just the front four coaches go through to Banksea Halt. I was beginning to relax by then,' Elizabeth explained. She looked up at Campbell with honest, searching eyes.

'Surely anyone could have got into your bag that went past it?' asked Campbell.

'It was in my line of sight and I was keeping an eye on it. But you are right. It could have been anyone around me.' Elizabeth smiled, relief showing on her face. 'I thought Gwen…'

'Do you remember when the other people got off the train?'

'There were fewer passengers after Cambridge.' She paused. 'The technician got off at Ely. I remember that.'

Campbell was confident he had enough information for Parnold to locate Elizabeth Rattagan on the train. Most of the people in that carriage would have reserved tickets and would be identified through ticket sales, others might take a little longer.

Inevitably the resource for identifying all the passengers who passed the luggage rack would be the security camera footage for the carriage. For those who bought their tickets from machines on platforms and unreserved cash purchased tickets would not be on the system and identifying them would take a bit longer still.

'If you don't mind me saying you have a certain professional air about you,' said Campbell reassuringly to Elizabeth Rattagan.

'I've been in the legal profession,' she replied her face flushing pink under her sun-caught cheeks.

Campbell nodded. That may be something they'd have to explore later just now it was time to deal directly with the letter. Still he had not opened it.

'We will need to take your finger prints and Gwen's for elimination purposes.'

'I haven't touched it. Have I, Lizzie?' complained Gwen entering the living room in her dressing gown. Campbell could see that her bleary eyes were taking in the tableau before her of himself sitting on a dining chair and her friend seated on the sofa. He thought he would let the interaction roll to see what was said.

'Yes, you have. You tweaked it out of my hand last night.'

'Sorry, you're right,' said Gwen. 'But you travelled up from Havensea and went across London on the underground,' insisted Gwen.

'I carried my bag with me all the time,' said Elizabeth. 'I was on the Victoria line from Victoria Station. I was heading towards Kings Cross.'

'And the time?' asked Campbell.

Elizabeth Rattagan turned to Campbell. 'It must have been about 9 am,' she said, paused for a moment. 'But I went into the side pocket in my bag when I got on the train to get out my ticket at Kings Cross. I'd tucked it in there when I got off the train at Victoria. I put the ticket in my handbag instead, which I kept on my lap. The letter wasn't in there then. I didn't go into the side pocket again until last night.'

'So, you might have left the pocket open on the side of your overnight bag when it was on the luggage rack?'

'Oh, yes I did. I remember now. I did it up when I put it in Gwen's car. It stayed in the boot until we came to the cabin.'

'You might not have been personally targeted for this letter,' said Campbell. 'It's possible that anyone travelling to Banksea Halt would do. Did you have a conductor check your ticket and ask you where you were going?'

'Yes, not long after the train had set off, before Cambridge I asked him if I was alright where I was for Banksea Halt,' Elizabeth confirmed.

Campbell could see she understood the connection.

She confirmed this with, 'Every-one nearby would have known where I was going.'

'And,' asked Campbell, 'where were you and Gwendolyn this afternoon?'

'Strath-Kind School, all afternoon,' said Gwendolyn. 'Just ask them. There was some talk on the history of the school. We were all expected to listen to that.'

Elizabeth Rattagan smiled, 'Yes, we were.'

Campbell held the letter in the vinyl glove he kept in his pocket for these occasions. At that point, there was another knock on the door.

'That will be a forensic officer who has come for the letter. Thank you, Miss, Rattagan for coming forward with this.'

Gwendolyn opened the door and Mary Brown came in and placed the plastic bagged letter in a brown paper bag with a grunt and labelled it. She pulled out her sampling case and moved on to take Elizabeth Rattagan's fingerprints.

'Do you think the letter's connected to the death on the beach?' asked Elizabeth Rattagan.

'Which one?' asked Gwendolyn. 'People die of heart attacks on the beach quite often. There could be lots of dead people every day on a beach.'

'Gwen, stop being so silly,' complained Elizabeth.

'Why do you ask that?' asked Campbell. He felt his gaze slightly narrow as he watched Gwen out of the corner of his eye. She seemed spot on about the death of Robert Epsy on Daneton Howe Beach, and he wondered if she had knowledge of it.

'One of the girls at the Gull Inn said about a death on Daneton Howe Beach,' said Gwen. 'She said the police didn't care. I think her name was Harri. Didn't like her much. Plunging neck line short skirt. Too much on display for a girl's night out. Perhaps she had something planned for afterwards. Not my business really.'

'You sound as if you don't know this girl well?' queried Campbell wondering whether this Harri was the same woman as the one he knew as Harriet Epsy from Daneton Howe Beach.

'Certainly not,' agreed Gwen. 'She was one of the old girls. Not our year though, a shade younger. You don't pay much attention to girls not in your year. I think she must've gone to the lunch. We went for the tea, we didn't see her there.'

'How did Harri know about the do at the Gull Inn?'

'I don't know really. She did turn up with that girl, Abigail Pilmer, was Peterson,' Gwen replied. 'You know the girl whose sister was in our year.'

'The one I saw on the train,' said Elizabeth. She looked at Campbell as if it all began to make sense. 'She's the one who walked past me with her baby and a man. He looked a bit younger than her. I didn't see what they did when they went by my bag as the lady in the suit was already making a fuss about her stain.'

'Have you got a contact number for Abigail Pilmer?'

'I haven't,' said Gwen. 'I asked her for it. She got distracted.'

'And may I take your full name and contact details too,' Campbell added.

'Gwendolyn Michelle Hawkesworth-Blythe.' Gwen gave him the phone to show him the number which was displayed. He copied it into his notebook.

Campbell stretched his shoulders. Rocked forwards onto the balls of his feet and thanked the two women for their co-operation. He heard a knock on the cabin door and Elizabeth let in Mary Brown who introduced herself in a friendly but abrupt way.

He was keen to look at the letter out of the way of prying eyes. If he wanted to tell Elizabeth or Gwendolyn anything about it to gauge their reaction, he could do that later.

'And we'll need your bag for forensic examination,' he said to Elizabeth Rattagan.

'You can empty it in the bedroom,' said Gwen.

'No,' said Campbell firmly. 'You must do it here.'

Reluctantly, Elizabeth Rattagan tipped out the contents of her hold-all and passed it to Mary Brown who placed it in an extra-large evidence bag and carefully wrote the details on the label.

Mary Brown invited Campbell into the front seat of her van where she handed him the letter in its bags with her broad strong vinyl gloved hand. At the same time, she placed a cardboard tray on his lap. Her leathery smile was encouraging. 'Let me see the envelope,' she said.

Campbell took out the unopened envelope from the bags as instructed and held it carefully in front of him turning it over in his gloved hands.

'It is made of good quality business paper,' said Campbell feeling the thickness of the envelope. He tapped it on one end to jostle the contents away from where he would open it. Keeping the letter upright to avoid anything falling out of the envelope, he raised his eyebrows at Mary Brown as a signal. She passed him a flat knife.

'Ready,' she said and nodded at him.

He used the knife to slice open the envelope flap and he drew out a folded piece of paper from inside the envelope and laid the envelope on the tray. The paper was lighter than the envelope and the sheet was ruled with horizontal lines and had a jagged edge down one side as if it had been ripped out of a notebook.

'Looks a bit like it's come from a ledger,' said Mary Brown pointing to the red vertical lines marking columns on the page.

'Aye,' agreed Campbell.

Campbell read the letter to himself first. 'It is unsigned and there is no detail in the wording. It may not be from the murderer, Watcher or Messenger Watcher, but it is possible that the author knows something of the murder. It could, of course, be an unrelated hoax.'

'Read it out, see how it sounds,' said Mary with firm direction in her voice.

'"Elizabeth Rattagan is responsible for his death,"' he read.

'Who's death?' asked Mary.

'That I don't know.'

'But the timing is suspicious. What is more, it was clearly meant for Elizabeth Rattagan. We will have to investigate the circumstances thoroughly,' insisted Campbell.

'Was it put in her luggage before William Cecil Broadgate's body was found?' asked Mary.

'Yes,' said Campbell. 'He wasn't found until six in the afternoon. The probability is that it was put in her bag during her train journey in the morning between nine and eleven-thirty.' Campbell placed the letter back into the envelope and the bags. 'You have seen the phone messages from Watcher?'

'I have,' said Mary. 'Watcher signed them both.'

'Watcher has gone silent since the murder of William Cecil,' said Campbell.

Mary Brown squinted at him thoughtfully. 'Campbell, I'll check the paper and the envelope and let you know anything I find. Rather like the cheques of eighteenth century England, a tear is always individual. You should be able to find out which book this page is torn out of.'

'We only have her word for the timing. However, I find her quite a credible person.' Campbell returned the bagged letter and envelope to Mary Brown. He opened the van door and got out awkwardly because he was fishing in his pocket for his phone at the same time.

Mary Brown swung open her driver's door and placed the letter in the evidence box in the back of the van.

'If we find the book the notepaper was taken from….' Campbell suggested the challenge to himself, moving the word "if" about on his tongue as if it was something dangerous. 'And, we'll have to check out all those in the train carriage who travelled with Elizabeth Rattagan. I'll contact Parnold right away.'

He was aware of Mary Brown starting the van engine as he set off to an area some distance beyond Elizabeth and Gwen's cabin, overlooking the bird sanctuary, to make the phone call.

The hands of the mantel clock pointed to eleven. They were stationary. The clock was not working and probably hadn't worked for some time. Parnold looked irritably at his watch. He was working his way through William Cecil Broadgate's bedroom drawers when his mobile phone interrupted his concentration. PC Howard was stationed outside the front door to explain or divert anyone overly interested in their investigations. Occasionally on these occasions a member of the public would turn up with something of interest to say – but not today.

Parnold's phone rang. He stopped to listen to Inspector Campbell telling him about his visit to see Elizabeth Rattagan, her letter and the need to check out the travellers on the London to Banksea Halt train on Friday morning.

'She's given us some good descriptions,' added Inspector Campbell.

'I'll bag up anything I can find here. There doesn't seem to be much about his first wife, just a picture of Georgia and her mother – says so on the back and that's about all. There isn't anything here about his second wife either so perhaps he's cleared all the stuff out when they died. Oddly, he's a man who has cleared out all his history.'

'That's not unusual,' said Inspector Campbell.

'There is a shot-gun,' said Parnold. 'PC Howard is going to deal with that.'

'Right,' said Campbell. 'There should be a gun licence.'

Parnold agreed and ended the call. He thought Inspector Campbell sounded officious. This was rare, but he didn't like his superior when he was in his all-knowing mode. He felt the fine hairs on the back of his neck bristle.

Parnold contacted the rail operators from his phone and asked for their security camera footage from the first four carriages for the duration of the journey including boarding and disembarkation at London, Cambridge, Ely and Banksea Halt.

'Did you want the footage for all the stops, sir?' asked the female voice at the other end.

'Surely,' said Parnold, 'that's all the stops.'

'No, sir. The train stops at Daneton before Banksea Halt.'

'I always go places by car,' said Parnold, mildly annoyed at not knowing about the London train stopping at Daneton. He thought of the small Victorian station at Daneton, with its wrought iron lamps and decorative roof trims. It was only used by the local volunteer run steam train line. He took a last look round William Broadgate's house and left, locking the door behind him.

'Do I need to stay here?' asked PC Howard.

'No, I don't think so,' said Parnold. 'You're taking the shot-gun?'

'Yes,' said PC Howard. 'It's upstairs.'

Parnold handed him the house key.

'I'll deal with that,' said PC Howard.

'Okay,' said Parnold and wondered if he would ever have the authority that Campbell carried so easily. The thought annoyed him. His fist clenched briefly. He shook himself out of it and strode with long energetic strides to his car.

After speaking to Parnold, Campbell chased away thoughts of his mother's flat and the cardboard boxes that Margaret had brought down to him from Scotland. They'd contained random items such as Christmas cards and birthday cards she'd given to him and his brother with Mum and Dad written in the same hand. He'd put them all to the recycle bin.

He stretched his shoulders back and called PC Grandler from the front of Gwendolyn's cabin. 'I have need of your services, Grandler,' he told her. 'I would like you to accompany me, so I can talk to Elizabeth Rattagan and Gwendolyn Blythe separately.'

Gwen Blythe opened the door when he knocked. He arranged for Elizabeth to sit on the sofa and he pulled up a dining room chair from the small table provided for meals in the cabin, so he could observe her reaction to the statement he was about to make. He asked PC Grandler to stay with Gwendolyn Blythe outside. They left together through the front door. Campbell looked around. There was no back door to the premises.

'And?' asked Elizabeth.

'The letter says that Elizabeth Rattagan is responsible for his death,' said Campbell.

Elizabeth almost visibly jumped, her eyes widened, and her jaw dropped. Her pallor became a shade greyer. 'It mentions me by name?' she stammered.

'Yes,' confirmed Campbell. 'So, your bag was not a random choice. Can you tell me what this means, Miss Rattagan?' he asked.

Elizabeth Rattagan shook her head. 'I have no idea at all.'

'Are you sure?'

'Absolutely sure. Who's death?'

'It doesn't say. Can you help us with that one?'

'No, how could I? I haven't killed anyone.'

'Have you had anything to do with William Cecil Broadgate?'

'The dead man? No, nothing.' Elizabeth face was looking increasingly horrified.

'Georgia Lomond?'

'Who's Georgia Lomond?'

'She went to Strath-Kind School.'

'No.'

'Any members of the Lomond or Broadgate family?'

'No.'

'Do you know a Fenella Florris?

'No, why should I?'

'This letter says you are responsible for someone's death? Are you?'

'No, certainly not.'

'This could well be a hoax,' said Campbell. 'Would anyone want to put you in an awkward position?'

'No, of course not. Why would anyone want to do that?' She looked towards the door, outside stood Gwendolyn Blythe with PC Grandler.

'Thank you, Miss Rattagan. I will probably have further questions for you. Campbell stood up and moved the dining chair back to the small table with studied care. 'Good day.'

He left her sitting there as he went outside to find Gwendolyn Blythe. PC Grandler stepped away from Gwendolyn.

'Miss Blythe?' asked Campbell. 'Is it okay to call you by that name?'

'Yes, it is,' said Gwendolyn Blythe. 'But please call me Gwen.'

'What do you know of your friend, Elizabeth? Would you know if anyone would want to harm her, in any way?'

'No, certainly not. Why should anyone want to harm Lizzy?'

'I hoped you could tell me that.'

'We fell out of contact when we left school. We met up really by accident at the reunion. I had this place booked so I asked Lizzy if she wanted to stay. And that's it really.'

'Thank you, Miss Blythe. We may ask you some more questions later. You gave me some of your details earlier. Please give PC Grantly your home address and let us know of any ongoing addresses and contact numbers.' Grantly stepped forward and opened her notebook.

Campbell usually found a certain rhythm to the routine questioning but when it revealed so little it became cloying and he felt as if a band had tightened around his head. He wanted to dismiss the letter but knew he could not. It was addressed to him and it arrived in the middle of a murder investigation. As he walked away he vigorously rubbed his forehead as if trying to make an answer materialise from his brain matter.

.

CHAPTER SIX

DC Garden couldn't get through to Inspector Campbell on the phone. She also tried Sergeants Jenner and Parnold without success. She wasn't sure if she was wasting time by following up the information about the burnt huts, but she would at least be at the scene of the murder of William Cecil Broadgate if she was at Banksea Beach.

Jess Barratt was bent double cleaning out the Banksea Beach kiosk following the scene of crime officers' checks. She was wearing a flowered print sundress and a red tabard. Her two-tone hair was scraped back into a tight pony-tail. She turned around on Garden's cheerful hello. She had a bulldog-about-to-fight expression on her sharp featured face.

'I know Sergeant Jenner has already spoken to you about what happened here on Friday,' said Garden in her best friendly voice. 'Your boss, Sarah Radley told me about the arson attacks on the beach huts here,' she explained after introducing herself.

'They've already been reported to the police,' Jess Barratt replied in a harsh tone. 'I could really do without this,' she added as she continued to scrub a shelf. Garden noticed her accent was local but mildly so.

'I wonder if you could confirm when the huts on this beach were burnt?' asked Garden in a pleasant but firm manner.

'The fire was last Tuesday,' Jess Barratt explained softening her tone slightly. 'It started in the one furthest away. It's the one on the end. The fire seemed to have spread to the next one.'

'That would be just three days before the murder,' observed Garden making a note.

'Why didn't it take more of the huts out?' asked Garden evenly.

'There's a gap between them and the next one in. Water runs through there. Surface water runs down from the caravan site; makes a little stream.'

'Could you show me?' asked Garden.

'You can see them for yourself. They're down to the left. There's just the two.'

'Can you think of any reason why they might have been burnt down?'

'You're the police.'

'Just one other thing. I understand that you know Harriet Epsy?'

'Yes, I do. Why do you want to know?' Garden thought Jess Barratt sounded defensive. The woman continued, 'Oh, I suppose you can't say. I used to work with her at the Gull Inn.'

'Did she go to Strath-Kind school?' asked Garden.

'Yes, but it didn't do her a lot of good.'

'What do you mean?'

'She got a taste for the high life. Her family weren't that well off.' Garden noticed her local tendency to say "were" instead of "was". 'Why they wasted what little they had on that sort of education I'll never know,' continued Jess Barratt. She paused and started rubbing the counter with a cloth. 'Harriet used to live in the flats behind the Gull Inn. I don't know if she's still there.'

Garden jotted that down and asked casually, 'Do you know Bradley Yorkman?'

'He hangs round the beach at Daneton Howe. I sometimes help Sarah down there when Kara's off. Sometimes he comes up here too.'

'Thank you,' said Sally Garden folding her notebook ready to put it away.

'I know where he lives,' offered Jess Barratt. 'He's down at Cricklestaithe. That's half way between Daneton and Banksea. I don't know the exact house, but I expect you could find that out.'

'It would be as easy to get to Banksea as to Daneton from Cricklestaithe if he has a means of transport,' suggested Garden reopening her notebook.

'He's got a trail motorbike he rides round the lanes,' said Jess Barratt.

'Thanks.' Garden stepped away from the kiosk and made a brief note of the information she'd just received.

She walked the way she'd been directed and noticed the scene of crime officers were still at work in William Cecil Broadgate and Georgia Lomond's rented beach hut. A little further on she found the burnt-out beach huts. She had to speak to someone who could make a decision. She tried Campbell again. This time she got through. Once she explained to him what she'd been told he agreed that the burnt-out huts ought to be brought in to the scene of crime investigations.

She thought she could see something lying among the dust and charcoaled timbers. She went to fetch it but somehow it was no longer there. She would have to leave it and let someone from Scene of Crime know.

As far as Jenner was concerned it had been a long morning at Strath-Kind School. It seemed that Georgia and the old girls on the list were at the school all afternoon, so they were out of the picture as far as being William Cecil Broadgate's murderer.

But she was also tasked with finding out about William Cecil Broadgate's second wife, Fenella Florris and her family which meant she had to push herself past her own tiredness. She was used to doing so and had taken some lunch to try and avoid a ragged temper. She hoped it would work as she had to face the dead man's granddaughter, Georgia Lomond. She knocked on the caravan door at Banksea Beach. Georgia opened the door.

'Hello, Miss Lomond,' she said evenly.

'Come in,' said Georgia. Her pale face was gaunt and tired. She showed Sergeant Jenner to the seating at the front of the caravan.

'It is really helpful that you have chosen to stay in the area. Are you on your own though? I understand you declined the company of the liaison officer,' said Jenner more crisply than she intended.

'It was just a waste,' said Georgia matching Jenner's tone. 'I don't need company for company's sake. I am hoping to organise Grandpa Will's funeral before I head home. I've spoken to my mother about it, my father is ill.'

'We have also spoken to your mother. And, she said she couldn't get away and she asked us to liaise with you over releasing his body.'

Georgia sighed. 'Aye,' she said.

'We need to know more about your Grandfather's family,' said Jenner bringing her tone down to something which was a little friendlier. 'Did Fenella Florris have any children that might have been put out by what happened to their mother?'

'I told your Inspector Campbell I didn't know. Nothing untoward happened to Fenella. Nothing illegal,' said Georgia defensively. 'She died. In hospital in the end. Grandpa Will didn't murder her. She trapped him in the bathroom for days. It was Grandpa who was frightened.'

'Didn't you say Fenella Florris needed to take medication?'

'Yes. She had a mental illness.'

'What happened with her medicine around the time your grandfather was attacked?'

'That was why it happened,' explained Georgia. 'She was crazy because she hadn't been taking her medication. When my Grandfather was eventually released she was visited by the health visitor who made her take her medicine. She took a reaction to it and died, just like I told Inspector Campbell.'

'We need to have her children's names and addresses and anything you might know about her previous history,' insisted Jenner.

'Her first husband's dead.' Georgia gave Jenner a sideways look. 'I know that. I don't know the children's names. I think they live abroad. I really didn't have much to do with her or her family. I didn't go to her funeral I was away working overseas at the time.'

'So, you don't have first-hand experience of the history between your grandfather and his second wife.' Jenner frowned. 'Were you jealous of her?'

'Certainly not. I was giving them space and getting on with my own life.' Her face was crimson and her tone suddenly angry.

Jenner put her notebook away, thanked Georgia and hoped Parnold had turned up something useful at William Cecil Broadgate's house. His phone had switched to answer messages on the couple of times she'd tried to phone him.

As soon as she left the caravan she relaxed her face allowing her frustration to show. Once out of view of the caravan windows she gave her body a little shake and looked forward to a long mind mending swim later in the evening.

A bright, 'Hello,' pulled her out of her mood. It was unmistakably Garden.

Jenner smiled.

'You look shattered,' said Garden with mild concern. 'I couldn't get hold of anybody, so I took it upon myself to visit Jess Barratt at the kiosk. I know you have already spoken to her but my interview with Sarah Radley sent me in this direction.'

'That's fine. I've just been to see Georgia Lomond,' said Jenner. 'We'll report back to Inspector Campbell at the office and hopefully that will be it for today.'

'What are you going to do after work?'

'I'm going to go for a swim at Cricklestaithe Bay.'

'Why there?' asked Garden frowning.

'Why not? I don't fancy Daneton or Banksea under the circumstances and Cricklestaithe isn't too far away.'

'I wouldn't mind coming and rinsing off the day in the sea.'

'That'll be great? See you back at the station and we'll have a better idea of timing then.'

'I need to pick up a swimsuit. I haven't brought one with me.'

'They've got a sale on in that lingerie shop in Banksea town centre.'

'Thanks. I'll try there.'

Garden parked her car next to Jenner's in the car park at the top of the cliff and changed in the back seat of her car into her swimsuit and tracksuit. She soaked up the view. On both sides of her were cliffs curling round both sides of the bay. Some broken timbers and dumped rocks protected the cliff in places. The cliff was not orange rock like the one at Daneton. This was made of soft red earth. Each winter more of it peeled away. Its very softness made it impossible to climb. The sea at high tide often scrubbed away at it. Some lumps of imported stone were now guarding its base. Jenner got out and joined her. Garden was pleased that she'd agreed to join Jenner at Cricklestaithe Bay. The dark waters of the North Sea invitingly reflected the evening sun.

They took the steep concrete steps which led down to the beach. Garden slid her right hand along the metal hand rail as she went down. Her feet landed on sand still damp from the retreating tide.

Jenner pulled off her tracksuit. She had her swimming costume on underneath. Garden too pulled off her tracksuit and they waded a few feet out into the water.

Garden squealed with surprise as the cold waves lapped about her legs.

I see you got sorted out with a costume,' said Jenner.

'Yes, just the job.'

'Have you been swimming here before,' asked Jenner.

'I haven't. Daneton is closer for me. The beach there is shallow. I've been here before -- the footing drops away. The water's deep quite suddenly.'

'I'm going to swim out past the groins and stay parallel to the beach. You okay with that?'

'Yes, that's fine. I'll come with you. I'm quite a good swimmer.'

'Right,' said Jenner and she dived forward in the water and kicked off into deeper water, her lean arms wheeling above her head as she front-crawled away into the waves. Garden followed.

Garden felt the water cold on her chin and salty on her lips. She peered into the green water. She could not see through it. She swam in the sea regularly in the summer, but she was tired. She knew she had to swim to escape the workday that hung about her even though she'd left work. She breasted a wave as she struck out with her first stroke. She found she was a different sort of swimmer to Bridget Jenner. Jenner was gliding away with a sleek front crawl while she was making progress with a steady breast stroke. She found she was already some distance behind her work colleague.

She stopped to tread water while Jenner continued to power through to the end of the bay. Garden thought she saw another swimmer in the water close to Jenner. This other swimmer was heading towards Jenner from the opposite direction with head down and arms wheeling at a tremendous rate. They were going to collide. Sally Garden shouted. Jenner disappeared under the water. Garden couldn't see what had happened for a moment. Arms and heads reappeared. One set headed away, the other set belonged to Jenner. She turned towards Garden and waved before swimming back towards her. Garden sighed with relief.

'See that?' asked Jenner, treading water.

'Yes,' said Garden. 'That idiot just cleared off.'

'No apology -- crashed straight in to me.'

'You'd think there was enough sea for everybody'

'Oh well, at least it wasn't a jet ski,' said Jenner.

'Hot chocolate?' suggested Garden.

Jenner nodded in agreement and they swam to shore. As they dried Garden asked, 'Was it male or female?'

'The swimmer?'

Garden nodded.

'I couldn't tell. That idiot wacked me with an arm and was gone.'

The tide was coming in and the beach was disappearing between the groins. They walked along the thin strip of damp sand that connected the end of the beach where they had left their clothes on a piece of concrete close to the steps.

Back at the top of the cliff Garden retrieved from the car a flask of hot chocolate she'd made at the Horseton Police Station. Bridget Jenner and Sally Garden sat and looked across at the vast expanse of the North Sea before them and sipped the drink out of plastic flask cups.

Campbell sat in the cupboard at the back of the cottage. It was almost big enough to be a room, at one time it would have been a wash house and coal house, but the cottage had been extended into the building. He'd promised to look through the items Margaret had brought down from his mother's flat when she'd moved into a residential home. Everything of his childhood was gone from the tenement and the place had been re-let by the landlord.

He felt tiredness overwhelm him. He lay on the concrete floor and pulled a patchwork blanket from under an old sideboard that was pushed against the end wall. He rolled himself up in it and went to sleep. It was warm and comforting in the same way it had been as a boy. He could almost hear his mother screaming and throwing knives and forks at his father followed by pots and pans and kitchen chairs.

He woke in the night and looked at the box with his mother's diaries and her photographs. He thought about opening it and then he thought about burning it without looking inside, then he rolled himself back up in the blanket and went back to sleep.

At Horseton Police Station Campbell drank his third mug of tea of the morning and stood up to give the briefing. 'This is the morning meeting of the second day of the investigation into the murder of William Cecil Broadgate,' he said.

He invited Jenner to tell the others what she had found out at the Strath-Kind School. Jenner stood up where she was and after she gave a quick round up of the old girls gathering and the information offered by the school, Campbell nodded. 'Good,' he said, 'that confirms Georgia Lomond's alibi and it also gives those that attended the history talk an alibi for the afternoon.' He moved on inviting his other sergeant to fill in the group on his findings with, 'And Parnold.'

Parnold stood up and walked to the front of the group. His height made him readily visible. 'We obtained very little from William Cecil Broadgate's house. The only pictures are the ones you see before you of Georgia Lomond and her mother, William Cecil's daughter. A real lack of information. We found a few other papers and collected a shot gun and that was all.' Campbell noted that Parnold spoke with his usual clear strong voice although, his local accent had lost some of its purity since his secondment to the Met. London accents were so easily picked up.

'The lack of Information is information in itself,' said Campbell.

Parnold looked annoyed at the interruption but nodded in agreement. 'However, after the letter in Elizabeth Rattagan's luggage was discovered,' continued Parnold. 'I started to check those who travelled up with her on the train.'

'It is just a possibility that one of them put the letter in her bag,' said Campbell, 'but we just cannot ignore this especially as the train stopped at Cambridge from where our Watcher phone messages were sent. Of course, Elizabeth Rattagan might have made the letter herself or put it in there herself. But somehow, I believe her, and the handwriting will be checked.' Campbell rocked onto the balls of his feet.

'Yesterday evening I managed,' continued Parnold, 'to view some of the security camera footage for the second carriage of Friday's nine fifteen am train from London to Banksea Halt. That's why I haven't been answering my phone. I've certainly not managed to see it all as well as the fact that the camera over the luggage rack was out of action. The fault had come up on the guard's screen. He considered it a minor problem as the area was partially covered by the camera further down the coach, which gives us the movements of the occupants, and the cameras at each of the exit doors, which give us identifiable images of the people as they get out. Apparently faults on security cameras are not uncommon.'

Campbell was impressed with Parnold's professional stance. He was no longer summing up the attractiveness of the women in the room while speaking. Perhaps, at last he had made a suitable attachment, Campbell wondered.

Parnold continued, 'Because of this, what we can't see is if anyone actually interfered with the luggage. I will have to check through every individual's movements to work out the possibilities. I haven't had time for that yet. I'll be having a go at that this morning.

Campbell nodded in agreement.

'Following the detailed descriptions, we were given by Elizabeth Rattagan, she and those travelling about her were readily recognisable. Their carriage was the second one from the front. So very few people walked through the carriage: only the mother, baby and her male companion, as described to Inspector Campbell by Elizabeth Rattagan. I located them in the front carriage sitting about half way up. After that pass through the carriage they stayed in the front carriage until Banksea Halt when they came back in and exited by the door next to the luggage rack.'

'Do we know why they did that?' asked Campbell.

'No, I'll have another look at that too.'

'Interestingly, Elizabeth only put her bag on the rack after the technician sat down next to her and he requested its removal from his seat.

So, was there an opportunity for the letter to enter her bag at that point?'

'I don't think so. I didn't see anything odd happen around the bag at that time. The bag was in full view of the carriage camera.'

Parnold made a finalising gesture with his arm and said, 'The rail operators are getting the names of all these people through ticket purchases and seat bookings.'

At that moment, the clerk, Lindy Greyling came in waving a piece of paper. 'From the rail people.' She was flushed with excitement.

'Thank you, Lindy,' said Campbell

She handed the list to Parnold. He looked down at it and said, 'The railways have come up with the names already.'

After a couple of moments, he started in a slow, meticulous way to give out the names of the passengers described by Elizabeth Rattagan, while Jenner marked them on the board.

'The "Technician" sitting by the window, next to Elizabeth Rattagan is Graham Aspen.'

Campbell passed him a pen so Parnold could mark the names up in their positions on the board to replace the alphabet letters marked against each person.

'The man with the studs sitting opposite to Graham Aspen, the "Technician", is Herbert Brandon.'

'Opposite Elizabeth Rattagan is her "Oriental Academic", Hye Woang.'

'The lady in the stained suit is Anne Crowlie, And, she is on the table on the other side of the aisle to Elizabeth Rattagan. Anne Crowlie is sitting opposite one of two seats booked by Louise Green. Presumably, baby Green is sitting on one.'

Garden put her hand up and said, 'Oddly enough the lingerie shop in Banksea belongs to Paula Green. I met her daughter Louise who was serving in there yesterday when I called in.' Garden reddened. 'We were just chatting. I didn't know that she was one of the people that was in Elizabeth Rattagan's carriage.'

Campbell acknowledged this snippet of information with a nod.

'Do we have pictures of these people from the door cameras?' asked Campbell.

'Still sorting them,' said Parnold.

'Can you go back and see her, DC Garden, and ask her about her day on and off the train?' asked Campbell.

'Yes, certainly.'

Parnold looked back down at the list of passengers. 'And the brown-haired man sitting opposite Louise Green is Sean Foragehall,' he added.

'The train took nearly two and a half hours to make the journey from London. I did an initial scan, so I could get the identities from the railway and banks. These names only came through quickly as they'd all booked seats.'

'And have they confirmed the name of the other group who settled in the first carriage?' asked Campbell.

'Yes, they were as Elizabeth Rattagan thought, Pilmer and Peterson.'

Campbell got up and thanked Adam Parnold. 'This fills in the detail very nicely. Do we know where these people alighted?'

'Some,' said Parnold with controlled evenness.

'Elizabeth Rattagan seems to have been fairly accurate,' said Campbell.

'Hye Woang with the lap top and tablet, Anne Crowlie with the suit got off at Cambridge. Graham Aspen, the technician, alighted at Ely as did Herbert Brandon with the ear studs, but Sean Foragehall got off at Daneton not Banksea Halt,' confirmed Parnold. 'Louise Green, Ralph Peterson and Abigail Pilmer got off at Banksea Halt.'

'Daneton,' said Campbell remembering his twisting road journey around the coast on Friday. Some places are just easier to get to by train than any other means of transport, he decided. He turned to the team arrayed before him.

'You all perhaps know that the letter I received yesterday was addressed to me.' He pointed to a copy of it pinned to the board. There were nods of agreement.

'It is being checked by forensics. I'm not holding out much hope regarding getting anything from that. However, I do think that we must pursue it. The letter appears to have been delivered prior to the murder of William Cecil Broadgate. It includes reference to a death which the writer says that Elizabeth Rattagan is responsible for. It says nothing about the victim or who the victim is or might be or how the victim met his end. It is not signed by Watcher. Never the less, it seems more than coincidence that this should turn up in the middle of a murder investigation. I conclude that we need to check-out the people from the train to see if any of them could have put the note in the bag.'

'We don't really know enough about Elizabeth Rattagan,' said Jenner.

'I agree,' said Campbell. 'Jenner, see what you can find out about her. We do need to talk to Elizabeth again. Despite what she has told us there must be something in her life to have triggered such a letter. To that end I will return and talk to her.'

Jenner nodded in acceptance of the task, and said, 'I did go back to see Georgia Lomond about her grandfather's second wife Fenella Florris. She said her children lived abroad and she didn't have much time for her grandfather, William Cecil, and his new wife.'

'Right. That could put the Florris children out of the picture. We need to confirm this with the local authorities where they live. Did she have any addresses for them?' Campbell stretched his elbow thoughtfully.

'No, she didn't. I'll look-into it and see what I can find,' said Jenner.

'Good. Superintendent Tarnish will liaise with any foreign authorities.' Campbell turned towards Garden. 'Now, DC Garden, the burnt beach huts.' He nodded at her.

'Bradley Yorkman,' she said. 'Is a local lad who spends a lot of time on the Daneton Howe and Banksea beaches. Jess Barratt has pointed the finger at him for recent beach hut fires.'

'Check what the fire officer has to say,' said Campbell. 'Scene of crime officers are still checking the incident site at Banksea Beach and have extended their search to the beach huts following your information. They have not found anything they can give us yet, but I hold out some hope there. Garden, have a look-into this Bradley Yorkman. There's no need to visit him just yet.'

Garden nodded.

'The crime of scene officers keep on complaining about the sand,' said Jenner. 'The wind and tide keep shifting it.'

Campbell said thoughtfully, 'That could well give rise to an issue. I will speak to Professor Mary Brown. She is now acting as Scene of Crime manager as well as co-ordinating the forensic team in the lab. In the mean-time if you see anything bag it and tag it, don't wait for sand and tide to take it away.' He turned to the board.

'So, Garden, you are starting by visiting Louise Green,' confirmed Campbell, 'and we will split up the other individuals from the train and visit them as soon as possible. Do we have their addresses?'

'Nothing on that from the banks yet. That information shouldn't take long for them to pull together,' said Parnold.

'We might find locally those who were travelling to Strath-Kind School,' said Campbell. 'Mother and Baby Pilmer and Ralph Peterson we know were on the train,' said Campbell. 'Abigail Pilmer, we know went to the school for the old-girls' day.'

Jenner said, 'When I spoke to the head mistress at Strath-Kind she thought some of the girls were staying at the Gull Inn. They have some converted barns. We could try the Pilmers there.'

Garden added, 'The Gull Inn. Harriet Epsy used to work there. Jess Barratt – the woman at Banksea Beach kiosk, knows her. She told me. They worked together there a few years back. She thought Harriet lived in flats behind the Gull Inn at the time.'

'Ah yes,' said Campbell. 'I'll call in there. Also, once we have the addresses, Parnold can you also contact our colleagues in other local police areas as we may be tress-passing on their jurisdiction because these folk from the train could be from all over?' Campbell paused and looked at the incident board. 'I'll wait to talk with Elizabeth Rattagan until Jenner has done her checks on her. In the mean-time I'll go on to the Gull Inn and see if the Pilmers are staying there.'

Campbell stretched his neck. 'Jenner, can you also find out more about William Cecil Broadgate and his first wife. He has got to remain central to our investigations.' He scrutinised the team. 'I shall just go on my own to the Gull Inn. We are thin enough on the ground as it is.'

CHAPTER SEVEN

The morning sun was bright as it bounced off the water. Elizabeth Rattagan sat on Banksea Harbour watching the boats moored for use in the gently moving sea and listened to the gentle clinks of cables on yacht masts. She needed time to think about the letter. She turned and squinted up as Gwen sat quietly down next to her.

Elizabeth felt disappointment at seeing her. She wasn't disappointed with her being there, she was expected, she would have found her eventually. She realised she was disappointed with their friendship. When she'd seen her draw up in her smart sports car on the school drive she'd been thrilled to see her. All the strength of close friendship had flowed around her, creating a warmth she couldn't remember the last time she'd felt. She had wanted support, but Gwen had been bright and distant, not as approachable as she had remembered her. Her doubts had grown with Gwen's behaviour at the Gull Inn. Gwen had spoken to everyone all pleasant and polite only to talk about them almost immediately using insulting terms when they could not hear.

'Why did you say such dreadful things about the old girls?' said Elizabeth after a cursory nod.

'What do you mean?'

'Before we even left the Gull Inn...'

'Shall we just go for a swim?' interrupted Gwen.

'Gwen!' demanded Elizabeth.

'I was just a bit drunk,' confessed Gwen.

'Did you put that letter in my bag, Gwen?'

'No. Of course I didn't. You put your bag in the boot of my car. I didn't touch it.'

Elizabeth agreed by turning away. The way she felt right now she could easily lose her only remaining friend, so she stopped herself from saying any more. At least her fitness was returning with each swim. Perhaps an improvement in her temper would follow. 'Yes, let's go for a swim,' she said.

'We could just collect the swimsuits from the cabin. I brought the car down.' Gwen said cheerfully.

'Just as well you brought two costumes as I've ended up borrowing off you.'

'This dry weather dries them off quickly. I brought two in case the weather was wet,' replied Gwen.

Elizabeth was pleased to return to a friendly atmosphere. She let her doubts about Gwen recede. Hopefully Inspector Campbell was right, and the letter was a hoax.

Elizabeth Rattagan was not answering her phone. Campbell thought she might have turned it off. He considered that he would probably do the same in the circumstances. So, Campbell thought he would try Harriet Epsy's number. He was already standing outside the rear of The Gull Inn and looking across at the flats where Jess Barratt had said she thought Harriet used to live. Her name nor her address had appeared on the list provided by the school of old girls' day attendees, so he used the number she'd used when she'd phoned the emergency call centre. Garden had checked Harriet's name had not come up for the flats or anywhere in Banksea or Daneton. He tried the mobile number several times. It did not respond. The number wasn't connecting at all. He put his phone away and entered the rear door of the Gull Inn.

Campbell was mesmerised by the scented atmosphere. He had chosen to take on this visit to the Gull Inn because this place contained memories of work that filled him with a sense of a job well done. He pushed his way around the chairs. The carpet was dark red. Several shades greyer than it had been from new. Dusty shelves displayed malt whiskeys. Cobwebs clung around the necks of wine bottles. A beautiful soft voice meandered through the heavy air from the furthest part of the room. Singing a popular song, often heard on the wireless, the singer had turned it into a ballad. It soothed his thoughts almost to extinction. He followed the curve of the bar dodging stools. He noted that the seating around the edge of the room was provided by backed benching, padded and covered in matching dark red plastic imitation leather.

And there spread across the bench at the furthest corner from the door was a woman. She looked to be of average height sitting as she was with her feet hidden behind one of the dark brown tables. Her width, however, covered enough space for three people.

The large woman stopped singing and stared at Campbell through the subdued light.

'Can I help you? ' she asked, a touch of suspicion in her voice.

'Inspector Campbell.'

'Oh, so it is,' exclaimed the large woman breaking out into a broad smile.

'I'm looking to talk to your visitors, Barbs: the ones that are staying in your barn.'

Campbell looked out of the etched glass windows. It was impossible to see anything distinctly through them. 'Barbs, is anyone about?' he enquired.

'No, just me, you lanky old beggar,' she said in a friendly tone.

Campbell inwardly chuckled but his face barely flickered at Barbara's greeting delivered in a broad sing song North Norfolk accent. 'Now Barbs, I'm not here about anything to do with how you run your business,' he reassured her.

'I should hope not,' said Barbs. 'Everything's above board now that I've got rid of that evil old man of mine. Glad you locked him up.'

'That was a while ago now,' said Campbell. 'I've come about another matter.'

'Okay,' said Barbs.

'Have you got anyone staying in your barn?'

'It's divided into four units. They are all taken. Who did you want?' Barbs unravelled herself from the bench and went over to the bar. She drew out a book from underneath the corner of the bar and licked her middle finger before flicking through the pages of the register with a studious expression on her face. She opened a page and passed it over to him.

'Thanks, Barbs,' said Campbell. 'I'll take all the names, if you don't mind?'

'Anything for you, Inspector. Putting that evil bastard away saved my life.'

'He'll be out in a few years, Barbs, you're going to have to be ready for him.'

'We all have people like that in our lives,' replied Barbs. 'He'll probably be after you as well.'

Campbell looked down at the list he'd been given. 'What time do the Pilmers generally get back.'

'I've got them coming back for tea today. Fish and chips if you fancy it?' She raised a questioning eyebrow.

'I'll just take their phone numbers and addresses.' Barbs took the book and photocopied the page in the small office tucked away by the kitchen. He could just see her from where he stood by the bar. She returned and passed it to him.

'And, I have a picture of a woman I am interested in talking to.' Campbell pulled out the photo from his pocket. 'I've been led to believe she worked here a while ago.'

She took the photograph and tilted it to catch the muted light from the window. 'The photo is taken at a funny angle. It could be a girl who used to work in here. She called herself Marie Claire. Black hair – looked dyed to me. She must have been in her early twenties at the time. She never said she came from Daneton. She said she came from Norwich. She didn't sound local, just a bit posh.'

'Did you ask her for any identification?'

Barbs looked at him and tutted.

Campbell took that as a no. 'Have you seen her since?'

'No, Inspector.'

'Will you let me know if you see her?'

'Why would that be?'

'I understand she lives nearby. She may be using a different name. Possibly Harriet Epsy.'

'Harriet Epsy was in last night,' said Barbs suddenly. 'I didn't connect the name with that photograph or Marie Clare. She'd organised the evening get together for the old girls from Strath-Kind School. I didn't recognise her. She was wearing one of those obviously false pink wigs. Some people don't seem to need much of an excuse to dress up.' She sucked her lips. 'Skimpy black dress as I recall. She's put on weight since Marie Clare days. The others were not dressed up in that way. It was almost as if she'd come to the wrong party.'

'Perhaps it was because she didn't want you to recognise her. Did you recognise her voice?'

'She booked on line. She never spoke to me directly.' Barbs frowned. 'Is this what this is about? Is it to do with that murder on the beach. You can't suspect the girls from Strath-Kind!' She looked at Campbell clearly searching for an answer. When she saw she wasn't going to get one she said, 'The Pilmer girl is the only one from Strath-Kind staying in the barn.'

'I didn't mention anything about the murder. Do not say anything about our chat, Barbs. If you see Harriet Epsy just let me know.'

'I can do better than that. I've got her information from the booking.'

Barbs pulled out a different register and copied a phone number on to a bar mat. 'Should I be scared of her?' she asked.

'Don't you go messing with her,' said Campbell, adopting a popular local phrase.

'Is she dangerous?'

'You know her better than I do,' said Campbell. 'What was she like when she worked for you?'

'Clearly, she was a liar: she was using a different name,' said Barbs putting her registers back behind the bar. She stopped looking at him and she half turned away, so he could not see her face.

'It's not just the name. You are holding out on me. Tell me what was going on, off the record.'

Barbs slithered around the front of the bar and nodded agreement to Campbell's proposition. 'I didn't like the way Marie Clare, Harriet, did her work. To be honest we didn't get on. She wanted to run this place as if it was her own business. I wasn't having it. I'd just got rid of my crooked old man thanks to you. She didn't understand that this is my business. I'm not having that kind of carry on here. I run a clean ship, Inspector, you know that. If you get my meaning?'

'I think I do.'

'She was selling counterfeit cigarettes and alcohol from under the bar on my days off. I had to let her go.' Barbs sighed with obvious relief at sharing the burden of her knowledge without any risk of prosecution to herself.

Campbell took the beer mat. 'Thanks Barbs.' He tapped it on the bar and stretched his neck. It was the same number as the one he had already tried.

CHAPTER EIGHT

Elizabeth and Gwen had wanted to take the footpath to the beach, but it was still closed by the police for their investigations. So, they walked along the marshland known locally as the Mere and with little conversation reached a tea room in a small flint barn situated against the road. They chose cakes and tea.

Elizabeth was burning with the desire to share the burden of the troubles that had happened so recently to her. She had to explain herself to someone, to make some sense of it. To talk it out may just help solve the problem. 'When we were at school, Gwen, my father had spoken to your father who was a lawyer. Your father thought it was a wonderful job and thought it would be a good career for me.'

'Oh,' said Gwen. 'My dad became ill quite early in his life. He passed away not long after I left school. He blamed his job, Lizzy.'

'I didn't know that.'

'You and I lost touch immediately after leaving school. We had our whole lives to grab.'

'So, what did you do, Gwen?'

'This and that,' said Gwen plunging her fork into her lemon meringue pie. 'You need to tell me what's going on, Lizzy. You really seem to be in trouble. I might be able to help.'

Elizabeth ignored her, using the moment to eat her cream and jam scone, carefully applying the cream to the small mountain of jam. 'I thought you might be dead when I was travelling up on the train.' Elizabeth looked earnestly at her friend.

'Why's that?' said Gwen. Elizabeth thought Gwen wasn't really listening to her.

'I saw your name in the will listing.'

'I haven't got any money, Lizzy. That's why I'm trying to get these women to invest.'

'Is that why you said those nasty things about the girls at the Gull

Inn?'

'They were not interested in investing, Lizzy.'

'You're not dead,' said Elizabeth going back to the subject of the newspaper.

'I certainly am not.'

'The person in the paper, she could be a relative?'

'What woman in the paper?'

'This woman with the same name as yours.'

'My grandmother has the same name.'

'Have you been in touch with her lately?'

'She's ancient. She's in a residential home due to her very great age.'

'Where?'

'East Sussex. I haven't been there for years.'

'I don't want to be the bearer of bad news, but I think she might well have passed away. Can you get internet here?'

'No signal,' said Gwen. 'We'll look it up later. I might not need investors after all!'

'Are you not sad?'

'Not yet. I'll wait till it's confirmed. So why, Lizzy, strong dependable Lizzy, are you in such a muddle?'

'Have you finished your cake?' asked Elizabeth. This time she didn't even feel angry at Gwen's question. Even though she wanted to share her burden there was only a limited amount she was prepared to tell her. Gwen nodded and reached for her purse.

'How are your funds then?'

'Getting low, Lizzy. But we're alright for now. After what you've just said, this lack of funds might only be temporary anyway.' Gwen paid, and they left the cool stone cafe behind and walked along the edge of the mere. The heat was beating down on the reed beds which seemed to throb with heat around them.

'I knew something was wrong when my boss Bernard challenged my procedures. He's always considered my actions and decisions to be very professional. My procedures are rock solid – always by the book. It was as if it wasn't Bernard speaking but someone else inside his skin. At the time, I was just upset. I had a think about it and told myself to get over it. Went out and bought a frock in the sales. I felt much better after that.'

Gwen laughed until she saw Elisabeth shaking her head.

'After that everything I said was wrong. Whenever I needed a colleague to back me up they did the opposite and eventually they stopped talking to me. It was very unpleasant. But I kept my head down and got on with the job. Work is not primarily a social club.'

'Oh Lizzy, I know how you feel.'

'No, you don't,' snapped Elizabeth.

'Okay I don't.'

Elizabeth frowned at her. 'Then I started being loaded with other people's work. I was working on an important case and I kept being given other priorities. I ended up getting three warnings and then I was dismissed.'

'Whatever for?'

'I lost my temper and threw some furniture about.'

'I'm sure you could get help towards a case for unfair or constructive dismissal.'

'I know it's a battle I will have to undertake. But at least I didn't die in a car accident like a colleague of mine.'

Gwen looked up startled. 'My boss …' Gwen paused. 'There's stuff you're not telling me. You're a lawyer tell me what was going on.'

'I can't talk about it.'

'Why not?'

'It's ex-judiciary.'

'To do with a case you were on?'

'Yes, it's waiting to go to court, so no-one can talk about it.'

'Which case were you working on?'

Elizabeth looked away as if someone had slapped her in the face.

'Have you been to the police?' asked Gwen.

Elizabeth thought Gwen had a strange wily look on her face, 'I dare not,' she said. 'What is it, Gwen?'

'I understand,' said Gwen. 'I have had a similar experience.'

'What do you mean?' Elizabeth frowned.

'The case you are talking about is the Dungrade case.'

Elizabeth's frown deepened.

'Lizzy, the Dungrade case has been dropped,' said Gwen.

'How do you know that?' Elizabeth's suspicions were starting to prickle at her again.

'I know someone in the office where you worked,' Gwen explained.

Elizabeth narrowed her eyes. 'Who do you know there?'

'It doesn't matter.'

'Yes, it does. I've been sacked on trumped up charges. How can I trust you now?'

'You have to believe me,' said Gwen. 'I know this man, Dungrade. I know what he's done, and it is more than your case.'

'Why are you involved?' Elizabeth felt hurt and angry. Would she never escape this tangle of deceptions? she wondered.

'Dungrade was a solicitor, he controlled people's lives. He advised my father to make him executor of his will. My mother ended up having to fight to get her own money back. She didn't get it all.' Gwen was breathless.

Elizabeth was beginning to realise that Gwen's situation was like her own, but more personal. Gwen's family had clearly been one of the Dungrade network's early victims. 'We didn't have any evidence from your family,' she said.

'There was no evidence to be had. His office got burnt down in the days of paper records, Lizzy. But you know he didn't stop. He grew tentacles, his network grew.' Gwen continued, 'All we had was evidence of low level stuff. The person I was involved in prosecuting was a lawyer in my area. He was almost struck off for stealing money from old ladies' wills. I believe he was connected to Dungrade. He jumped in to working for the local council and the investigation was never completed. What exactly was Dungrade being prosecuted for down your way?'

'Again, nothing terrible, embezzlement. He had got hold of people's money. It was a club. The local council had given them money for renovating the old buildings. The money disappeared-from-view for about ten years. The council made no effort to retrieve the money. It was eventually investigated by the police after a complaint was made by a member of the club. The complaining member of the club died in a road accident and the money reappeared magically. The treasurer for that time was a solicitor. He also worked for the local district council.'

'And?' asked Gwen.

'Dungrade seemed to have connections with him through investment companies,' said Elizabeth. 'I suspected this involvement was only the tip of the iceberg. There were rumours that other donations may have gone astray. This man helped-out with the book keeping at several places.' Elizabeth stopped for a moment and caught her breath. 'Dungrade was working for a lot of criminal clients. Yet I felt they were really working for him from the stories we were hearing. But we had no hard evidence.' Elizabeth stopped and stared at Gwen. 'So, you setting up a business and looking for investment is happening because you've been pushed out of your job?'

'Yes, strange how our experiences are so similar.'

'I fear my contact with you may have brought Dungrade to your door,' said Elizabeth.

'They know me as Madeline Franklyn, not Gwendolyn Blythe. Dungrade and his colleagues will not spot me. But I'm sure that they pursue you still.'

'You mean the letter in my bag to that Inspector Campbell?'

'Yes,' agreed Gwen. 'How easy has it been for someone to put you in an awkward situation with the police.'

'Why me and not you?'

'As well as having two names I only have suspicions, you have some evidence. They think they've dealt with me. As far as Dungrade is concerned I've disappeared off the map.'

'So, you came to the old girls' day to find me?'

'Yes, I did. I got you to come.'

'The messages about the old girls' day came from you?'

'Yes, through the girl in the office I knew.'

Elizabeth grabbed Gwen's forearms. 'Thank you, Gwen. Thank you so much.' Relief rushed through her.

'Don't thank me yet,' said Gwen.

Campbell tried Elizabeth Rattagan's phone number again. Jenner was still checking her back history, but he felt he had too many questions for her not to speak to her as soon as possible. The phone went straight through to answer message. He was just returning his phone to his pocket when Parnold came up to him at his desk.

'I've checked the footage from the carriage,' said Parnold. 'I've made a list of any one who stood by the luggage rack for long enough to interfere with Elizabeth's bag. That's all of those around Elizabeth and the couple who walked through with the baby, Ralph Peterson and Abigail Pilmer. The others, because, perhaps, of the way the train positions itself on the platform, walked towards the back doors of the carriage. Fortunately, we now have the names and addresses of these people from the card purchases of their tickets. Their details have been forwarded to their local police offices.'

'Good,' said Campbell. 'Whose first on the list of those that overlap with other people in the investigation and/or have an interest in the area?' he asked Parnold.

'I've got the address for Sean Foragehall. The camera footage showed him getting on the train in London and off at Daneton,' said Parnold. He sat on the table across the aisle from Elizabeth Rattagan and he sat opposite the mother and baby who spilt the drink and next to the woman in the suite, Anne Crowlie.'

'Anne Crowlie got off at Cambridge.'

'Yes, that's right.'

Campbell had stopped listening. 'I was called out to Daneton by Watcher,' he said thoughtfully.

'From the security camera Foragehall passed the luggage when he got on at Cambridge and when he got off at Daneton.'

'But you said he got on in London, now you say he got on in Cambridge,' said Campbell.

'He was on camera getting on in London and Cambridge,' said Parnold, his neck reddening.

Campbell stretched his aching shoulders. 'We really need to see Sean Foragehall especially as he got off at Daneton in the morning. He had plenty of time to go through to Banksea Beach. Let's try him first.' Campbell drew out his Edinburgh accent in emphasis of the last phrase.

'I have his address, sir. He's at Cricklestaithe Farm.'

'That place is on the way between Banksea and Daneton just by Cricklestaithe Bay. I've passed it many times. It advertises a farm shop at the end of the drive.' Campbell chucked the car keys for Parnold to catch. 'It will be interesting to hear Sean Foragehall's timetable for Friday.'

Parnold caught the keys by stretching out his left hand. With a nod Campbell walked across the open plan office with Parnold. He pressed a security button to open the heavy wooden external doors. Out in the car park Campbell went over to the passenger side of the car. Parnold's driving was abrupt but Campbell was not a natural driver and he disliked the whole process. No matter how often he drove the experience never improved so he was happy to leave it to someone else. Parnold revved the engine and the car lurched forward.

'You lead on this interview,' said Campbell. He turned to look out of the windows and fell into a reverie.

The road ran through undulating fields of bright pink-yellow wheat. A combine could be seen working in the distance from the cloud of dust billowing up over the crest of the hill on the horizon. Parnold drew the car up outside a brick and timber barn advertising itself as a farm shop.

Campbell gave Parnold a long hard look before entering the building, trying to check his tendency to go racing after his prey with the abandon of a hound in full cry. On introducing themselves to the young woman inside she advised that Sean Foragehall was on the tractor and trailer filling the silo with grain from the combine harvester.

'He's the farm manager,' she explained. 'Lives in the farm house. She waved vaguely towards the back of the shop.

'Has he been away recently?' asked Parnold.

'You must be kidding. This time of year, he's far too busy with the harvest,' replied the girl.

'He caught the train on Friday,' said Parnold firmly.

'Well he would,' she snapped.

Campbell looked at her quizzically.

'It was his day off.' She looked cross. 'I'll get him on the radio. You can talk to him directly yourself.'

She turned on her heals and went back to stocking the shelves with locally brewed beer.

Campbell and Parnold went outside and around to the back of the farm shop. The tractor came around the cattle shed in front of them, stopped and swung open the door. A brown-haired man jumped down from the vehicle and approached them.

'Sean Foragehall?' asked Parnold.

'Yes,' answered the driver.

'Massive tractor,' said Parnold, impressed.

'It's designed to tow a large trailer of grain to reduce the number of trips between the combine and the silo,' said Sean. 'How can I help you?'

Campbell noted the hint of aristocratic tones that mostly seemed to have been levelled to give an acceptable neutral, non-accented voice.

'We're police,' Parnold said firmly showing identification. 'Have you always lived in this area?'

'I was brought up in Sussex and went to school there. We moved here eight years ago. Our old farm became a housing and an industrial estate.'

'We're investigating the death on the beach. You probably saw it on the news. We need to ask you a few questions,' continued Parnold.

Sean Foragehall frowned. 'Yes, I did. Someone on Banksea Beach. Of course, I'll help where I can. May I ask, why me?'

'I can't give out that information. But bear-with us, please. Do you run the farm?'

The young man got down from the tractor. He ran his hand through his mid brown hair shining in the sun. 'I'm manager in name only, Dad still runs the farm. That's him out there on the combine harvester and he'll need me back with this trailer to unload the grain.'

'Why did you alight from the train at Daneton on Friday?' asked Parnold.

'Because it's the nearest station to here. Neve picked me up. That's my sister. The girl in the shop.'

'Did you know anyone on the train yesterday?' asked Parnold.

'I didn't see anyone I knew. But who can say? The train was four carriages and I only saw the people travelling in the same one as me. I didn't recognise anyone there'.

'You got on in London?' asked Parnold.

Campbell shot him a glance for drifting into asking a question with a suggested reply in the answer.

'No,' replied Sean Foragehall. 'I got on at Cambridge, but someone was in the seat from London before me.'

'How do you know?' asked Parnold.

'I saw him sitting in the seat as the train drew up. He passed me in the doorway as I got off.'

'Which door did you get out of?'

'The one at the front of the carriage.'

So, both Sean and the other brown-haired man who sat at the table on the opposite side to Elizabeth passed the luggage rack, Campbell deduced. That made sense. Elizabeth Rattagan must have been mistaken about the man getting on at King's Cross and staying on until Daneton. Two similar men, Sean Foragehall and the first man who got on in London. This first one will want to be checked out too.

'Where were you on Friday morning and afternoon?' asked Parnold.

'Here with Neve. We were updating the monthly accounts.'

'Did you have anything on the luggage rack?'

'No.' Sean Foragehall looking confused.

'Did you touch anything on the luggage rack?'

'No,' said Sean Foragehall, his tanned face starting to flush.

'Did you see anyone else touch anything on the luggage rack?'

'No. My father will be waiting for me and the trailer. He'll need to download the grain in the harvester's tank, I'm holding him up standing talking to you,' said Sean Foragehall, his face twisted with barely controlled temper.

'Thank you, Mr Foragehall. That's all for now,' said Parnold. 'We may need to ask you some more questions later,' said Parnold.

With a nod Sean Foragehall turned and went back to his tractor. Campbell watched him go.

CHAPTER NINE

Campbell stood with Parnold outside the Cricklestaithe Farm Shop, a warm breeze nudging around them smoothing their curled tempers.

'Elizabeth Rattagan could have had her eyes shut or been turned away occupied by something else on the Friday morning train to Banksea Halt,' said Campbell.

Parnold watched as Campbell stretched each of his feet upwards in turn while he left the heel of the foot on the ground slightly in front of its partner. 'She won't have memories for those times. She might not even realise she's been asleep or in deep thought.' Campbell followed the toe turning up exercise by stretching each of his feet and pointing his toes, then he returned each foot in turn to a normal standing position.

'I'll check it out,' said Parnold, surprised that he wasn't as annoyed with his Inspector's foot exercises as he expected to be. He had become aware that his boss allowed himself these small stretches as a release from tension, in the same way as he swore and went to the boxing gym.

'The idea of the man on the train being, in fact, two men fits in with what I saw on the video recording,' said Parnold, 'though my interpretation of it only being one man sitting next to the woman in the suit, Anne Crowlie, and opposite Louise Green was similar to Elizabeth Rattagan's on a first viewing.'

Campbell and Parnold returned to the farm shop once Sean Foragehall had driven the tractor back towards the field where the combine was working.

'Hello, Miss Foragehall,' said Campbell conversationally. 'I wonder if you could tell us what you were doing last Friday?'

Without hesitation she said, 'I picked Sean up from the station and we came back here. We were doing the accounts.'

'I thought you said it was Sean's day off.'

'Thursday was Sean's day off not Friday. He stayed over in Cambridge and returned to work here on Friday.'

'Do you know what he was doing?'

'He was seeing his girlfriend, Chief Inspector.'

'He's coming in now. You can ask him yourself.' She turned away to finish filling the shelves.

'Do you know his girlfriend's name?'

Sean Foragehall had clearly changed his mind about returning to his father and the harvest.

'Are you still here?' he asked, glaring at Parnold.

Parnold stood a little straighter.

'Just one more thing while we're here: when you were in Cambridge on Thursday who did you visit?'

'My girlfriend,' Sean Foragehall snapped. 'do you need to know her name?

'Not at the moment,' Campbell interjected. 'We might later.'

'Neve,' said Sean to his sister, 'I've just had a call from Mum. She needs you to go over to the house and fetch her purse, she left it in your car.'

'Whatever for?' asked Neve.

'I'm sorry, Sergeant, Inspector, we have to go. Neve will have to shut up the shop.' The interview was clearly over. He and Parnold left the shop and returned to the car.

'Do you think that we heard the truth about their mother needing her purse?' wondered Campbell as they approached the car.

'I doubt it,' said Parnold. 'What about this girlfriend of his?'

'We're after alibis for Friday's events just now. And Sean has an alibi for Friday – he was with his sister, so he is not the killer or Messenger Watcher, as he was not in Cambridge.' Campbell stretched his neck and rotated his shoulders before opening the car door. 'Distractions, like sand in your sandwiches,' he pondered as he got in the passenger seat.

Parnold gave him a long look and wondered why he had to say such random things.

'I think we'll have to check what time the baby-drink incident occurred,' said Inspector Campbell. 'And double check who went to the baggage area then.'

'You're not saying that it was orchestrated as a tactical distraction, are you?' asked Parnold. 'I can check the time from the video.'

'Good point. I doubt if such a thing as a baby's spilt drink can be organised with babies and drinks. I think it might be more of an opportunity to put the note in the bag. Och, if this is a side issue, let's get it eliminated by investigating it,' said Campbell making a straight wiping action with his right hand across the air in front of him.

The policemen drove up the drive dust swirling up around the car from the dry track.

Parnold glanced at Campbell as he drove. 'Now there's the London to Cambridge brown haired man to find as well,' he said. 'He must have bought his ticket with cash as we don't have any information on him. I'll get all the available records checked. Paying cash for a ticket is unusual these days with the use of bank cards.' Parnold was looking annoyed with himself. 'I should have realised about the two men.'

'It's impossible to pick up every detail on an initial trawl,' said Campbell.

'He might be difficult to find,' said Parnold. 'I'll double check the video and see if we can get a recognisable image.'

'Someone else can check that out on the security camera footage from the train. You still have the interviews to organise for us with the other train passengers seated around Elizabeth Rattagan.'

'Thank you, Sir, but I'd rather check it out myself.' Parnold paused, then asked, 'Don't you think all this stuff about a note left in a bag is a bit random. We could be doing a lot of chasing about for nothing.'

Campbell nodded in acceptance of this possibility. 'Hopefully Jenner will be coming up with some information on Elizabeth Rattagan. We just don't know enough about her. If for instance she has more of a connection to William Cecil Broadgate than just going to the same school as his granddaughter – and not even at the same time – then we might have a greater reason to believe the message is more than coincidental. In any case this new brown-haired man may be of no consequence. We'll continue to pursue these train passengers. It should not take long to check out those we already know about. And, they are the people who went by the bag. I am not ignoring other possibilities in the inquiry. If something occurs to make us change our priorities, I will do so.'

'Right,' said Parnold in agreement. His expectations of his own work performance were exacting but his enthusiasm when he and Campbell started working together was still there.

'Let's look at those that got out at Cambridge because the Messenger Watcher was messaging from Cambridge,' said Campbell stroking his chin.

Without warning Parnold exclaimed loudly and swung the steering wheel round to the left and braked hard. A middle-sized trail styled motorbike swung out from behind them and cut across their car from the right showering up shale from the side of the lane onto the car.

Parnold warned Campbell with, 'Watch out.'

Campbell grabbed the door pull to prevent himself from being rattled about.

Once Parnold halted the vehicle, he removed his notebook from his pocket and jotted the number of the motorcycle down. He jumped out and tried to clear the layer of dust from the windscreen.

'Private road,' said Parnold leaning over the driver's seat from outside and wiping the surprise off his face with his forearm. 'There's a limit to what we can do.'

'Aye,' said Campbell heavily. He gave an impression of being totally unchanged by the experience. He languidly removed himself from the car and stretched out his legs.

Parnold agitatedly shook himself down. 'I'll see if I can get hold of some of these Cambridge passengers and someone can chase this motorbike's number up.'

Garden paused on the edge of Banksea Market Square and looked across at the lingerie shop where Louise Green worked. She'd been pleased with the swimsuit she'd bought there yesterday. Garden thought it strange that the shops looked just as they did when she'd first visited the town as a child. Just different owners. Louise Green's mother instead of Harriet Epsy's, as Campbell had said. And no longer were kin from the kiosks running the tea shop opposite. The shape of the town had barely changed: the little cottages of the fishermen taken over by incomers, the coaching inn with its ancient timbers. But now all was smart and clean for the holiday makers and the thread of shops running up from the harbour was full of gifts and garments of good cloth and smart design. She'd seen the old photographs of the town showing that for decades upon decades small rendered and painted buildings had stood against flint cottages in a double arc around the market place. Garden opened the door to the lingerie shop and a bell tinkled above her as she stepped in.

'It's mum's shop,' explained Louise after Garden had introduced herself.

'I'm here about an incident on the train,' said Garden.

'That can't be a police matter,' said Louise. 'My baby just spilt a drink.'

'In itself, it's not. There is a connection with another enquiry.'

'The murder?' asked Louise. 'How is it connected?'

'I'm sorry I can't discuss any police business with you,' said Garden gently, feeling that Louise's sudden leap to the murder on the beach was a bit large, but she guessed that everyone in the town would be talking about it.

'I made a bit of a fuss about being able to pay the dry-cleaning bill because money is tight. I have to take Lilly down to specialists in London on a regular basis. It costs a lot of money. There's only mum and me. We take turns with the baby and the shop. I didn't dare tell her about the dry-cleaning bill. I'll pay that Elizabeth Rattagan back at the end of the week when I get my wage packet.'

'How long has your mum had the shop?'

'She's had the shop for, must be at least, five years. When I was at high school my mother bought this shop from Gillian Epsy, I was about thirteen. I was still sixteen when I had my baby.'

'May I ask you if you went to Strath-Kind School?' Garden felt she was sticking to the list of questions quite well.

'No, I didn't go to Strath-Kind School. Do I sound like I went to school there?'

Garden lowered her head to concentrate on her notebook. She looked up and asked, 'And, what did you do on Friday when you got off the train?'

'I took Lilly down to the beach. We came off about 3pm'

'Did you see anything unusual?'

'No, I didn't.'

'And your Mum?'

'She was in the shop.'

'A few years ago, did you know a Fenella Florris?'

'The name isn't familiar.'

'Did you know Harriet Epsy?'

'Yes, I did. She used to come in and help Mum with the shop sometimes even though her mother had sold it to my mother. But the shop didn't have the profits that the account books showed when Mum bought it. There was a bit of a scene one day and that was the last contact we had with the Epsys.'

Garden made up her notes.

Louise offered, 'I did recognise William Broadgate. His picture was on the TV last night. But he was local.'

'So, you didn't know his second wife?'

'Oh yes, she used to come in here.'

'Fenella Florris was William Cecil Broadgate's second wife.'

'Oh, I didn't know her name. Everyone in the town knew William Cecil Broadgate.'

'What was she like?'

'She was nice.'

'Can you describe her?'

'English looking, quite posh English accent, medium height, brown hair, might have been dyed at her age, but she never had it any different. I couldn't tell you about her eyes.'

'How was she with her husband.'

'Fine, but he wouldn't stop in the shop, he would just wave and go over to the café opposite until she had finished shopping.'

'We are trying to trace Fenella's family and friends, we believe she had two children from her first marriage.'

'Oh yes, she used to talk about them. They went to New Zealand to live.' That confirmed what Georgia had said, thought Garden. New Zealand was not such an unusual journey to make. They could have been here, done the deed on William Cecil Broadgate and returned already. But, she knew that Tarnish was liaising with the New Zealand authorities.

Garden didn't like to pry but she thought it best to enquire further about her reasons for being on the Friday morning train from London to Banksea Halt. 'Do you have any record of the hospital visit? Did you go with anyone, with Lilly's father, perhaps?'

'My baby's condition is inherited through the maternal line. I don't see the father. He was a mistake.'

'Did you have any luggage on the train?'

'Just the baby buggy on the rack.'

'Did you check the buggy?'

'It was fine I could see it well enough from where I sat. There was another buggy on the rack. I think it belonged to the people who came through the carriage with their baby just before Lilly spilt her drink.'

'Did you see any bags on the luggage rack?'

'There were a couple of bags on there I seem to remember.'

'Did you notice if any of them looked open.'

'One had the side pocket open.'

'How do you know?'

'I caught my hand on it when I went to the rack to pick the buggy up at Banksea Halt. It flapped.'

Garden produced a picture of Elizabeth Rattagan's bag.

'Yes, that one, or one just like it,' confirmed Louise.

'Thank you,' said Garden. She thought Louise looked tired or guarded. She wasn't sure.

Campbell returned to the Gull Inn. He hadn't been able to get hold of Elizabeth Rattagan and Parnold had returned to his video footage of the train and his list of passengers. The pub was already busy with those seeking an early tea and Barbs smoothly flowed between the maze of rooms delivering plates of mouth-watering fish and chips. Campbell asked after the Pilmers. Barbs pointed Campbell in the direction of a family sitting in a corner. The young woman's long auburn ponytail swung round as she gave her baby a chip on his high chair table. The young man who was with her had his head down eating. All Campbell could see of him was a crown of black hair.

Campbell introduced himself and drew up a seat from the table behind them. After explaining his enquiry regarding their travel on the train to Banksea Halt he checked their names.

The young man looked up briefly and said, 'I'm Abigail's brother, Ralph Peterson.'

Campbell asked, 'Where did you travel from on Friday?'

'My sister came up from Seachester and I met her in London and we travelled up together.' Ralph returned to his food.

The girl with the auburn hair turned to Campbell from settling down her baby in the high chair and said in a soft rich voice, 'Abigail Pilmer.' She extended her hand to him.

Campbell shook hands with her. 'Could you tell me about your journey?'

'Me and Bertie changed trains in London and we met up with Ralph,' said Abigail Pilmer. 'We decided to have a holiday without the car as we were only coming up for a few days. We used to live up here, so my brother has friends here and I was coming up for the school reunion. I used to go to Strath-Kind School. I was in the same year as Georgia Lomond. I was shocked to hear about her Grandfather on the news.'

'Is this what this interview is about?' asked Ralph briefly looking up from his food.

'I can't discuss that,' said Campbell. 'Do you remember much about your train journey from London to Banksea Halt?'

'It was busy in London and we were a bit late getting on,' explained Abigail. 'So, we jumped on the train at the back, when all the carriages were together, as that was the nearest bit to the gate to the platform. Then we walked up the train to our seats. But when we got there, there wasn't room in our carriage for the buggy. The racks were full, so Ralph put ours in the next carriage.'

'Were you not worried about it?'

'I was a bit, so I had my brother go and check it at each stop. There was another buggy there and I didn't want ours picked up by mistake.'

'Ah, Mr Peterson, may I ask you if you noticed any bags on the rack with the buggies?' Campbell enquired.

Ralph Peterson looked up, cleared his mouth of food and said, 'No, can't remember a thing about it,' and returned to his chips.

Campbell made a note of the information and turned again to Abigail Pilmer. 'Did you know Georgia Lomond's grandfather, William Cecil Broadgate?'

'Very vaguely. He used to come and pick her up from school. I was a border. Georgia used to stay with him.'

'And did you know Harriet Epsy?'

'Is that the girl who organised the do here on Friday night? Harri she called herself, pink wig?'

'I believe so.'

'I hadn't met her before. She was a funny one. I ordered a pudding, but when it came in the waitress said who ordered the sticky toffee puddings and she put her hand up. She hadn't ordered one. I pointed out we were one short, so I got one, but because she hadn't ordered one she didn't get billed for it. As far as I know she probably did the same with the wine.'

'I understand she was an ex-pupil of Strath-Kind School.'

'She would have been a bit older than me. Just four or five years. If she was a day pupil I might never have really seen her in any meaningful way.'

'Your family lived locally at that time.'

'Yes, but I boarded in the week. My parents were busy people.'

'Where were you both on Friday afternoon?' asked Campbell.

'I was at Strath-Kind School,' confirmed Abigail.

'I was on Banksea Market Place painting the scene,' said Ralph.

Campbell confirmed the Peterson/Pilmer contact arrangements, thanked them and walked towards the door.

'Are they dangerous?' asked Barbs as he made his way out of the door.

'Do they look dangerous to you?' asked Campbell as baby Bertie sucked on a chip.

.

CHAPTER TEN

Campbell met Parnold on the way in to the office. Parnold joined him and returned into the team room where Jenner and Garden were at their desks. Campbell said 'Hello,' and addressed them, 'This Harriet Epsy is appearing to be living some sort of lie. And for what reason?'

'She could have nothing to do with this,' said Parnold. 'Lie or no lie.'

Campbell sucked in his cheeks thoughtfully. 'She is mentioned by everyone we talk to. And no one has an accurate address or telephone number that works,' said Campbell. 'The phone she contacted the emergency services on is no longer working.'

'Both of Watcher's phones and Harriet's phone have been deactivated,' agreed Garden.

Lindy Greyling came into the meeting room and walked past the case information board and straight up to Campbell. He bent over to talk to her. 'Tarnish wants to see you, Sir,' she said to Campbell quietly.

'Aye,' said Campbell without commitment.

'The Superintendent is absolutely steaming with temper this morning,' Lindy advised him.

'Thank you, Lindy,' said Campbell as if he hadn't heard her comment about Tarnish.

Tarnish's door felt like a safe solid barrier between him and the always angry Superintendent.

Campbell opened the door. Tarnish stood behind his desk tapping the woodwork with the index finger of his right hand. His eyes narrowed, and his shoulders hunched like a rhinoceros about to charge.

'I've been reviewing this case, Campbell,' he said.

Campbell said nothing.

'You seem to be wandering around the subject. Chasing after this letter looks to me like a complete waste of time. Is it your ego?'

Campbell raised his eyebrows questioning whether Tarnish was discussing his ego or Tarnish's own.

'If your lines of inquiry do not tie up this will prove to have been a complete waste of man power.'

'I did not invent such a connection,' said Campbell.

'Of course not,' snapped Tarnish.

'We are sticking to those from the train that have a tighter connection to the circumstances of the murder of William Cecil Broadgate.'

'And then there's this interest in Harriet Epsy. It is way off centre. She was nowhere near William Cecil when he was murdered. She was on a different beach.'

'Watcher sent me there. Robert Epsy died. He wasn't her uncle.'

'Put her to one side.'

'She is tangled up with the old girls from Strath-Kind School, Georgia Lomond's old school, William Cecil Broadgate's granddaughter,' Campbell persisted.

'This looks like a professional job on William Cecil Broadgate. This has not been carried out by a bunch of school girls.' Tarnish wiped his hand over his smooth tanned pate. 'Work from the centre outwards. The Broadgate family will know more about William Cecil Broadgate.'

'I have been working on that side of the investigation as well,' said Campbell. 'The Broadgates haven't been easy to trace. William Cecil has left little trace of his family. We've spoken to his daughter, Georgia Lomond, and her mother, Shirley Lomond. She's not come down from Scotland to arrange the funeral or attend the inquest. She seems to be leaving that to Georgia.'

'Where does she live?'

'Bathdale.'

'Where's that?'

'Central belt of Scotland, between Glasgow and Edinburgh.'

'Fly up and see her yourself,' demanded Tarnish.

'But...' started Campbell. His voice sounded a bit whining to him. He couldn't defend his resistance about going to Scotland against the tight neck muscles of this rhino of a boss. 'Parnold could go,' he said.

'Sort this out yourself, Campbell,' demanded Tarnish. 'The others stay here. I will direct them in your absence. It shouldn't take more than half a day. Go now.'

Campbell walked out of the office. His shoulders and chest felt tight. He tried to turn his mind off. He realised his hands were shaking. He stuck his hands in his jacket pockets. This was work. He would make himself control his inner turmoil.

Within hours he was at Edinburgh airport. He had not dared sleep on the flight in case the fears came to him. The last time he'd been here was when he left Scotland. The things from his mother's flat had been brought down to him by his wife. He had not told Margaret that he was coming up to Scotland. He stood in a cold sweat. He knew Margaret and his children were not far away. He closed his eyes briefly and thought of Victoria studying at her books and Edmund gaming on his computer. He wondered if that was what they were doing or whether they were out in the hills with their maternal cousins. All these thoughts were much more pleasant than the thoughts he had expected to flood his mind.

He opened his eyes and saw his father walking towards him. Tall, slim but with dark brown hair turning to steel grey. He blinked. No, it was a trick of the bright lights on tired eyes. A burly policeman was striding across the arrivals area towards him. His size increased by his uniform stab vest.

Campbell's vision cleared as the man spoke to him. Other than the colour of his hair he was nothing like his father. Campbell pulled on a business-like attitude. He would not allow his history to envelop him.

When Sergeant Proud viewed Edinburgh airport and scanned the new arrivals from the internal flight from Stanstead, he saw every sort of humanity. He'd been told to look out for a tall, thin man. Never-the-less he had written Campbell on a placard. He thought the man he was approaching must be Inspector Campbell, but his face was set and his movements were tight. He'd been told Campbell was quite a languid man, a little unpredictable but generally relaxed. This man did not look relaxed.

'That's the new part of Bathdale you'll be wanting?' he asked Campbell once they'd established that they'd met up with the right people and checked the destination address.

'You know better than me,' said Campbell. 'I've not lived this way for more than twenty years.'

'You've not lost much of your accent,' commented Sergeant Proud.

Campbell nodded. 'Right, let's get on.'

An hour later Sergeant Proud drew up outside a modern four-bedroom house with white pebble-dashing.

Shirley Lomond opened the door.

'Hello,' she said. Any North Norfolk accent she'd had had faded into a whisper of water lapping a beach, but she still sounded English rather than Scottish. On production of their police identity, Shirley Lomond introduced herself.

'Who's that?' demanded a Glaswegian male voice from the kitchen area.

'Police,' answered Shirley Lomond.

'I told you they would come and talk to you anyway,' replied the Glaswegian a little softer now. 'Matthew Lomond,' he introduced himself when he came through to the living room. He was stocky with greying sandy coloured hair and beard.

Neither Georgia's mother nor her father had a criminal record, so Campbell didn't fully understand why they were reluctant to talk to the police. It was clear that Georgia didn't like them, and they did not give the impression that they had the sort of money that would pay for a school like Strath-Kind.

'I'm worried for Georgia,' said Shirley Lomond.

'Your father, William Cecil, spoilt that child rotten from the day she was born,' complained Mr Lomond to his wife. 'She looked like your mother, so he said.'

'She did look like her,' said Shirley Lomond. 'Lovely red hair.'

'Yes, I suppose she did,' Mr Lomond agreed reluctantly.

'Do you have some photos, Mrs Lomond?' suggested Campbell.

'Yes, yes, I do,' said Shirley Lomond. She scurried out of the room and up the stairs.

'Your daughter said you weren't well, Mr Lomond,' said Campbell.

'I'm quite well thank you,' said Matthew Lomond.

'Were you reluctant to talk to us?' asked Campbell.

'Not in the least,' explained Matthew Lomond. 'Georgia is a little ashamed of us. She would rather we didn't really exist. She wanted to deal with the funeral arrangements, so we let her.'

Shirley Lomond came downstairs with a photograph album in her hand. 'I wanted to go down to Norfolk and see to my Dad,' she said. 'It seemed right and proper.'

'Her father used to rubbish me and Shirley,' explained Mr Lomond, 'and how we brought up Georgia. We have three sons. He's never shown any interest in them, but Georgia had to have the best and he paid for it.'

'Did you not object?' asked Campbell.

'It was pointless. The man was Shirley's father. She was in awe of him. I could have lost her and the boys.'

'What are your sons doing at present?'

'Two are in the army and one is in the navy. They are all on postings abroad right now,' said Mr Lomond. 'Alex is away with his ship.'

Campbell made up his notebook. Enquiries could easily be made.

Shirley bit her lip and looked down at her photograph album. She seemed too emotional to speak.

'Did you fear for Georgia's safety at all?' asked Campbell.

'Not while Shirley's mother was alive,' said Mr Lomond.

'Were you in the armed services?'

'Yes, I was in the army,' said Mr Lomond. He seemed to grow a little taller as he spoke, thought Campbell.

'And what about when William Cecil's first wife died?'

'It all changed then,' said Mr Lomond showing a little relief. 'Georgia came home for a while but then she went off travelling before he remarried. Perhaps she might come home now.'

Campbell paused and examined Mr Lomond's face before turning to Shirley, who was sitting very quietly clutching her album on her lap, and asked her, 'Did you see your father when he was having difficulties with his second wife, Fenella Florris?'

'I understood there were problems, but they happened in Norfolk. They came up here to visit once or twice. They seemed happy enough,' said Shirley.

'That seemed false to me,' grumbled Matthew Lomond.

'Georgia was away at the time?' suggested Campbell

'Yes, that's right,' she replied, 'it was the most normal time we had with my dad,' She opened the photograph album at a page filled with wedding photos. 'That's my wedding. There's my father and my mother. You can perhaps see the likeness to Georgia?' Shirley turned the page, 'And this is my father's wedding to his second wife, Fenella Forrest. This was in a registry office.'

'He poisoned Georgia's mind against us,' complained Mr Lomond.

'When my mother was alive I trusted her, so I let Georgia live with them. It's not like she's ours at all now. As soon as Fenella died she moved back in with him. He'd moved to a new house from where he used to live with my mother, but Georgia made herself completely at home and shut us out again.'

'She'll come back one day,' said Mr Lomond, comforting his wife.

'May I?' said Campbell taking the photograph album from Shirley and examining William Cecil's wedding photographs. One took his attention, it was a good picture of both Fenella and William Cecil. He turned the page and spotted a picture of a woman with Fenella Florris. 'Do you know her name?' he asked pointing at Fenella's companion.

'I'm sorry I don't remember. I didn't really speak to her. That's Fenella's half-sister. She wasn't on my table. Do you remember, Matt?' Shirley Lomond asked her husband.

Matthew Lomond came over and looked at the picture. 'I think that's Judy Wong.'

Shirley Lomond picked up a photograph of Georgia from the sideboard. 'Mum's been dead years, and now dad's dead and Georgia's not back.' Shirley Lomond was in tears.

'Thank you, Mrs Lomond, Mr Lomond. May I take a copy of this photograph. It has Fenella Florris on it.'

'Yes certainly.'

'Thank you, Mrs Lomond.' Campbell paused and turned to Matthew Lomond. 'Where were you last Friday, Mr Lomond?'

'I was at work. I work just down the road. I can give you the details.'

'Thank you, Mr Lomond,' said Campbell evenly. 'And Mrs Lomond, where were you?'

'I was at the bakery in Bathdale High Street. I work there three days a week: Thursday Friday and Saturday.'

'We might need to contact you again,' said Campbell as he got up to leave. Sergeant Proud followed him.

'Of course. I'm sorry I was reluctant before,' said Shirley Lomond. 'I'm not comfortable with such matters on the phone.'

'Is there any reason why you are leaving the details of your father's death to your daughter?' asked Campbell.

'Georgia insisted she handled all of that,' said Shirley Lomond confirming Matthew Lomond's statement. As if the last of her strength had left her, Shirley slumped against her husband.

Campbell looked carefully at Matthew Lomond. He was well built, neat and showed no sign of alcoholism. What was Georgia Lomond up to? Had she not said, implied her father was not well, incapable. What had she really understood about her parents?

She had barely told the truth about anything, yet she had a firm alibi for the time of her grandfather's murder.

Campbell stepped out with Sergeant Proud. The interview was almost as if it had taken place in Norfolk. The house was like many built in Norfolk and once inside he could have been anywhere. And the job had kicked in, like it always did.

'I'll check out their alibis,' said Sergeant Proud.

'Aye, thanks,' said Campbell.

He found Sergeant Proud straight forward and helpful, yet he unnerved some historical part of his past that he was trying to keep under control, so he spoke to him only briefly and tried not to count the minutes to his flight back down south.

CHAPTER ELEVEN

'Hello,' said Parnold. 'Back by tea time, that's good going.' Parnold looked at Campbell. He may have returned to the Horseton office, but his superior officer looked bedraggled. However, Parnold could detect a steely determination in him.

'I need to see that lady who sat near to Elizabeth Rattagan,' replied Campbell.

'Which one?'

'The Oriental Academic,'

'Hye Woang?'

'Yes,' confirmed Campbell. 'Can you show me a picture of her?'

'Yes, sure. Here it is.' Parnold brought up her picture on the computer screen.

'Can you print one of those off?' asked Campbell.

Parnold did as he was asked while saying, 'We have her home address and a works address for her in Cambridge.'

Campbell picked up the sheet from the printer. 'I thought Tarnish pulled us off that area of work?' he said with just the smallest hint of amusement on his face.

Parnold produced a wry smile. 'He didn't say anything to me.'

'I want to visit her this evening,' said Campbell. 'I'll take both the addresses.'

'I can come with you,' said Parnold. 'I'll just contact her. We've got her mobile number and so I can find out where she is.'

'Yes, that's fine. There is no reason to surprise her.' Campbell studied the photograph he'd just taken from the printer.

After a couple of minutes chatting on the phone Parnold came back to Campbell with, 'She is working late at one of the research facilities in Cambridge.'

Campbell stretched his aeroplane cramped shoulders.

'I'll drive,' said Parnold, making a grab for the car keys.

'Thank you,' said Campbell.

Once in the car Parnold looked uncomfortable. He started the car. 'I phoned Anne Crowlie earlier too,' he confessed, explaining that she was, 'The lady who got the baby's juice over her clothes.'

'I won't tell anyone,' said Campbell, almost conspiratorially.

'Once she left the train at Cambridge she bought another suite. She said she was in meetings all day in Cambridge,' said Parnold.

'If that's true that would rule her out as William Cecil's murderer.' Campbell turned away. He would not directly criticise his senior officer's decisions in front of one of his sergeants. Campbell wanted to interview Anne Crowlie also, as he knew Parnold did. But Campbell's thoughts were drifting. He let his head roll towards the window and closed his eyes.

Hye Woang sat at a large desk. The sun brightened white venetian blind fully screened the window against the view of several of the Cambridge language schools which were opposite.

She invited Campbell and Parnold to sit down. Campbell noted her neat features and bony face. He thought her too thin. Perhaps she was the sort of academic that was too busy thinking to eat.

After the introductions Campbell asked her, 'Initially, we are here to talk about you being on the train on Friday morning from London to Cambridge.'

'That day I was coming back from a conference. I was in a hurry to get back here. I should have caught an earlier train, but for some reason I must have known I would be running late because I had booked that train. Anyway, I stayed with my first arrangements in the end. We had been to a conference dinner the night before. The train was busy. I was a bit twitchy.'

'There were a lot of people going up to Strath-Kind School for an old girls' day,' said Campbell.

'Ah yes,' said Hye Woang. 'I know the school myself. I wasn't a student, but I did some teaching there.'

'How come?' asked Campbell.

'A few years ago, I was waiting for this post to become available. The job was in line for funding. These things take time to come through, so I went to Strath-Kind School. I was a house mistress there as well as doing some teaching.'

Campbell nodded and Parnold made notes.

'On Friday, I actually saw one of the girls I taught. Abigail Peterson, now Abigail Pilmer, I believe. I saw her in one of the shops at the station in London. We had a brief chat. She was caught in the queue trying to pay for something for her baby. I think she ended up having a bit of a dash to the train because I saw her walk from the back of my carriage through to the front carriage.'

Parnold raised his eyebrows. It was as if Inspector Campbell was shaking a tree of cherries and they were all falling out into his lap.

Campbell leaned forward slightly. 'That sets the scene in the railway carriage very nicely.' He paused, becoming more serious. 'Did you pass the luggage racks at the front end of the carriage that you were seated in?'

'Yes, I did. I didn't have anything on there, myself. I came in and left by the front door of the carriage.'

'Did you see anyone interfere with the luggage?'

'No. I was sitting looking in the other direction, towards the back of the train, and I didn't see anything as I entered or exited the train.'

'Do you know anyone called Elizabeth Rattagan?' asked Campbell.

Hye Woang showed mild surprise. 'No, I don't, Inspector,' she said. She leaned forward the policemen and frowned at Campbell and Parnold. 'But I thought you might be here to talk about the murder of my brother-in-law.'

Campbell was aware that Parnold's mouth had dropped open. He was looking at Campbell. Campbell had said nothing to him about Hye Woang being related in any way to the victim. Campbell knew he should have told him about his suspicions. He had meant to, but he had only woken with a start when Parnold had drawn the car into the carpark of this nineteen seventies office and laboratory building. Parnold would get over it, he decided.

'That was, in fact, my main reason for coming,' confirmed Campbell. 'But I need some confirmation that you are William Cecil Broadgate's sister-in-law?'

'May I ask where you got my details from?' asked Hye Woang.

'I only found out about your relationship with William Cecil Broadgate earlier today, 'said Campbell. 'I was told you were Judy Wong.'

'Yes, that is my English name,' explained Hye Woang. 'Only my mother calls me Hye Woang, and of course, the Bank.'

'And your receptionist knows you are also known as Hye Woang.'

'Yes, and my receptionist. I didn't say about being Judy Wong earlier as you were using my correct name.'

'You didn't approach us about your connection when you saw the murder mentioned on the media,' said Campbell.

'I thought it might just seem like nosiness,' said Judy. 'I have had nothing to do with William Cecil since my sister died. I wasn't sure that I could tell you anything that would help. I expected if you had anything to ask me you would find me. And here you are.'

'We had the video recording from the train and the rail records of your tickets and a photograph from the Lomond family,' explained Campbell. 'I didn't say any more earlier as I wasn't sure it was you. I was about to ask you the same question when you asked me. Can you confirm your family connections to William Cecil Broadgate?'

'I have so few pictures of my sister. She was my half-sister really. You can probably tell. We have the same mother. But my father was Henry Woang. Fenella's father was Frederick Florris. He had died, and mother married my father. I have the same photograph Shirley probably showed you.' She picked up her handbag and pulled from her purse a folded down photograph of her sister at her wedding to William Cecil.

When Judy opened it up Campbell noted that it was, indeed, identical to the one he had seen of Judy Wong with her sister Fenella at Shirley and Matthew Lomond's house

'What about your mother, is she still alive?'

'Yes. My father has also passed away, but my mother remarried some years ago and lives abroad. I see very little of her. This was even before Fenella died. Mother didn't come to Fenella's wedding.'

'Where is your mother?'

'She settled in South Africa. I visit her occasionally.'

'What about Fenella's children?'

'I do keep up with them myself. They are in New Zealand. They visit my mother regularly.'

'Have you heard from them lately?'

'Yes, just last week we spoke on a video call.'

'We would be grateful for contact details for them,' said Campbell.

Parnold leaned forward ready to take the information.

'Yes of course.' Judy Wong rummaged in her handbag and took out a phone. She found their details and passed them across to Parnold.

Judy Wong rubbed her thumb over the photograph of her sister. 'I blame myself for William Cecil and Fenella meeting. It was just by chance that there was a swimming event that Georgia Lomond was in, and her grandfather had come along to watch. Fenella was recently widowed herself and was staying with me. Neither of us were interested in the swimming so we walked along the beach where the event was taking place -- where she met William Cecil. Two lonely people I suppose.'

'I hear that their relationship deteriorated. What happened between them?' asked Campbell.

'Fenella wasn't schizophrenic. William Cecil Broadgate said she was. I had no evidence of that. She had a life-threatening illness. She was delaying surgery because her daughter was also having surgery and she wouldn't have hers until her daughter, Holly, was sorted out. They had the same illness. They gave Fenella pills that would help until she had her surgery but William, got angry. I suppose he was frightened of losing her. I was there. He attacked me. Fenella managed to drag him off, then he attacked her.'

'Did anyone report the attack?'

'Fenella begged me not to. She said there was enough stress without getting the police involved.'

'Was Fenella's daughter in England when she and her mother were ill?' asked Campbell.

'Yes, she was. The situation was complicated. The ailment was thought to be genetic in some way. Holly, was in hospital herself when the second incident happened.'

'Another incident?' queried Campbell. 'Was William Cecil involved?'

'Yes. He told Fenella he would get a new wife as she was allowing herself to die. And then he said that he could speed up the process and tried to force a quantity of her pills down her throat. They were very strong. They could have killed her, but when she started to choke he went and hid in the bathroom. She was frightened of him, but she managed to clear herself and bring up the pills. He was waiting for her to die cowering in the bathroom, so she found the key and locked him in.'

'What about you?'

'Fenella phoned me. I asked her to leave William Cecil and come with me, but she said it was all her own fault. She asked me to continue keeping Holly company while the girl underwent surgery.'

'How old was your niece?'

'Twenty-five.'

'So, did Fenella stay in the house with her husband locked in the bathroom?'

'Until the neighbours rescued him. By that time, he'd come up with the schizophrenic story to hide his violence. I don't know what he said to Fenella after that, or what she said, but shortly afterwards she shut me out.'

'How did you feel towards William Cecil Broadgate?'

'I didn't understand my sister, Inspector. Why did she let herself die? Her son and daughter needed her. She never had her treatment.'

'How is her daughter now?'

'Holly had the surgery and treatment and made a full recovery.'

'How did her daughter and son feel about William Cecil after that?'

'I don't know. Holly was already married to her New Zealander husband. She recovered well from her operation. She'd returned home before her mother died. She thought Fenella was going to have the treatment and so did her son. So, did I. Fenella had insisted I must never tell them about the incidents with William Cecil.'

'And your feelings towards William Cecil Broadgate?' insisted Campbell.

'People thought he was nice, but he wasn't: he was wilful and manipulative. My sister could not see that before they were married, but neither did I. Fenella was too nice, Inspector.'

'Do you think he had some hold over her?'

'How could he? I don't know what he could have on her that would make her give up on her own life and family.'

Campbell nodded and with his elbows on the desk grasped his chin thoughtfully. 'And lastly, Miss Wong, you have been most helpful. I wonder if we might go back to the matter of Strath-Kind School?'

'Yes, of course,' said Judy Wong. Parnold looked up from his note taking. She was becoming weary.

'Do you remember that I asked you about Elizabeth Rattagan earlier?'

'Yes,' replied Judy Wong frowning slightly.

'Elizabeth Rattagan was in fact a pupil at Strath-Kind School. Did she have anything to do with your sister?'

'I'm sorry inspector I wasn't there long, just one school year, September to September.'

'Elizabeth Rattagan was the woman you were sitting opposite on the train.'

'The blond curly hair?'

'Yes.'

'I do remember her vaguely from the train because there was an incident with a baby and a drink she got involved in, but otherwise I do not remember her. She seemed to me to be too old to be among the girls I worked with at Strath-Kind. I'm sorry, Inspector, I'm exhausted. I wonder if I might rest.'

'Yes, certainly. Thank you for your time. May we also have your itinerary for the Friday you came up on the train from London.'

'Yes, of course, when I returned from London I was here all day, working with colleagues.'

'And lunch time?'

'I worked through lunch.'

'And in the evening?'

'I was here until eight pm. A day away at a conference means work must be caught up. Let me print out my schedule.'

As they left the building with her schedule Parnold said, 'We should have looked at her computers.'

'Perhaps. I hadn't organised a warrant. I didn't really know if it was going to be Fenella Florris's sister. I only had the name Judy Wong from the Lomonds. I just had the old photo to go on. Her employer would never let us have her computers without a warrant with the sort of work that she does. And, any mention of her computers might have alerted her. Also, I suspect if she does have anything she wants to hide from us she has the skills to do that.'

'So, we would be looking for a separate computer or phone.'

'Yes, I think she would if she has organised William Cecil's death,' Campbell yawned. 'That's it. I can do no more today. Even if we had been allowed to see Anne Crowlie, I couldn't manage it now. We can check out Judy Wong's story tomorrow. Medical records might tell us which of these stories of Fenella's death is the truth. You are right, Parnold: Judy Wong does have a strong motive for murdering William Cecil Broadgate.'

CHAPTER TWELVE

The next day, after the morning briefing and lunch at her desk, Jenner found herself on the doorstep of Georgia Lomond's caravan with Inspector Campbell. Fenella's medical history had been accessed and read by them both.

'I'm not getting much information out of Elizabeth Rattagan's old office,' said Jenner.

'I see,' said Campbell. 'Seaminster isn't it? I think Lindy Greyling is from that area. She might know someone.'

'You might like to lead on this one,' said Campbell. Jenner thought he looked like a man who had only had a short night's sleep.

She nodded.

'How long will you be staying here?' asked Jenner after Georgia let them in.

'I'm moving in to my grandfather's house tomorrow. I've heard from the solicitor and he tells me that it's okay as I've been left everything in his will. The whole thing will have to go through probate before it's officially mine, but I think it suits them to have someone in to look after the property.'

'Your grandfather has left nothing for your mother, his daughter?' asked Jenner.

'Apparently not,' said Georgia. She sounded very Scottish to Jenner's ears.

'Did you know about the will?' Jenner looked across to Campbell with the meaningful look of a relay runner passing over the baton. She placed her attention on her notebook.

'Yes, of course I did,' said Georgia. 'Grandpa Wills told me everything.'

Campbell shook his head very slightly at Jenner while Georgia's back was turned. He gave no hint from his outward appearance of his thoughts at learning this information. It gave Georgia a motive for arranging the death of her Grandfather. Jenner made a note of this information and looked up at Georgia with deep seriousness. 'We've heard a different story about Fenella Florris,' confirmed Jenner.

'I don't know what you mean?'

'Georgia, Fenella had a genetic condition. It gave rise to a condition that required an operation. She didn't have schizophrenia. She refused treatment for her condition. That is why she died.'

Georgia said, 'That's rubbish Fenella had schizophrenia. Why would she refuse treatment for that sort of condition? She would have to be mad.'

'Initially she refused because she wanted to give her daughter her full attention because she had the same condition,' explained Jenner. 'But she asked her sister to look after her instead and in effect allowed herself to die.'

'That just doesn't make sense,' said Georgia.

Jenner looked at Campbell and asked him to intervene with a sharper than she intended, 'Inspector Campbell…'

He unravelled himself from his thoughts and said, 'I would be grateful if you would accompany us down to the police station to answer some questions.'

Georgia nodded, looking confused. She waggled her head slowly as if trying to clear an internal mist. 'I would like to bring a legal representative with me,' she said.

'Yes, that's fine,' said Campbell, noting her familiarity with police procedure. 'You are not under arrest, Georgia. Can you contact the individual now, so we can go directly to Horseton Police Station and you can meet your solicitor there?'

Georgia nodded and took out her mobile phone to make the call.

Campbell paused before entering the interview room with Georgia Lomond and Jenner to ask Garden to visit the lad on the motorbike who'd pulled across him and Parnold at Cricklestaithe.

'Parnold checked him out from our records,' said Campbell. 'Turns out that the boy on the motorbike is also your boy on the beach, Bradley Yorkman.'

'The one Sarah Radley and Jess Barratt from the kiosks pointed out as possibly causing the fires to the beach huts at Daneton Howe?' asked Garden.

'Looks like it, or a lad by the same name. Can't be too many of those. Didn't you say he had a motorcycle?'

Garden agreed with a sideways nod. 'Did forensics find anything in the burnt-out huts?' she asked.

'I'm not aware of anything but you could check that one out before you go.'

'Yes, Sir,' said Garden.

'Ask Parnold to go with you when you visit the lad,' said Campbell. 'Oh,' he added, 'no connection, but Bradley's not as young as you might think -- turns out he's twenty.'

'I'm sure he'll be quite cooperative,' said Garden.

'He might not be the arsonist, but he might have seen something suspicious on these beaches if he regularly spends time at Daneton and Banksea,' said Campbell. He was sure Garden could keep Parnold in check in her persuasive way.

He turned towards Jenner, who was standing by the interview room door where Georgia Lomond and her solicitor were waiting.

Georgia's solicitor introduced himself as Mr Godfrey and settled down to make notes.

'There is no record of Fenella having schizophrenia,' explained Campbell again to Georgia Lomond. 'Why did you tell us that she had schizophrenia?'

'That is what Grandpa Wills told me.' Georgia looked at her hands on her lap.

'Why do you think he said that when it wasn't true?'

'I don't know.'

'Did he want you to return to him once Fenella was dead?'

'Yes, he did.'

'Do you think your grandfather wanted to put himself in a good light, so you would return to him?'

'I suppose that's possible.'

'Did Fenella leave William Cecil Broadgate any of her money in her will?'

'Yes, she did. There was quite a bit I understand. She left all of it to Grandpa Wills.'

'Did her children contest the will?'

'They were both abroad. It would have been too costly for them.'

'Is that what William Cecil said?'

'Yes, that's what he said to me.'

'Is that why you returned to him after Fenella's death?'

Georgia looked at her hands. 'He said we could live well.'

'When did you discover your grandfather had not told you the truth about Fenella?'

'I didn't know anything about it until today when you told me.'

'There was a lack of papers in William Broadgate's house. Had you removed any papers?'

'No. I had nothing to do with his papers. I said once about the lack of photographs and he said he didn't want to carry any memories around with him. I accepted that.'

'Did you kill your grandfather for his money?'

'No,' she said.

'You knew about the money. And it was a large amount. Did you want it sooner rather than waiting for the old man to die?'

'No. He never said how much, nor did he tell me exactly what he owned.'

'Did you find out what he'd done to Fenella and feared he might bully you also?'

'These are lies. Grandpa Wills didn't bully anyone.'

'We have heard that he attacked Fenella when she was ill.'

'No, I'm sorry. I just don't believe you. I would never hurt Grandpa Wills and he would never hurt me. I was at the school all afternoon at the old-girls' day. I came back to the beach and he was dead.'

Mr Godfrey said, 'You are fishing, Inspector.'

'She may not have murdered her Grandfather herself, but she may have had him murdered by an accomplice.'

'I suspect you have no evidence for that,' said Mr Godfrey with finality. 'My client has not been arrested, she is just helping you with your enquiries. She can leave at any time.'

'We did state that at the beginning of the interview,' said Campbell.

Georgia made no comment and gave a negative gesture with her hand to the solicitor. 'I want to talk about this. I don't really understand what's been going on.'

Campbell changed his line of questioning. 'Can you go over again what he told you of Fenella's illness?'

'He said she had schizophrenia. He said she attacked him and locked him in the bathroom. The neighbours had to rescue him.'

'Did you ever speak to the neighbours.'

'They moved shortly afterwards. Why wouldn't Fenella have her treatment. It doesn't make sense?' Georgia started to cry. 'Grandpa Will wouldn't hurt anyone.'

'He hurt your parents.'

'No, he didn't.'

'He took you from them.'

'No, he didn't. They didn't want me.'

'Is that what William Cecil told you?'

'I suppose so. I don't remember. They are rubbish parents. Perhaps they killed Grandpa Wills.' Georgia blew her nose with a tissue offered by Mr Godfrey. 'I didn't expect to be a suspect,' she said quietly.

'My client has answered all your questions fully,' said Mr Godfrey, 'as she agreed to do. Is that all for now, Inspector.'

'Yes, thank you, Miss Lomond. We may have more questions later,' said Campbell. 'You do understand, Miss Lomond, that we have to look at every angle of your grandfather's death because it appeared someone wanted him dead and killed him. And the person who wanted him dead did not necessarily carry out the murder.'

Jenner closed the interview.

Outside the room Campbell stretched. Old Tarnish was right; the family had turned out to be an interesting line of enquiry.

But was the infighting enough for the family to turn in on itself and murder an elder member of its group? He would wait and see what the New Zealand police had to say about Fenella's offspring's whereabouts in the last few weeks.

CHAPTER THIRTEEN

At Cricklestaithe Farm Cottages Bradley Yorkman was investigating the chain on his motorcycle. Parnold was bristling with temper. Garden felt that she was going to lose her opportunity to connect with Bradley Yorkman if Parnold started the conversation.

'Hi Bradley,' she said.

'Hi,' said Bradley Yorkman looking up. Garden noted his sandy hair and blue eyes and a ruddy complexion, but he had a square bony face. 'Yeah, you look like police to me.' His tone was relaxed with a noticeable local accent pulling 'like' into 'loik'.

'We are police,' said Garden quickly before Parnold could say anything.

'I've not been on any public roads with the bike,' he said.

'We're not really here about that,' sad Garden feeling Parnold's tension beside her.

'What are you here about then?'

'We understand you spend quite a bit of time on the beach at Daneton Howe and Banksea beaches?'

'Yes, so do a lot of people.'

'That's true. But your name has come up in conversation.'

'That'll be those old cows from the kiosk. They think I'm arsonist.'

'And are you?' chipped in Parnold.

'No, I'm not. Everyone thinks you're a wrong'un just because once when you was twelve you wanted to make a fire on the beach.'

'You're not very careful with that bike,' said Parnold.

'I don't know what you mean?' said Bradley Yorkman defiantly.

'I mean, you careered along the driveway to the farm shop in front of us the other day.'

'It's also the driveway to the farm cottages where I live,' replied

Bradley Yorkman.

Garden noticed Bradley's accent was even broader in defiance.

'You have a responsibility even on private land,' said Parnold.

A large man in his fifties came out of the house. 'Excuse me, can I be of any help to you people. If you're looking for the farm shop, it's down the right fork in the lane'. He looked at Bradley with concern and asked him, 'Alright, Son?'

'Fine, Dad.'

Garden wondered if she ought to introduce themselves as police but decided that there were too many ways the conversation could go and none of them would be helpful. She didn't want Bradley to be in trouble with his dad. She didn't want Parnold to escalate the issue with the motorbike and she wanted to retain a passable connection with Bradley Yorkman she might be able to use on another occasion.

'Thanks,' she called out to Bradley's father. She started to walk away and said firmly to Parnold to come with her. She heard the door shut behind Bradley's father as he went inside. Parnold reached the car.

Bradley came up to her. 'Thanks for that. He didn't need to know you were the police. It wouldn't be so good for me.'

Garden nodded and gave him her card. 'I'd like to have a chat soonish. Perhaps down at Daneton or Banksea.'

'I'll let you know,' said Bradley. 'I really don't take the bike on the roads. I take it as far as the road. There's a barn down there where I can hide it when I walk across to Daneton Howe Beach. It's not far that way. At Banksea Beach I push it across the road and then I'm back on farm tracks.'

'Gwen, why have we moved?' asked Elizabeth as she unpacked her few items from a carrier bag, most of it borrowed from Gwen. Her friend's clothes were much more fashionable than her own and they fitted her better as she'd lost weight over the last few months.

'I think it's for the best. We were lucky to get this caravan at this time of year. We only got it because the girl that was in here was the one whose grandfather was murdered on the beach. She left early.'

'That's awful. This is a crime scene.'

'No, it's not. The police would have kept it taped up if they'd wanted to.'

'We ought to tell the police that we are here.'

'If they want to find us they will.'

'Gwen, you know something about what's going on here, don't you? You knew about me and somehow you know about this.'

'And, so do you.'

'No, I don't.'

'Well someone thinks you do, because of the note saying you caused his death.'

'I don't even know this William Cecil Broadgate man.'

Gwen started moving cushions about.

'What are you looking for?' asked Elizabeth.

'You're right. I do know a bit about what is going on here. I did recognise the dead man, William Cecil Broadgate,' confessed Gwen. 'When he visited Sussex, he went under a different name.'

'What do you mean visited Sussex?' asked Elizabeth suspiciously.

'I've been watching him for some time,' Gwen explained, without turning around from the cupboard she was delving into.

'In Sussex?'

'Yes, Sussex and Bedfordshire.' Gwen explained reluctantly. 'I know William Cecil Broadgate is not Dungrade, but he was an associate of Dungrade's. I know him.'

'We need to tell the police,' said Elizabeth. 'This could be dangerous knowledge. William Cecil Broadgate was murdered.'

'How short is your memory?' said Gwen. 'How much joy have you had dealing with Dungrade? You worked for the prosecution service and you got sacked. You and I both don't trust the police. It could be more dangerous to contact them than…'

'Than what?'

'Just help me search this place.'

'There won't be anything to find. The police would have searched it.'

'Yes, but I know what I'm looking for.'

'You should know where it is hidden as well then', said Elizabeth sarcastically.

'Very funny,' said Gwen flatly. 'Of course, I don't know where its hidden. You've got to trust me on this, Lizzy. You do trust me, don't you, Lizzy?'

'I don't really have a choice, do I?'

Gwen continued to turn everything out of the drawers and examine the bottom of each. She went back into the cabinet under the sink.

'You've already looked in there,' said Elizabeth.

'There's a gap between the back of the cabinet and the wall of the caravan.'

'We're going to look guilty, Gwen. The police have already been sent a message about me. We don't want to be in possession of any more incriminating evidence.'

'But it was a hoax? You said you had not caused the death of anyone.' Gwen turned from her task, still crouching, and looked quizzically at Elizabeth.

'Of course, it was. But, supposing I caused the death of someone unknowingly?'

'I assumed the note was connected to the circumstances of your harassment.'

'So, did I. You have turned the conversation around to me, Gwen. 'How do I know you're not lying.'

'So, you don't trust me?

'I have been involved with the Dungrade case for a while. You have not been investigating in Sussex yourself or I would have known about you.'

Gwen sat down next to her. 'No, I'm not. I'm Bedford based. My investigations have led me to here and to you. I can find out about Sussex with a phone call. I had to go under an alternative name. I didn't deal with you directly. I mostly spoke to Madeleine. That is why you don't recognise my involvement.'

'What name were you going under?'

'My full name is Gwendolyn Michelle Hawksworth-Blythe.'

'Oh, that's what you told the police. I didn't take it in at the time,' said Elizabeth.

'Using Gwen Blythe was arranged at school for simplicity. I never liked the rest anyway until I needed it. Yes, you have sent me letters asking to look-into various cases linked to Dungrade's activities.' Gwen turned back to her task.

'Shelly Hawkesworth? I should have guessed that,' Elizabeth declared. 'So, all this setting up of a business was a lie then?'

'Oh Lizzy,' said Gwen with an edge of despair in her voice. 'No, no it wasn't, is not. I'm really getting short of money the same as you. But now thanks to your eagle eye, it looks like Granny might help me out with that one after all.'

Elizabeth curled her eyes upwards and shut them until Gwendolyn started rummaging back behind the sink cupboard. 'What are you looking for?'

'This,' said Gwen. 'look what I've got.'

Elizabeth opened her eyes and looked at a plastic bag that was holding a black hard backed notebook.

'That is evidence,' said Elizabeth.

'I'm not handing this over to the police,' said Gwen. 'We'll never see it again. Okay, for you,' she said as she went into her handbag and came out with a pair of the sort of plastic gloves which are in garages as hand protection for filling cars with diesel. What?' she responded to Elizabeth's click of the tongue. 'I always have a pair.'

Elizabeth gave Gwen another long hard look, 'How did you know this place was coming up for rent?' she asked.

'When I go for my morning swim down at Banksea beach I talk to the woman in the kiosk. I told her I was looking for something cheaper and she told me about this place. You still don't believe me?'

'Come on, you knew what you were looking for in the caravan. You wanted this caravan.'

'Ok I did ask her about Broadgate's caravan. I was just going to break in and look but then she said she'd heard that the granddaughter was moving out.' Gwen was looking earnestly at her. 'It is cheaper than the hut,' she insisted, and then she smiled slightly. 'We need to pursue this. This Dungrade case will not go away. Don't you want your job back? I want my life back. I want to always use my real name not just the middle bit. And, this little book can help us do that.'

Elizabeth shook her head. 'As you say I have heard so many lies, I'm not sure now when I hear the truth. Are you going to open that bag?'

Gwen peeled open the top of the plastic bag with her gloved fingers. The black book fell out onto her lap and Gwen picked it up and opened it. She turned each page looking intently at each one, and she smiled. 'You're right Lizzy it is evidence and we need to put it in a safe place immediately.'

'What does this book mean?'

'I think it means Lizzy that we have proof that William Cecil Broadgate could well have been Dungrade. It is evidence against Dungrade.' Gwen handed Elizabeth the book.

'But you didn't recognise him on the telly?'

'I don't know why that is. I thought William Cecil Broadgate was Dungrade's money launderer, but this shows him to be Dungrade.'

'At last, evidence,' said Elizabeth. She looked through the pages of the book. 'We really do need to go to the police with this.'

'Not yet. We need more evidence otherwise it looks as if you are involved in some way. Isn't that really why you got pushed out. They tried to make it look as though you were not following proper procedures? In fact, they tried to show that you were somehow influenced by Dungrade and his associates.'

'Yes, you are right,' said Elizabeth sadly. 'How do you know?'

'The same method was used on me when I went by the name of Gwen Blythe every day. I changed offices and rejigged my name but, in the end, the same thing happened to Shelley Hawkesley as happened to Gwen Blythe.'

Elizabeth looked away from her friend. Her emotions were rising, and this was not the time to let them get the better of her. She breathed deeply and thought about the black notebook. 'Did you ever come across Broadgate's granddaughter?' she asked. 'She was mentioned on television, but not by name. I don't ever recall coming across her.'

'I never came across her either,' said Gwen.

'Do you think she was involved?'

'She could have been,' said Gwen.

'They said she was an old girl from Strath-Kind School,' said Elizabeth.

'Do you remember seeing her on Friday at the school?' asked Gwen. 'She wouldn't have gone on Friday evening to the pub.'

'I don't know,' said Elizabeth. 'They haven't shown her on the TV just spoken about her.'

'She must have been there on Friday afternoon,' said Gwen.

'She couldn't have known about the book otherwise she would have taken it – she was staying here,' said Elizabeth, beginning to feel like she was starting to unravel the puzzle that had wrecked her life.

'She might have left the book there as it was well hidden. She might be expecting to come back here when it's gone quiet.'

'Gwen, that is not reassuring.'

'Yes, but we'll catch her when she comes, and we can hand her over to the police.'

'Oh, Gwen,' said Elizabeth in despair. But she could see Gwen's mind already working on another idea.

'I'm going to photograph each page. It will be easy to keep the memory card separate from the camera.' Gwen set about the task and Elizabeth moved away to the bedroom to settle her clothes in the drawers. Gwen had elected to sleep on the bed in the living area.

She heard Gwen gasp.

'What is it?'

'Nothing,' said Gwen.

'Yes, it is,' insisted Elizabeth as she came out of the bedroom.

'Look,' said Gwen. 'There's a page torn out.'

'Oh,' said Elizabeth staring at the jagged edge of paper protruding from the book's centre-fold, the remains of where a page had been ripped out.

'Does it look familiar? Does it look like your note, Lizzy?'

'I didn't see it for long and now the police have it. But yes, it is very similar.'

'This means for certain that Broadgate's murder and your note are connected.'

'No, it means my note and Broadgate are connected; not his murder.'

Gwen took a photograph of it, and insisted, 'We have to eat. I'm starving.'

'How can you even think of food,' complained Elizabeth from the bedroom.

'Do you think Dungrade might be involved with my grandmother's money?' While waiting to listen to Elizabeth's reply she returned the book to its packaging and its hiding place.

Elizabeth came out of the bedroom and considered the suggestion for a moment. 'I think that it could be time to step up and claim your inheritance. If he is involved, we might be able to flush him out of the undergrowth. Your father became entangled by them with his own last will and testament. It is possible that his mother's will could be with a linked firm of solicitors.' She breathed deeply. She felt she'd taken a further step towards clarity.

Gwen brought out a tablet device which Gwen hadn't seen her use before and started searching the internet. 'You are right. The solicitors are now part of the same chain of businesses that my father used. They must have merged. I think I shall be making that phone call and see what happens.'

'Gwen, supposing it is they who are trying to flush you out?' asked Elizabeth.

'I'll phone up Granny's home first and check she's really dead, Lizzy,' Gwen said smiling broadly. 'At least then we'll know where we stand.'

Elizabeth felt relief spread through her.

'What's that smile for?' asked Gwen. 'You're not allowed to smile,' she teased.

Elizabeth chucked a pillow at her.

Parnold found Campbell at his desk. 'I've double-checked the passengers on camera on the train with Elizabeth Rattagan. There is only one family that could have had the opportunity to access the luggage rack while the baby was having the drink incident. The Pilmers/Petersons. The chaos just about blocked the passage in that carriage.'

'Oh yes,' said Campbell sitting up straight. 'More work we shouldn't be doing.'

Parnold thought he sounded pleased about going against Tarnish's instructions.

'Ralph Peterson said he was coming back after each station to check on the buggy,' added Campbell.

'Yes, but there wasn't a station until Cambridge and there he was hanging around the luggage rack. The security camera footage for the time of the baby incident in the front carriage confirms Ralph Peterson came back into the carriage and put the buggy on the rack at that time.'

'Thank you for that.'

'But we are no further on,' complained Parnold. 'He still might have put the note in the bag.'

Campbell stood up and walked into the atrium. It was probably the best feature of Horseton Police Station. Sergeant Jenner was coming down the stairs in the centre. 'We've just received a phone call giving us advance-warning of the report from the pathologist arriving about the man known as Robert Epsy.'

Campbell stopped and stared at her.

'Professor Brown wants you to phone her. She couldn't get through to you.'

'I was at my desk,' complained Campbell pulling his mouth into a downward curve and wrinkling his brow in disbelief. He went back to his desk, stretched his shoulders and lengthened his back. He reached for his phone and turned up the ring volume, which he'd turned off earlier, and dialled Mary Brown.

She answered promptly, 'Hello, Campbell,' she said without waiting for him to introduce himself.

Mary Brown launched into her usual energetic wall of words and Campbell waited for his instincts to be confirmed. She paused for breath and said: 'I heard you wanted to know about Robert Epsy?'

'Aye.'

'He died of heroin poisoning. We carried out the blood tests for Colin Lincoln, so it will be on his report.'

'Does it look like murder?'

'He has sent you a copy of his initial report as well as me,' said Mary Brown scathingly. 'The heroin was administered by injection between the toes. He could have done it himself. There's little sign of arthritis for his age in his joints.'

'Haven't seen it come through on my emails,' said Campbell.

Mary Brown tutted. 'I'll forward you mine.'

'When I saw him on the beach he had sandals and socks on,' said Campbell.

'It need not have been self-administered as you are aware,' said Mary Brown, adding: 'We have tested his hair for drug use and there was some history of drug taking but not for a few months. Goodbye, Campbell.' Mary Brown put the phone down.

Campbell went into the team office and found the photograph of Harriet Epsy from the tea kiosk at Daneton. He phoned through to organise an alert. Now Harriet Epsy was a person of interest to the police. And she would have to be found.

Georgia Lomond stood on Daneton Howe beach. She was glad to be away from Banksea. She didn't think she would ever go back there. She couldn't go back to her parents; she felt too old for that. She wandered along the sand looking at the far distant sea and then in the opposite direction at the beach huts nestling against the sand dunes.

A breeze ran through the sharp grasses making them rustle. The huts here were far larger than those at Banksea Beach. They had areas underneath where an effort had been made to keep them above the sand, but the sand had blown in and tried to fill the space between the supporting posts. As she worked her way through the deep sand heading towards the kiosk for a drink, she stepped over a rivulet, but she sank in the soft, wet sand on the far side and her canvas shoes were soaked. She bent down and took them off. A shadow cast over her and still crouched she looked up.

A silhouette was standing over her.

'Hello,' said the silhouette. 'You won't remember me.'

Georgia stood up. The owner of the silhouette seemed to be male and probably about the same age as herself. She flicked her long red ponytail in a defiant gesture as she stood up.

'I'm Bradley, Bradley Yorkman,' he said.

She looked at his soft blond hair and smiling face. He looked friendly enough. 'Do you fancy a drink at the teashop?' she asked.

Bradley's smile broadened. 'Yes, that would be great,' he said.

He turned and walked beside her up towards the kiosk. As they did so they passed a couple of burnt out beach huts. Another rivulet ran across the beach. They both jumped it and laughed, and Georgia said, 'I'll race you.' She set off to attempt to beat Bradley to the kiosk.

CHAPTER FOURTEEN

The woman stood facing the pool. The pool was still busy but not crowded. She liked to swim at this time of day. The late evening sun raked beams of light across the water's surface even though there was rain outside. She swam some forty lengths with a business-like rhythm. She paused for a breather and noticed that people were leaving with no more people arriving. She swam another five lengths, more slowly to cool down, and got out. She always thought it strange that she didn't feel wet while she was in the water, only once she was out of it. She showered in the public area and wrapped her towel around her. She took one last look at the pool and marvelled briefly at the invisible mechanics that produced this clean blue water. Like the effect she thought her lover had on the world.

She had played her part in Watcher's mechanics, and that she now regretted.

Watcher had said wait here, at the pool. All would be good. She would be released from her obligations. The safety guard had his back to her tidying the floats and ropes at the corner of the pool. She went out into the unisex changing room. She was feeling increasingly uncomfortable as she stripped off. She could hear a man in the next cubicle. Unnecessary, she thought, for him to come into the next cubicle when there were so few people in the pool and so many other cubicles he could have chosen. She looked up at the top of the cubicle: it had been fitted with a kind of racking that could be used for hanging towels but also prevented entry to the cubicle from the top. She could hear swing doors opening and closing with a whoosh and a click. She dried her legs.

She didn't like these mixed-sex changing rooms. Strange really. Perhaps because the rest of her life was so ordered that when she swam she didn't want to think about the disruptive element of there being humans of the opposite sex there. That is, she thought, her life was ordered except for Watcher. She must have been mad to get involved with him. She should have just been honest. And, she realised she wasn't even sure if Watcher was a man for she had never met him. As she rushed to dress, her clothes fought against her damp skin.

She could still hear the man in the cubicle next to her. Once fully dressed she came out of the cubicle, went over to the mirror and lifted the hair-drier.

She would have done anything Watcher had wanted with the information that evil person had on her. She'd done everything Watcher had asked her to do. She'd had enough. Well, soon she would be phoning the police and ending Watcher's little game and she would take the consequences. "Watcher", indeed, at least she deserved to know his real name. First the internet and then phone messages on a phone that arrived in the post. "The excitement of the operation" as Watcher had called it before "the operation", now he used what she'd done as another threat. She had nearly been exposed. Watcher had said not to panic. "We'll sort something out."

"Everything was legal, Watcher was allowed to clean up," Watcher had told her in the messages. She was less sure of the legality of her actions now. She wished she hadn't deleted all the messages as Watcher had told her to do.

She finished dressing and went to dry her hair. She caught a movement in the mirror. She guessed it was the man from the cubicle beside her. She tried to dismiss the disquiet that gave her.

The man went into the toilets and a few minutes later he left.

Content that her hair was dry, she dried it a little longer to allow enough time for the man to have left the building. She hung up the hair dryer and left the changing area. The door swung shut behind her. She was in a corridor that arched three quarters of the way around the swimming pool. At one point, there were windows looking into the pool area, then the route took her past many different doors on the way to the entrance lobby. One of the pool attendants passed her with a friendly nod. She expected to meet Watcher in the car park. That was the arrangement. There was a finality about it for her. The death on the beach hadn't made any sense to her. Watcher denied all knowledge. She hadn't heard from Watcher since.

There were three doors on her left and one on her right. The one on the right was slightly open so she could just glimpse some very ordinary office equipment.

She felt herself falling, but she didn't feel her body hit the floor.

Early the next morning Campbell and his team arrived at Banksea Swimming Pool. The site including the car park was completely cordoned off. They parked on the road. Campbell glanced across the coast road which, here, was separated from the coast by an area of marshland crossed by tracks. When he entered the area, Campbell found Scene of Crime Officers were swarming in their ordered fashion over the premises.

'This way, Sir,' said a uniformed policeman showing Campbell the corridor that went around the swimming pool. From there another uniformed policeman directed him through the middle of three doors. A concrete stairway with metal railings took him down ten or so steps to a lower level. Pipes and pumps and switchgear surrounded him in the swimming pool machine room.

He and Parnold approached the body. The Forensic Pathologist was crouching over the body in his disposable overalls. He lifted his hooded head and introduced himself as Colin Lincoln and continued with, 'We'll be taking her away shortly, she died from a broken neck.'

'Is it someone who works here?' asked Campbell.

'I think she's a swimmer. The Scene of Crime Officers found a bag of swimming stuff, towels and costume.' Colin Lincoln nodded towards Mary Brown who was marshalling the scene of crime officers with their bags of swabs into an area where they were being boxed ready for transport to the laboratory.

'The victim has a blow to the head, but it is slight.'

'Any phone?' asked Campbell.

'No, I don't think so,' said Colin Lincoln. 'There was no phone on her body. There were no personal items on her.'

Mary Brown approached to speak to Campbell and at his enquiries about phones and identity she looked around at the swarm of people logging bags of swabs. 'The place was relatively clean,' she said. 'There's no phone in the swimming bag though. It was left quite close to the body, just by those pipes there. It looked placed rather than dropped, being just a carrier bag. I would have expected it to be spilled if it had been dropped.'

'Thank you,' said Campbell but Mary Brown had already returned to her officers.

'Do you know who that is?' asked Parnold, with a mild swagger, as the pathology team started placing her in a body bag.

Campbell frowned questioningly.

'The car she came in is out in the car park,' said Parnold. 'The staff noticed that it was the last one in the car park last night and that it was still there this morning. Jenner's getting the ownership of the vehicle now.' Parnold's face was full of knowledge.

'Right, Parnold?'

'It's Anne Crowlie, Sir. The lady on the train who had drink spilt on her by Louise Green's baby.'

Campbell looked down at the dead woman as her face disappeared into the body bag. 'She certainly looks like her photograph from the train. Identification will be clearer when she's been cleaned up,' he said to Parnold. 'She is a fair way from home for an evening swim. She could have been meeting someone. This does not look like a random killing.' He shook his head sadly.

Jenner came in. 'It's Anne Crowlie,' Parnold said for her benefit gesturing towards the body already wrapped in the body bag and being removed to the pathologist's mortuary.

'No! Is that who she is?' replied Jenner, incredulous.

'I think so,' said Parnold, with less confidence than before.

'The car belongs to, Frank Norton,' announced Jenner.

'Who is Frank Norton?' asked Parnold with a hint of irritation at the apparent challenge to his identification.

'I pulled up his driving licence picture and he's very similar to Sean Foragehall,' continued Jenner. 'But it isn't Sean Foragehall.'

'You mean he might be the extra man on the train?' asked Campbell.

'If so he was sitting next to Anne Crowlie all the way to Cambridge,' said Parnold with excitement. 'I'll double check that footage when we get back to the office and try and confirm whether or not he is the man on the train.'

'Interesting,' said Campbell. He felt an almost familial pleasure in the team's smooth functioning. He had a strange surge of hope. Campbell paused and looked at Jenner. 'Did you find any handbag or identity in the car, Sergeant Jenner?' he asked.

'No,' said Jenner. 'There was nothing in the vehicle at all. It had been broken into, so if there had been anything it was probably taken. They're checking security camera footage for the car park now.'

On the way out of the pool, the receptionist passed Jenner a copy of the security camera recording. 'I'm afraid it's the usual: an individual wearing a hoodie,' she said.

'Could this be Messenger Watcher?' asked Jenner of her colleagues once they'd moved away from the reception desk.

'Do you think Messenger Watcher wears a hoodie?' asked Parnold. 'He seems more sophisticated than that.'

'Might not be a man,' warned Jenner. 'We might get some clues from the car park recording.'

Garden came up. 'I've been in the carpark with the scene of crime officers. They haven't found anything obvious and they're going to take the car away for further examination.'

'Let's borrow a room in the swimming pool,' said Campbell. 'We can have a brief meeting in there.'

'I'm sure the staff will point us in the right direction for the coffee machine,' said Parnold.

The receptionist unlocked the room and invited Campbell, Jenner, Garden and Campbell through the door. Campbell gave a brief résumé and drank three cups of the strange liquid the staff of the swimming pool had managed to persuade out of the machine.

'If our deceased lady is indeed Anne Crowlie from the train she could have seen something she wasn't meant to see; or, there could have been some reaction by others following on from the spilt drink incident on the train,' suggested Campbell. There was general acceptance of this, so he continued, 'Garden, if you could go back and have another word with Louise Edge, perhaps she's said something about the drink-spill incident to someone and they've got overexcited.'

Garden nodded. 'I'll go after this meeting,' she offered.

'Yes, that would be useful,' Campbell confirmed. As she left he continued, 'We need to know more about Anne Crowlie. You've already got her address?' he enquired of Parnold.

'Yes,' said Parnold. 'I had got her details for home and work before the embargo on those lines of enquiry was in place. You might remember I spoke to her on the phone and she'd bought a new suit and been in meetings all day. Or so she said.' Parnold frowned.

'We can't worry about the embargo. We might not have picked up anything from her if we had visited her before this,' said Campbell.

'But we might have,' grumbled Parnold. The faces of Garden and Jenner agreed with Parnold.

'Jenner can you go to Anne Crowlie's workplace and then her home and round up her computers phones etc. and do the usual trawl. We need to look for connections to William Cecil Broadgate and Robert Epsy and

Elizabeth Rattagan.'

'Yes, certainly,' said Jenner.

'We have the man in the car park who could be just a thief, or he could be Watcher,' considered Campbell. 'There is nothing to say the person who broke into the car was not Watcher. After all we don't have any of Anne Crowlie's things. That could be significant.'

'And, we have the name of Frank Norton, the owner of the vehicle in the carpark. He could be Watcher, or at least one of those calling themselves Watcher. If he was the man on the train in Sean Foragehall's seat, he got off in Cambridge and so could have sent the messages. Parnold, check out Frank Norton.'

'Then there's still this business about Elizabeth Rattagan's note.'

'Surely, this murder makes that less relevant,' said Parnold.

'Lindy has found out more about Elizabeth Rattagan,' said Jenner. 'She got the impression from a friend who works there that she was dismissed from her job at Seaminster prosecution office. Apparently, she was discredited.'

'Get Lindy to do some more digging on that one. Have you seen Elizabeth Rattagan lately or her friend, Gwendolyn Blyth?'

'I called round to the cabin. Apparently, their rental had run out. The owner thought they had moved into somewhere local, but she didn't know where.'

'And they haven't seen fit to let us know where they've moved. We did ask them to.' Campbell raised himself up on the balls of his feet and stretched his chin out with irritation.

'I've checked Elizabeth's phone. It's not been on for several days,' said Jenner. 'There's no location on it.'

'What does that look like to you?' asked Campbell.

'They're hiding,' said Parnold.

'They might be holding back information,' suggested Jenner.

'That'll be two more for the list of those we need to find,' said Campbell.

As they left the room to attend to their tasks, Campbell asked Parnold, 'What is happening with the hoodie in the car park?'

'We'll run through the CCTV as well as this recording from the car park. There's also security coverage for the rest of the place but the cameras seem to have not functioned for the period of the murder,' replied Parnold.

'Aye,' said Campbell, 'We ought to look into that.'

'It's just the way it is. These cameras are really temperamental,' said

Parnold as he left.

Garden followed Parnold saying, 'I'll see what I can do,' to Campbell.

Jenner said to Garden, 'We can ask for more detail from the pool manager.' The two of them headed towards the reception desk.

Campbell stood just inside the door on his own. He visually examined the room from his vantage point. On the room side of the doorframe he found a hair. He got out his phone and rang Mary Brown.

'Has anyone looked in the function room from Scene of Crime?' he asked her.

'No, the room was shut and locked when we arrived, we were told it was always kept locked unless it was in use.'

'I think the initial attack may have taken place here. We've just had a meeting in here. I'll check with reception whether this room was locked yesterday evening.'

'Someone will be with you right away,' said Mary Brown.

Campbell thanked her and finished the call. Once the scene of crime officer arrived Campbell went to the reception desk of the swimming pool. He had to wait until a girl appeared at the desk in an unhurried fashion. He asked her about the room.

'No, it wasn't locked this morning when I came in,' said the receptionist. 'It should have been, so I locked it, so no-one would get into trouble. That was before…' The words tapered away.

'May I have the key?'

'Certainly,' said the girl.

'No-one is to enter that room. We will be cordoning it off.'

The girl flushed, clearly embarrassed. Campbell found PC Howard and arranged for him to guard the room.

Jenner arrived in the centre of Cambridge to meet the uniformed policeman from the local office who was to accompany her. He was waiting by the gates of one of the colleges. He introduced himself as, 'Sergeant Percival from Cofen Police Station.'

'It's just a short walk from here,' he said, and he used the distance to chat continuously about the search for Watcher and the Watcher phones. He stopped suddenly and turned to Jenner. 'I thought we were going to catch him.'

'You don't know Watcher is a him,' she said conversationally. 'Nor do you know how many Watchers there are.'

'There were two phones sending messages out of Cambridge,' said Percival. 'After the first message, we thought we'd caught up with the messenger but there was no-one there.'

'Bicycle?' queried Jenner, looking at a dozen of them passing them on the narrow, cobbled streets not far from the colleges.

'Bit fast for your average pedaller. It would have to be someone really quick on a bicycle or even a moped or small motorbike to escape us.' Sergeant Percival stopped walking and pointed out a glass and concrete office block. 'The office you're after is here.'

'Anne Crowlie's?'

'Your dead woman in the swimming pool,' confirmed the officer opening his hand towards a modern styled office across the street. 'So, do you lot think this is connected to the Watcher incident?'

'There is a strong possibility, but we don't have any positive connections,' explained Jenner. She walked into the office where Anne Crowlie had worked with Sergeant Percival. A man came over to the reception desk from a bank of desks and computers. He slid the glass screen to one side. Jenner noted and appreciated the sparkle of the diamond studs in his ears. The purple striped shirt falling loosely over his plump belly was crisply laundered and well styled. His eyes were red, and the flesh of his face looked pinched. She guessed he'd been crying. He introduced himself, 'Herbie Brandon at your service.'

Jenner stared at him, recognition tickled at her; she had to confirm her suspicions. 'Hello, are you Herbert Brandon?'

'Of course,' Herbert said cheerfully despite his pallor. 'I think that's kind of what I just said.'

Jenner continued, 'Were you on the nine-fifteen am train from London to Cambridge and the North Norfolk coast with Anne Crowlie the other Friday?'

'Yes, we were,' he said, taking half a step back and looking puzzled.

'We?' asked Jenner, already writing in her notebook.

'Would you like to come into the office?' asked Herbert Brandon.

'That is probably a good idea,' said Jenner.

'We can continue the conversation in our little office in the reception area.' He said as he came out of a door next to the reception window and opened another door opposite, into a room with a single desk surrounded by four chairs. Once settled Herbert Brandon continued as if there had not been a disturbance to their conversation.

'Yes,' he replied. 'Myself, Graham Aspen and Anne Crowlie were on the train together.'

'Anne didn't exactly sit with you,' objected Jenner.

'There were more people going down to London for the conference originally, but some cancelled and the seats were reallocated, presumably, by the railway company,' explained Herbert. 'I like a window seat at a table myself. Just because you all come from the same company and you've been at a conference doesn't mean that you have to talk to each other on the train journey back. We'd been shoved together for long enough.'

'Anne Crowlie too?' Jenner asked.

'Yes, Anne Crowlie too,' confirmed Herbert.

'Does Frank Norton work here?'

'No, I don't know a Frank Norton,' Herbert said tilting his head as if curious about the question.

'Are you sure? He was on the train.'

'No, he doesn't work here,' said Herbert.

'He was sitting next to Anne,' explained Jenner.

'Ah, I see. No, I definitely don't know the name and I only recognised my colleagues on the train.'

'Do you think he might have anything to do with Anne?'

'I didn't see them speak,' said Herbert. Jenner could see he was focused on her questioning now. 'But I wouldn't have noticed anyway. I look out of the window and plug into my music.'

'Did she have a boyfriend?' asked Jenner.

'Anne? I don't know. I don't know anything about her private life. We're all devastated by her death. I mean murder. What is anybody wanting to murder our lovely Anne for?'

'I want to find that out as much as you do,' said Jenner. She looked back on her notes. 'Is Graham Aspen here today.'

'No, he's working up in a factory in Ely again today. They're having some machinery fitted. That's what we do here. Design and fit equipment into factories.'

'Do you deal with security lights here?'

'No, not at all,' said Herbert Brandon.

'Have you got Graham Aspen's work plan for the last few weeks?'

'Yes, of course, I'll pull up his diary from the computer. We all share diaries.' Herbert Brandon got up and entered the office again. Jenner and Sergeant Percival followed him over to his computer. He opened the diary page. 'He's been at Ely most of this last month. I went through with him on that Friday you were talking about.'

'Can I have a print-off of that?'

'Yes, sure,' said Herbert.

'Can I have your diary and Anne's too?'

'Yes, of course,' said Herbert hitting the print button.

'Can we have the details of the factory.'

'You want to check up on us,' said Herbert with a twinkle in his eye. 'We haven't done anything naughty.'

Jenner said sternly, 'We have to check your whereabouts.'

'Of course,' said Herbert losing his brittle-bright manner.

'Can we get access to Anne's emails?' asked Jenner.

Herbert looked suddenly weary. 'You will have to go through our computer people for that. I'll just call them up and you can arrange it.'

'Would she have any other system for communications?'

'Just her phone,' said Herbert. Sadness pulled at his easy-going expression. 'I'm sorry,' he said.

'Where would she leave that?'

'You could check her desk. She would have a work phone and a home phone. That's what most of us do. If not, they could both be in her handbag.'

Sergeant Percival searched Anne Crowlie's desk. He shook his head. 'No phones, no handbags.'

We haven't found her handbag anywhere, thought Jenner. There was no handbag in Frank Norton's car, anyway. Perhaps the man wearing the hooded sweatshirt had taken it. She turned to Herbert Brandon. 'I'm sorry this has been distressing for you but thank you for your help,' said Jenner.

Herbert Brandon found a large brightly coloured handkerchief in his pocket and moved away with an 'Excuse me.'

Jenner joined Sergeant Percival at Anne's desk.

'Empty,' said Sergeant Percival.

'Paperless office,' said Herbert to them as he passed by on his way out of the room.

The email and computer records were quickly arranged, and Jenner and Sergeant Percival left Anne Crowlie's place of work.

'What did you think of Herbert Brandon?' asked Jenner of Sergeant Percival on the path outside.

'Nice chap, in his own way,' said Percival.

'Do you think he was being over helpful and friendly?'

'No, I think that was his normal way.'

Jenner nodded. She would ponder and discuss Herbert Brandon at the team meeting in the morning.

'Let's see if we can get Anne Crowlie's handbag and phones at her home,' said Jenner.

Anne Crowlie's home was a ground floor flat on what had once been a nineteen thirties semi-detached house in the suburbs of Cambridge. Sergeant Percival was quiet. Jenner could feel his tension. Yet, she always felt strangely relaxed when entering a premises. There could be someone there, but the likelihood was that the deceased's home was empty. After buzzing around the other flats in the building they were let in by a resident who knew nothing of Anne Crowlie and was not aware of anyone in the building having a key. Despite the lack of answer from the buzzer on the outer door she knocked on the door of the flat, perhaps Frank Norton might answer.

No reply. Jenner turned back to Sergeant Percival and shook her head. As no keys had been found for her house in Frank Norton's car, the swimming pool or Anne Crowlie's office, Percival fetched the locksmith who'd been arranged and was waiting in his car parked by the roadside. Jenner viewed the yard and noted a red car parked out on the tarmacked area in front of the building.

When Sergeant Percival returned she asked him, 'Could you find out the owner of that car on the driveway, please?'

'Sure,' he said.

The locksmith arrived with his tools and opened the door. Jenner entered. She had to consider everything she saw and keep foremost in her mind Frank Norton, William Cecil Broadgate, and Harriet Epsy's supposed Uncle Robert as well as any information relating to Elizabeth Rattagan.

It was too late to ask Anne about these people. Why couldn't Superintendent Tarnish just trust Campbell? His instincts for crime were uncanny. She tried again to focus on her search. She also had to look with an open mind.

The house was in darkness. Heavy curtains were shutting out the afternoon light. She opened them carefully. Light fell on elegant furniture and pale carpets, but the room contents were in disarray: drawers were open, cushions tipped off chairs, items raked out from under shelves and the television unit.

'Someone's beaten us to it,' she said to Sergeant Percival. Jenner knew now that their search would be a waste of time. 'We'll have to call in Scene of Crime.'

'Yes,' agreed Sergeant Percival.

She looked at him. She liked his straight forward manner. 'I think we can carry out a careful search,' she said.

'I agree,' said Sergeant Percival. He made the phone call to Scene of Crime and Jenner took out her investigation gloves from her pocket. She viewed the room before her and moved into the kitchen area, the bedroom and bathroom without touching anything.

'Scene of Crime are on their way,' said Sergeant Percival, pulling his gloves out of his pocket and putting them on.

Disturbing as little as possible for the benefit of the scene of crime crew they searched the flat and made careful notes. As they finished Jenner said, 'Someone must have beaten us to it. No computer or phone. No sign of Frank Norton in any shape or form.'

'Not only a paperless office but a paperless life,' complained Jenner lifting the corners of one of the piles of odds and ends that were left where the drawers had been emptied. 'Someone made a very thorough search.'

Sergeant Percival nodded and looked at his phone messages. 'The car outside belongs to Anne Crowlie,' he said.

'Ok,' said Jenner enthusiastically, already heading for the flat door.

They went outside. The locksmith had already reinstated the door lock and provided them with a key. They locked the door and affixed "Police No Entry" tape across it.

At the car Sergeant Percival tried the driver's side door. 'It's unlocked,' he said opening the door and putting his head inside the car.

Jenner opened the boot and looked inside followed by the rear passenger doors and finally the front passenger door.

'The keys are in it,' said Sergeant Percival. 'Perhaps the battery is flat.'

Jenner looked at him. 'There's nothing in the boot, it's completely empty.' She looked in the glove compartment and they both felt under the seats. 'Nothing,' said Jenner.

'Coffee?' asked Sergeant Percival.

'I'm a bit of a tea person,' said Jenner at last allowing herself to relax and smile.

CHAPTER FIFTEEN

Garden was about to leave her car when she heard the news of Anne Crowlie's death broadcast on the national radio. She sighed and opened the door. She'd parked in Banksea's market place, not far from The Gull Inn. The lingerie shop was along the street where she hoped to talk to Louise Green.

'Hello,' said Louise recognising her instantly.

Garden told Louise Green, 'Anne Crowlie has been murdered.'

'I heard about the suspicious death at the swimming pool. It's being treated as murder, so they say. Who is Anne Crowlie?'

'Anne Crowlie was on the train. She was the lady over whom your baby Lilly spilt her drink.'

'I never got her name,' said Louise. Her face sagged. The girl looked troubled. 'I wrote down Elizabeth Rattagan's name, so I could pay her money back,' she replied. After a thoughtful pause she continued, 'Well, I'm not going to have killed her for the sake of a dry-cleaning bill.' She waved at the radio behind the counter. Her lower lip trembled. 'It's terrible. Another murder.'

'Did you say anything to the baby's father about the incident?' asked Garden. 'You need to tell us who the baby's father is now, Louise.'

'If you must know the father is Sean Foragehall. He has absolutely nothing to do with Lilly. I haven't seen him, and I have nothing to do with him.'

Garden drew in a sharp breath. 'Sean Foragehall was on the train from Cambridge. He sat opposite you.'

'That was a coincidence.' Louise Green looked down at the counter.

'No, it wasn't,' insisted Garden.

Louise shuffled her feet. 'Okay, so it wasn't a coincidence. Mum said he messed up my life. He's a bit older than me. I know it takes two to make a baby. I wanted Sean.'

'Why didn't you say this earlier?'

'Because I thought it would get back to my mother that I'd met him. She does a lot for me. I didn't want to quarrel with her.'

'Sean got on at Cambridge. So, he didn't see the drink incident. Did you tell him the story?'

'Yes, I did but I didn't tell him I had borrowed the dry-cleaning money. I've tried to pay it back, but I can't get through to the number that woman gave me.'

'Perhaps she's run out of battery,' suggested Garden. 'When you told Sean about it, could you have exaggerated the events?'

'Yes, I did tell him. I did exaggerate a little bit, I suppose.' Louise hesitated. 'He wouldn't do anyone any harm. He hasn't done anyone any harm, has he?'

'Has he, Louise?' returned Garden raising her eyebrows.

Louise burst into tears and shook her head and Garden sighed and pulled out some tissues from her pocket.

Garden drove up the sandy lane at Cricklestaithe to the farm and found Sean's sister, Neve, in the shop.

'Why didn't you tell us about Sean's baby, Miss Foragehall?'

'It wasn't relevant,' said Neve.

'It was the reason he was on that train,' said Garden recalling Parnold's résumé of events. 'He didn't go and see a girlfriend in Cambridge on the Thursday night before William Cecil Broadgate's murder on the Friday, did he?'

'No,' confessed Neve.

'When did he go down to Cambridge?'

'He went that morning.'

'Friday morning?'

'Yes, he took the early train.'

'Where was he yesterday evening?'

'He was harvesting with his Dad. His Dad would never cover for him, but don't mention the baby. Dad's still angry about it. He reckons the pauper, Louise Green, was just after Sean's money.' Neve paused and then scoffed, 'As if there is any.'

'Marriage?' asked Garden a little surprised at Neve's agitation.

'Yes,' Neve shook her head despairingly.

'Honesty would have helped our investigation, Miss Foragehall. The fictitious girl-friend could have led us down a very different path.'

'I'm sorry. I'm in the habit of doing what I'm told in this family.'

Garden nodded. She mentioned the possibility of prosecution for wasting police time and followed it with, 'Where is Sean and his father harvesting today?'

'Just over the hill. If you go back to the coast road and turn left for about half a mile. I'll phone them, so they will expect you. Nothing will stop them working at this time of year.'

As she left the shop to make her way up to the harvesters Garden was thinking about Elizabeth Rattagan sitting on the train on that Friday. She decided that Elizabeth must have been very wrapped up in her own thoughts or asleep to not notice the interaction of Sean Foragehall sitting opposite Louise Green from Cambridge to Daneton.

Elizabeth Rattagan strode across Banksea Beach with her towel tucked under her arm. She was trying to ignore the taped off area with the blue and white beach hut.

She slipped off her shorts and top and left them on the beach. She was ready for swimming with her costume already on. She thought she would have a hot chocolate from the kiosk after her swim.

She waded into the water. The tide was in and the water wasn't particularly deep here. It chilled her until she started to swim. She set out, planning to head along the coast away from the harbour and in the direction of Daneton. She didn't plan to swim as far as that, just round to the next beach.

She was delighted at how quickly her fitness had returned and she soon found herself well away from Banksea Beach. Here the coast was also sandy and backed by pine trees, like Banksea. This was Brene Beach. She hadn't been here for a long time.

She thought it would be a pleasant place to stop and have a rest, before returning for her hot chocolate and her clothes. The beach here was free of beach huts and very few people were on the sand. When Elizabeth had said she would like to swim to Brene Beach, Gwen had reminded her that the only way was a long walk opposite the swimming pool and the entrance to the lanes were chained-up, so cars couldn't generally go down the edge of the marshes from the coast road. So, as ready access to the woods and the beach was blocked, she would have to swim back.

She drew up onto the sands and lay down enjoying the sunshine. She closed her eyes and let her body go limp. She sat up after a few moments and viewed the beach. There were woods between Banksea Beach and here and in the other direction she could just make out the creak where the boats went out for trips to view the seals. She lay back on the sand and relaxed.

A shadow drew over her. She opened her eyes. The figure above her was in silhouette. She sat up on her elbows.

'Hello,' said Elizabeth guardedly. She vaguely recognised something about the silhouette. 'Is that Harriet? Harriet Epsy?' she asked tentatively. She didn't recognise the shaggy black mane of hair tied into a bandeau above her, but she did vaguely remember the heart shaped face. 'I don't know why you wore that pink wig on Friday night,' she said flatly.

'Just a bit of fun,' said Harriet. 'Thought that was you. I was just up the beach.'

'I just swam round from Banksea.'

'I thought you had. I'll race you back.'

'I don't think I'm up for a race,' replied Elizabeth.

'Well, we need to be swimming back while the tide is still running in, it will be dangerous once it starts to run out.'

'That's true,' said Elizabeth. 'We had better leave now. But I'm not racing. How will you get back from Banksea Beach?'

'I'll get a lift in your car.'

'I don't have a car. Gwen has a car.'

'I'll ask Gwen when I get there then,' said Harriet.

'Okay,' said Elizabeth, laughing at Harriet's audacity.

Harriet was dressed in a green swimsuit with no apparent over-clothing. She produced a swimming-hat in Strath-Kind School colours from the leg of her costume, pulled her bandeau off her hair and tied the hair tie around her wrist and crammed her hair into the cap. Suddenly Harriet looked serious and Elizabeth knew the race was on as far as Harriet was concerned.

They ran into the water and set off in the direction of Banksea Beach. Harriet's flesh had been dry, her green costume had been dry. She was shaped by her pronounced muscles, Elizabeth knew she hadn't got a chance, but she was already warmed up from her earlier swim and Harriet had not been in the water recently, so Elizabeth more easily moved into her stroke. For a while she was ahead until the coastline turned to Banksea Beach.

Harriet swam out in front and Elizabeth responded with a surge of speed. It was not quite enough. Harriet was already running up the beach to reach the kiosk when Elizabeth found her footing and followed her. Harriet reached the kiosk just four strides in front of her.

'My friend is buying, Jess,' said Harriet. 'She lost the race. Two hot chocolates please.'

'Can you put it on the slate?' asked Elizabeth. 'I'll fetch the money as soon as I get back to the caravan.'

'Tomorrow will do,' said Jess, pouring hot water out of the urn over hot-chocolate powder in two plastic cups.

Elizabeth and Harriet sat near Elizabeth's clothes on the sands with their drinks.

'Bit creepy here with the murder and all,' said Harriet.

'We could go back to the caravan,' said Elizabeth. 'But that's a bit creepy too. It's the one where the dead man was staying.'

'Oh wow, I'd like to see that!'

'Would you?' said Elizabeth wrinkling her nose in distaste.

'I need that lift back in any case as the tide is changing.'

'Let's check it out with Gwen.'

'That's great,' said Harriet, standing up. 'I'll take your cup.'

Elizabeth handed her the empty cup and Harriet deposited them at the kiosk as they walked by back to the caravan.

Harriet wandered about in the caravan. She touched the seats and the table as if she were caressing them and stroked the kitchen cabinets. Her behaviour made Elizabeth feel uncomfortable. She glanced at Gwen and she could see she was feeling the same as herself.

'I'm just going to put some clothes on,' said Elizabeth taking her shorts into the bedroom. She left the door open, so she could hear what was being said in the living room.

'Harriet, what have you been doing with yourself all these years?' enquired Gwen.

'This and that. I've worked in the Gull Inn.'

'That Barbs woman didn't seem to recognise you at the old girls' night. Had you had a falling out? Hence the pink wig?'

'You're very shrewd, Gwen,' said Harriet. 'You're quite right. And it worked. She didn't work it out that I was the girl who worked there a few years back.' Harriet looked pleased with herself.

'To be honest,' said Gwen, 'I don't remember you from school either.'

'I was a day pupil. Borders never remember day pupils and I think I was a few years below you, so you wouldn't remember me at all.'

'Harriet wants a lift back to ... where exactly?' asked Elizabeth.

'I left my car on the road outside the swimming pool and walked through the marshes and woods to get to that beach. That whole area between the coast road and the sea is riddled with lanes for miles along the coast. The main road only gets close to the sea at a few places.'

'We'll both take you back,' said Gwen. 'And you can fill us in on all the other things you've been up to.'

'Yes,' said Harriet rising her eyebrows. 'That sounds great.'

Elizabeth noted a slight reduction in enthusiasm for the proposal from Harriet. She looked questioningly at Gwen: her car was essentially a two-seater with a tiny shelf like seat behind the front passenger and driver. Gwen returned with a glance of suspicion in the direction of Harriet.

'Do you want to borrow a skirt until you get to the car to put over your swimming costume,' asked Elizabeth.

Gwen very slightly shook her head at Elizabeth.

'We haven't got much else,' said Elizabeth.

'No, you're fine,' said Harriet. 'I've got my clothes back at the car.'

At the car Gwen, without a word, directed Elizabeth to sit behind the passenger seat. Harriet said, 'Oh no, I'll be fine in the back.'

Gwen's eyes told her to stay put. 'I'm fine, thanks,' said Elizabeth climbing in the back.

Harriet got in the front passenger seat a little reluctantly.

Within a few minutes they were by the swimming pool and Gwen was saying a little sharply, 'Here we are.'

Harriet thanked them and got out.

'She's well lost the school accent,' said Gwen.

'Well, so have I,' said Elizabeth.

'I don't think she was ever at Strath-Kind,' said Gwen. 'She's not got in her car yet, so I'm going to turn around and see what she does.'

'It'll be one of the cars along here,' said Elizabeth.

'You'd soon get in your car if you were just wearing a swimming costume, Lizzy.' Before Elizabeth could answer Gwen had driven up a side road and turned the car around. 'And she hasn't.'

As they came down the side road they looked across and along the main coast road to where they left Harriet.

'She's walking down that lane to the beach,' observed Elizabeth.

'Her car must be down there, Lizzy. Let's park up and see what she does.'

'Why?'

'Because I don't think she is who she says she is,' said Gwen.

'How come?'

'You asked me, Lizzy, why I was so rude at the Gull Inn the other night at the old girls' get together. The business thing was real, by the way. But I thought I'd seen the girl who I remember as working for Dungrade. It unsettled me, and yet in some way that was what I'd hoped for.'

'You mean Harriet?'

'I wasn't sure. Oddly enough, it was the pink wig and her outfit, so over the top. It was meant as a disguise, a deflection from who she really was. And then today, in daylight without the wig I recognised her instantly from the visits to Dungrade's office when I was involved with the team that was investigating him. She had blond hair then.'

'Does she recognise you?'

'I don't think so, I was in uniform. I wore a hat.'

'You weren't a detective?'

'No, not then.'

Elizabeth shivered as they parked close to the entrance by the swimming pool and waited. About fifty minutes later a car came up the lane.

'That's Harriet,' said Elizabeth and Gwen almost at the same time.

'She drove down the lane to the coast,' said Gwen.

'She said she walked. It's meant to be all locked up.'

'She must have access.'

'What is she up to?' wondered Elizabeth.

'I don't know, but she seems to have targeted us.'

'Perhaps she does recognise you, Gwen.'

'No, she's after you. She didn't show any recognition when she looked at me. I bet she saw you leave Banksea Beach today, Lizzy, and drove round here hoping to interact with you on Brene Beach in some way.'

'That's really unlikely,' said Elizabeth. 'Shall we follow her now?'

'No, she said she would give us a ring. Let's wait for her. She will contact us soon enough. She looked like someone with a scheme from the expression on her face as she came up that lane. If we follow her she will surely notice us.' Gwen paused. 'In the meantime,' she said, 'I intend to pursue my inheritance.'

Elizabeth looked at Gwen with surprise.

Georgia sat on Daneton Howe beach. Bradley Yorkman sat next to her. She gave him a kiss and he hugged her sensing her sadness. Their red and fair hair mixed together in the breeze.

My grandfather lied to me,' she told him at last. 'I believed everything he told me and now the police are questioning me like I'm some sort of criminal.'

'They're questioning everybody, and you were the closest to him.'

She smiled thinly. 'I was totally taken in by him.'

'You were just a child.'

'Why didn't my parents stop him?'

'Perhaps they were taken in too?'

After some thought Georgia said, 'It's possible. But what about you. I can see the trouble in your eyes.'

'You do one small wrong thing when you're young and people think that every bad thing that happens is down to you.'

'I'm going to start again,' said Georgia, 'As from today. It should be easy to do. You can do the same. We're young enough. We've got the rest of our lives.'

Bradley smiled. She knew he liked her and she knew she liked him.

'Oi!' shouted a man striding up the beach. 'What are you doing with Georgia Lomond?'

Bradley stood up. 'Sean what are you doing here?' he asked the new arrival.

'What are you doing here, more like: with Georgia?' retorted Sean.

'I just met her here by chance,' said Bradley.

'I doubt that,' said Sean moving towards Bradley with his hands working into fists.

'What do you mean by that?' asked Georgia looking at Bradley and Sean in turn.

'I arranged to meet you here,' said Sean. 'So, what's he doing here?'

'We met by chance,' confirmed Georgia.

'I doubt that,' repeated Sean.

'Our meeting was because you had something important to discuss with me,' Georgia reminded Sean.

'You really don't know do you?' asked Sean of Georgia.

'Know what?'

'Bradley used to follow you about when you used to be at that Strath-Kind School.

'So, did you,' said Bradley.

'That was different,' said Sean with a growl in his voice.

'In what way? You had a girlfriend already, Louise Green, and you still came after me,' said Georgia.

'You spoilt my relationship with Louise and my daughter,' complained Sean turning towards her.

'I had no knowledge of it until Louise told me,' said Georgia.

'What do you want to talk to Georgia about?' asked Bradley defensively.

'That is none of your business.' Sean moved towards Georgia his face colour darkening.

'I'm not leaving her here with you in this mood.' Bradley stepped between Sean and Georgia.

Sean lifted his arm to strike Bradley. Bradley picked up a piece of drift-wood from the beach.

Georgia went between them and tried to wrestle them apart. Sean jostled her, and Bradley let his drift-wood fall from his hand. Bradly immediately heard a clear female voice behind them say, 'Police.' Detective Constable Garden was running down the beach towards them.

'What is all this about?' she asked.

Behind the police officer an older man, thick set and red in the face from sun and exertion came running up. Bradley recognised him and felt uneasy.

'Dad,' said Sean.

'This is my fault,' said Mr Foragehall senior.

Sean dropped away from Bradley.

'He has nothing to do with this,' said Mr Foragehall senior nodding at Bradley Yorkman.

'He's an arsonist,' said Sean accusingly.

'You are just angry, Sean. You know full well he's not an arsonist,' said Mr Foragehall senior.

Sean looked at his feet. Then he looked at his father angrily.

'I went to speak to you in the field and I found your father on his own with the combine,' said DC Garden. 'He said you had gone to the beach and feared you might be in trouble as you and he had had a terrible argument. So, we came to find you.'

'You led me to believe the farm was ours. And it's never been ours,' complained Sean.

'I'm sorry, son. When we had financial difficulties down South I sold our farm down there to clear our debts. Developers bought it. I thought we could maintain our life-style by becoming tenant farmers here.'

'So, there is nothing for me to inherit? All this work has been for nothing.'

'Who owns the land?' asked DC Garden.

'She does now,' said Foragehall senior nodding at Georgia.

'What did you want to see me about?' asked Georgia of Sean.

'I wanted you to tell Louise that nothing happened between you and me,' said Sean.

'Well, I can't do that can I?'

Bradley surged forward towards Sean.

'Enough,' said Detective Constable Garden, firm and calm. Uniformed police officers strode up to them. 'I am taking you two into the station,' confirmed Garden acknowledging the arrival of Sergeant Howard and PC Grantly with a nod. Sean Foragehall and Bradley Yorkman were escorted away by Sergeant Howard and PC Grantly.

Garden watched the two young men being led up the beach, their heads bowed. 'I would like you to come along and make a statement about this incident, Miss Lomond,' said Garden.

'You saw everything that happened,' Georgia replied. 'There was nothing else.'

Garden nodded. 'I realise that you might not want to come back into the police station just now. Perhaps you can tell me, how did this start?'

'It was a fight over me,' said Georgia. 'Sean and I had a relationship. It was the reason he and Louise split up. Bradley thought he was defending me.'

Sean's father looked despairingly at DC Garden.

'Sean will be out fairly soon I expect,' she said to him reassuringly. 'What's this about the ownership of the farm?' she asked Georgia.

'I inherited everything from my grandfather. He owned this stretch of land that the Foragehalls leased off him. I thought that was what Sean wanted to see me about.'

'And the other business with Louise.'

'I lied just then and back when Louise became pregnant. I was angry with Sean. He always wanted more but he was always too old for me. I know Louise is a bit younger than me, but we're all different about the men we like.'

'Will you tell Louise the truth?'

'Aye, I will.' Georgia turned and wandered away up the beach.

'So, there were no fortunes for Louise Green to have been after?' asked Garden of Foragehall Senior.

'No, I was never against Louise Green. And I had absolutely nothing to do with Sean's break up with Georgia Lomond. He said all that nastiness about me being to blame, even to my own family, to hide his hurt.'

'And you said nothing in all this time?'

'I'm his father,' said Foragehall Senior. He glowered at Garden. 'How do you expect me to get a harvest in now? He won't come back after this. I'll have to get Neve to shut the shop and drive the tractor.'

'Thank you for your help,' said Garden. 'Your son will be out from the police station in a while.' She left Foragehall Senior to his harvest. She returned to her car going in the opposite direction to the one which Georgia had taken herself in.

Georgia looked to re-settle herself further down the beach after Bradley and Sean had been taken away by the police. She turned away from the sea and clambered up through the dunes beyond the beach huts. She laid back knowing she was hidden away, surrounded by the sharp reed-like grass and the mounds of wind-blown sand and she closed her eyes. Perhaps she would go and see the place where the upside-down tree had been found. Some ancient site, so the archaeologists said, revealed by a storm washing the sands away from it. Her grandfather was like that. Now he was dead she had learnt so much more about him. She rolled onto her stomach and peeped at the sea through the folds of the dunes.

'You look comfy,' said a male voice behind her.

Georgia swung round and stood up all in one swift movement.

'No need for alarm.'

'Ralph Peterson,' said Georgia with a tremble in her voice.

'You're open country now with that old devil of a grandfather's out the way. And rich too I understand.'

'How do you know?'

'I was enjoying the little excitement on the beach earlier.'

'You were watching?'

'Yes, it was excellent entertainment.'

'You want to mind your own business.'

'Oh, I will,' said Ralph Peterson. 'You are my business.'

'Of course I'm not.' Georgia started to walk away. She glanced back to see Ralph Peterson wearing a vicious grin on his face.

'You just wait and see,' said Ralph Peterson.

Georgia started to run back towards the Daneton Howe Beach carpark. She didn't look back.

CHAPTER SIXTEEN

Campbell came in to interview Sean Foragehall with DC Garden. Sean had asked for his solicitor to be present.

Garden started by asking Sean Foragehall, 'Why were you fighting with Bradley Yorkman?'

'The little creep was always following her about a few years ago when Georgia was at Strath-Kind.'

'When she was about seventeen/eighteen?'

'Yes.'

'Is Bradley not about the same age as her?'

Sean Foragehall nodded.

'So, what's this really about?'

'How dare that Bentley Yorkman make a move on Georgia,' stormed Sean Foragehall.

'Georgia is a wealthy woman who owns the land you want. Was it William Cecil Broadgate who saw you off, Sean?'

'From Georgia?' Sean looked down. 'Yes.'

'You could have murdered William Cecil Broadgate thinking you could not only revenge him for not allowing you to have anything to do with Georgia, but the process would have provided you with the land you so desperately want.'

'I only found out today: that was what I was arguing with my father about. Neve had been doing the accounts and she opened a letter explaining that the ownership would be changing.'

'Neve didn't know either?'

'No, she didn't.' Sean Foragehall paused for a moment. 'But Georgia is interested in that Bradley Yorkman boy.'

'She told me,' said Garden, 'that she'd never been interested in you.'

His body sagged over the table. 'Georgia has ruined my life. She took Louise and Lilly away from me. I was infatuated with Georgia. I see that now. I wish she'd told me then.'

Garden wanted to say that Georgia was very young, but she held her council, hopefully someone else would say that to him.

'I wish my father had told me then the business was worthless, and we didn't even own it,' he said.

Campbell leaned forward. 'Do you know Anne Crowlie at all?'

Sean Foragehall looked surprised, 'No,' he said. That's that murdered woman at the swimming pool.'

'Where were you last night?'

'Doing the harvest with my dad all evening and most of the night. We got back to our beds at about one in the morning.'

'Thank you, Mr. Foragehall.' Garden closed the interview and turned off the recording machine.

'We can let Bradley Yorkman go too,' said Parnold as Campbell and Garden came out of Sean Foragehall's interview room. Jenner and Parnold's faces told him that they had collected the equivalent of bottle tops instead of gold coins from that trawl through the sands of Sean Foragehall's mind. 'Bradley was just on the beach chatting up Georgia Lomond,' he confirmed to his colleagues.

'Did Bradley know Anne Crowlie?' asked Campbell.

'No,' said Jenner, 'and there was no defensiveness in his replies.'

'Where was he last evening?'

'With his dad watching the cricket on the telly,' said Parnold.

'It was worth asking them especially as Sean could have had a motive. They did bring themselves to our attention,' said Campbell, 'and around Georgia Lomond too.'

Campbell looking carefully down in thought and then he raised his head. 'I'm sure the deaths of William Cecil Broadgate, Robert Epsy and Anne Crowlie are linked in some way. We need to get to the truth of it.'

Elizabeth saw Gwen Blythe return from her phone call to her grandmother's residential home. She came from the Banksea Halt direction of the coast road and turned up the side street where they were parked. Gwen opened the driver's side door and slid into her car next to Elizabeth. 'Lizzy, I'm going to have to put my phone on again,' she told her. 'All this phone activity might bring the police to us.'

Elizabeth could see from Gwen's blotchy complexion that she had confirmed with the home that her grandmother had died. 'Here's the car keys, Lizzy. There aren't that many street cameras around here. I'll meet up with you in a couple of hours at the cafe by the bird sanctuary – the one near where we were staying. Try and park out of the way.'

Elizabeth frowned.

'The Manager at Gran's home said the solicitor was called Pilmer,' explained Gwen.

'Could that be Abigail's husband?' asked Elizabeth.

'I believe he is a solicitor. I'm sure I heard her say that at the Gull Inn. She was telling some story about someone taking the pudding she'd ordered.'

'But could he be dealing with your grandmother's will, Gwen?'

'I checked him out on the internet. I'm sure of it. They both work in Seachester on the south coast.'

'Are they both solicitors?' asked Elizabeth. 'Seachester is two counties away. I haven't come across him in my work.'

'Abigail Pilmer is a clerk there,' explained Gwen. Their names are listed on the company's contact details.'

'Okay, I'll meet you at the café. I'll walk there so I can hide the car first.'

Gwen nodded and left.

Harriet waited and watched Gwen and Elizabeth. They must have thought her totally stupid if they had thought she hadn't seen them watching her. From their behaviour they certainly hadn't seen her double back and park alongside the coast road, perhaps they had been preoccupied parking up that side street. Watching them meant that she had to take time out from watching the police, but this was a priority. Gwen Blythe had made a phone call on her mobile and returned up the side street to where her and that Elizabeth Rattagan had thought they'd parked their car discreetly. It might have been away from the police, but it was not away from her. Silly women.

Gwen Blythe reappeared from the side street and turned in Harriet's direction, along the coast road towards Daneton. Harriet swore under her breath and slid down in the seat in the hope that Gwen was too lost in thought to notice her car. Harriet had parked in among many parked along the street, so her number plate was hidden from view. But before Gwen reached her she crossed the road with her phone to her ear. Harriet relaxed.

Over an hour later, Gwen walked through the coastal marsh to the café and book shop and disappeared inside. Harriet wondered from her vantage point on a protective bank within the bird sanctuary whether Elizabeth was in there. She guessed she must be.

Perhaps, thought Harriet, she ought to make her way to the café and confront the women. But that could be a dangerous strategy, she wasn't prepared. A moment later Harriet noticed the pair of them leave the café through its garden and exit across a footpath running along the edge of the wheat field at the back of the café garden.

Harriet saw a motorcycle careering towards Cricklestaithe on the opposite side of the field to the path taken by Gwen and Elizabeth. Again, Harriet swore under her breath. She'd lost her opportunity. She felt her phone ring in her pocket. She answered it, listened. 'Ok,' she said and closed the call. Harriet smiled and walked back down the bank towards her car. Whatever had Gwen thought she was achieving by walking around the bird sanctuary, Harriet had been able to watch her all the way without having to move far. Anyone would think the woman was an amateur.

Gwen stopped along the track and watched the motorcycle disappear behind some trees and looked back at the tea shop. 'Let's go back to the creak and get one of those seal trips,' she said to Elizabeth.

'Why?' asked Elizabeth.

'We used to go on those sandbanks when we were at school. Do you remember?'

'Yes, it was all very organised. The Head Teacher's daughter, Arabella Macfine, used to take those excursions with a guide. Strange to see Maccy as head mistress now,' said Elizabeth.

'We need something to lighten our moods, Lizzy. As I've arranged to see the solicitor tomorrow in Cambridge, we've got the rest of the day to unwind. Your nerves are getting really strung out. I feel you might snap any moment. I thought it will do us both good to see the seals again.'

'Yes, you're right.'

On arrival at the jetty the boatman welcomed them and twenty others onto his craft which looked like an oversized rowing boat with an outboard motor mounted on the back.

'Are you old girls from Strath-Kind?' he asked.

'Yes,' said Gwen.

'We've had a lot of you lot this week.'

Gwen and Lizzie smiled and nodded.

'Reunion,' said Lizzie.

The boat moved out from the creek from the far end of Brene Beach where Lizzie had met Harriet in the middle of her swim from Banksea Beach. It turned away from the beach at the end of the creek and travelled in the Daneton direction. Lizzy and Gwen nestled down on the side benches fitted around the boat's wide flat hull.

'Boats don't come as close as this usually,' said the boatman. 'The water's too shallow near the sandbanks.'

'I remember Arabella Macfine bringing us to a bungalow out here for nature studies,' said Lizzy.

'Yes, Lizzy, you know that this bit isn't a sandbank as such,' said Gwen. 'It's actually a long spit of land, a peninsula, if you like.'

'So why exactly did we come out here?' asked Lizzy.

'That's right,' said Gwen, replying to her previous statement about the bungalow. 'I expect they sold it. An asset like that must be worth good money.'

Around the bend of the shore line half grown pups and adult common seals basked in the sunshine. And, back from the beach, an old timber bungalow came into view. There was no car parked beside it but there was a boat trailer. 'I thought Harriet might be staying out this way,' confessed Gwen.

'From what we can see on this trip we would not be able to tell if she is or not,' said Lizzy.

'Oh look,' said Gwen. 'The seals are lovely.'

Lizzy frowned at her and turned her attention to the seals.

The boatman said, 'There's someone swimming. What an idiot! The currents here are treacherous, let alone the seals. They don't like you near their young. And, anyway, it's not allowed because of the seals.'

'We were never allowed to swim down here,' commented Gwen. The passengers peered with Lizzy in the direction of the swimmer.

Gwen borrowed a fellow passenger's binoculars and looked at the head moving smoothly through the water.

'Can you make out who it is?' asked Lizzy.

'No, I can't but whoever it is wearing the school hat.'

Their boat turned around. Gwen could see the swimmer's head bobbing along towards the shore some distance from the seals but before she could see who it belonged to, their boat had travelled back around the bend, and their view was blocked by sand dunes.

Campbell viewed the team of police officers before him. They were looking exhausted. The leads created by Anne Crowlie's murder investigation seemed to have stalled. All the usual efforts were being made to find Frank Norton, but until he was found no further progress seemed likely. Campbell decided that a normal length of working day would help everybody including himself recover some energies.

After giving out these instructions he went down to Daneton Howe and parked by the promenade. He stood in the same place, leaning over the promenade railings where he had observed Harriet and the man described by her as Uncle Robert Epsy, before becoming involved with that man's death.

He watched the people walking along the beach. He joined them and walked down past the café and along the cliffs until he reached the beach huts nestling in the sand dunes. He sat for a while contemplating the vast sea and sky before him. His head lowered, and he examined the dunes. He thought about the sand whipping along the beach in the evening sea breeze covering and shifting the litter and reshaping the beach itself. He liked to sit for a while quietly and absorb the place. This activity always settled his thoughts and helped the pieces of the puzzle move about in his head.

His mind drifted unwantedly to his personal circumstances and echoes of old Edinburgh invaded his thoughts. He felt that as time passed the wind was eroding the protective sand of everyday life he had gathered about him to protect himself. He could not have his mind wander so destructively from its task. Yet to assuage the increasing need he had to confront his past he decided he would spend an hour going through the cabinet of his mother's things before bed. He stood up and knocked the loose sand from him and started to walk back towards the town with his jacket slung over his shoulder. The sun was low in the sky and the far distant lands of Lincolnshire formed a silhouette along the western skyline.

Out of the dunes he found the wind keen. In the distance, he saw a lone hooded figure running, parallel to the beach huts and using the hard sand left by the retreating tide to head up towards the promenade. Campbell continued, his face stung from the sharp sand in the wind. He dipped his head against it as he progressed back up the beach towards the promenade.

Level with the beach huts Campbell became aware of a sound that was not wind, sea or shrieking gulls. The sound of crackling alerted him to burning wood, too loud for a beach fire lit to cook a meal, a beach hut on fire? He ran as best as he could over the deep sand in the direction of the noise. He phoned the emergency services as he ran. He felt the heat of fire and then he saw it. Flames licked and lapped the wood at the back of the painted beach hut, quickly turning the bright colours to black as the vicious flames spread.

Someone was rattling the door from the inside.

Campbell scrambled as best he could across the remaining soft sand between him and the hut. The heat was becoming fierce and the door rattling stopped. The metal handle of the door was untouchable. He wrapped his jacket around his hand and grabbed it and levered it down. He pushed the door. It wouldn't open. The timber door was too hot to touch even through his jacket which fell away singed. He felt the pain from the burn on his hand.

He lifted a foot and kicked the door. Campbell guessed a human was caught behind but his only way of releasing this person before they were all engulfed in flames was to break down the door. He tried again. This time his foot struck the catch breaking it. He used his foot to break down the remains of the door. A man was slumped inside. He dragged the man out. The victim had been clutching a laptop computer under his arm which came out with him as Campbell dragged him down the steps and away from the fire. The computer tumbled down the beach hut steps with the man.

Campbell checked him. He was blackened by smoke, but he was still breathing. He seriously needed help, more than Campbell could provide. He knew he might harm the man to move him further. He found a water stand pipe with a tap a short distance away for the use of the beach huts. A large plastic bottle was caught in the grass nearby. He filled it, allowing the splashing water to run on to sooth his hot feet and burnt hand. He returned to the man and soaked him as best he could to reduce the heat of his body. He continued to do this until he heard the welcome sound of sirens. Physical exhaustion overwhelmed him. He sat on the beach next to the victim, his mind racing.

The beach hut was rapidly disappearing before his eyes. He noted a nearby petrol can and realised his presence on the beach had disturbed the arsonist. Campbell mentioned the loan hooded runner to the first officer he saw. Perhaps at least one crime could be solved with quick action and, if not, with some careful investigation of the security footage. He and the victim were soon surrounded by knowledgeable help. As the paramedic and ambulance driver lifted the man, Campbell lifted the computer.

The ambulance driver passed Campbell a wallet. 'Found it on him,' she explained.

Campbell opened the wallet and found the man's picture on his driving licence. He looked a bit like an older version of Sean Foragehall. He had seen this picture before. Jenner had shown it to him. This man was the owner of the car used by Anne Crowlie to bring her to the scene of her death. The man's details were listed by the photograph. His name was Frank Norton. Campbell sighed. At last. He hoped he would be able to be questioned at some point. He asked the paramedic, 'How bad is he?'

'It's bad,' she said, as she closed the back doors to the ambulance on Frank Norton. Campbell dug out his phone from his pocket and arranged for a uniformed officer to remain at the hospital with Frank Norton. He wanted to know the moment that he would be able to talk to him.

He continued to look through his wallet and found a picture of Anne Crowlie but no other evidence of next of kin. He'd get Lindy Grey in the office to check that. He looked at the phone. He picked up the laptop and took it back to the car where he had a selection of evidence bags in the boot. He picked up one that would fit, filled in the form on the back and placed the laptop inside. He was tempted to look at it but knew he could not and should not without forensic computer advice.

Parnold arrived and glanced at the scene before him. He was on the rota for call out. The scene of crime officers had secured the site and set up lamps to assist them. He found Campbell by his car shuffling evidence bags. 'I'll take that back to the office, Sir?' he suggested nodding at the computer.

'Victim's Frank Norton,' said Campbell. 'His wallet.' He waved vaguely at the other package in the boot of the car. 'Yes,' said Campbell finally responding to Parnold's suggestion. 'I'm in no fit state. I've been checked out by the paramedic. I'm okay. They've just dressed a small burn on my hand.'

'I'll drive you,' said Parnold, ignoring the reassuring tones which were in opposition to the Inspector's sagging shoulders and smoke blackened face.

'No need to look at the computer now.' Campbell said. 'Looks like arson. Saw someone running along the beach towards the prom – wearing a hoodie.'

'Uniform are on to it already, as soon as you said,' said Parnold reassuringly. Campbell wasn't inclined to not form full sentences. Parnold took his reduction in words to be a sign of exhaustion. 'Home.' Parnold's statement was more demanding this time.

Campbell didn't argue. 'Thanks,' he said.

At home Campbell poured sea salt into his bath water, undressed and wedged himself into the bath. Other than his dressed hand which he left out, the minor burns he had not told the paramedic about stung in the bath and were then soothed by the water. He closed his eyes and slept. He woke about an hour later, dried, covered any sore places with cream and took himself to the cupboard at the back of his house. He pulled out an old coloured rug his mother had hooked herself and a patchwork blanket made by the same hand. He lay on the mat and covered himself in the blanket. He immediately fell into a deep sleep.

Parnold returned to the burnt-out beach hut at Daneton Howe after dropping off Campbell at home. The hut remains were still too hot to approach so he returned to the car. He immediately received a call from the station telling him that Jess Barratt had been arrested for suspicion of arson. 'She smells of petrol,' complained the Duty Sergeant. 'We're giving her something to change in to and sending her clothes to forensics.'

'Was she wearing a hoodie when she came in?'

'Yes,' replied the Duty Sergeant

'I'm coming in to book in some evidence, but we'll interview her in the morning,' Parnold advised, looking at the laptop sealed in its evidence bag.

CHAPTER SEVENTEEN

The morning sunshine was dazzling Elizabeth and Gwen as they stood outside the office in Cambridge in readiness for the interview with her grandmother's solicitor. They stepped into the porch of the old stone-faced building to read the list of businesses within. Elizabeth was looking around the street behind her, on her guard. This building contrasted sharply with the office block built in the flat style of the nineteen sixties next to it. She noted that it belonged to an engineering firm.

'Please concentrate, Lizzy,' said Gwen. 'There are a lot of names on the menu for the building.'

'Are you sure this is the place?' asked Elizabeth.

'Of course, I'm sure,' replied Gwen. 'Michael Pilmer was quite clear. He even described the building next door.'

'Do you want me to record the conversation?'

'No, I told you, I'll do it.' Gwen ran her finger along the listing again. 'Got it,' she said.

Elizabeth grabbed her friend's arm as she was about to press the buzzer for the office. 'These people might be dangerous,' Elizabeth said gravely. 'The police are investigating two murders.'

'So?' asked Gwen with irritation in her voice and a twitch of her shoulders

'There's that woman murdered at the swimming pool.'

'We have no reason to believe she is connected.'

'She must be,' insisted Elizabeth.

'Do you know her?'

'They gave out her name as Anne Crowlie. I don't know that name. But I might have met her. Supposing she was on the train on Friday? The television didn't show a picture of her.'

Gwen frowned. 'Lizzy, we don't know her. For goodness sake concentrate,' she said, while double checking the address on her piece of paper.

'Why didn't Michael Pilmer want to meet you in Banksea? His wife and brother-in-law are staying in the barn at the Gull Inn. Surely, that would have made sense?'

'I didn't say we were there. He doesn't need to know we are here. He doesn't know we know Shana and that we met Abigail on Friday.'

'Oh right,' said Elizabeth, wondering if Abigail would be in the office anyway.

'Michael Pilmer said he was borrowing the office from a colleague.' Gwen pressed the buzzer.

Elizabeth, unseen by Gwen made her phone ready to record despite Gwen's protest.

Michael Pilmer was tall, slim and wore an elegant suit with a crisp shirt and tie. He introduced himself and expressed his pleasure in meeting them. He spoke pleasantly about the deceased and pointed out that her grandmother had left everything to Gwendolyn and that his firm were executors to the will. There were aspects of the estate that required winding up and the assets would have to be ascertained and probate would have to be applied for and granted.

'What aspects are outstanding?' asked Gwen.

'We need to trawl for all the bank accounts she might have. Usual procedure.'

'When will the monies be released?'

'That could be some months.'

'I see, thank you,' said Gwen politely.

Elizabeth and Gwen left. Outside the office they sighed with relief.

'Nothing unusual there,' said Elizabeth to Gwen. 'Although I thought they would have pulled together the banks by now. Perhaps it is a delaying tactic, they might drag it out to maximise charges on their services'

The office door opened suddenly, and Michael Pilmer came out. 'I've got a friend who advises in investments, all above board you understand. Let me give you his card.' He pushed a business card into Gwen's hand. 'This guy is really worth a look. He's done some great deals for me.'

Gwen sounded enthusiastic as she said, 'Thank you very much,' and put the card in her pocket. When he left she said, 'I turned my recording off just before Michael Pilmer made that approach.'

'I didn't,' said Elizabeth. 'This time we go to the police.'

Gwen nodded. 'We could just check out the name on the card?'

'No,' said Elizabeth firmly. 'We can give it to the police.'

Gwen agreed, and they started going down the stairs. Elizabeth looked up at the sound of footsteps approaching them rapidly. Harriet Epsy was bouncing up two steps at a time towards them. 'Hello girls,' she said, tossing her black curls as she reached them.

'What are you doing here?' asked Gwen.

'I work here.'

'For the solicitors?'

'No,' she breezed. 'I saw you loitering outside earlier and so I've been keeping an eye out for you. Do you fancy a coffee?'

Elizabeth frowned. She had been scanning around them for just such an occurrence.

'Yes,' said Gwen.

Elizabeth's expression asked her why as Harriet Epsy left the building in front of them.

'She's knows something,' whispered Gwen.

Elizabeth reluctantly agreed.

In the coffee shop Harriet unravelled her crossed legs and smiled at them. It made Elizabeth feel more uncomfortable. 'I'm not going to insult your intelligence,' said Harriet. 'I know that you, Gwen, have worked for the police and you, Elizabeth, for the prosecution service. I know that you no longer work for either of these institutions and I know why.'

'And how would you know all that?' asked Gwen.

'I have been following your careers,' said Harriet.

'In what way?' asked Elizabeth.

Harriet ignored Elizabeth's question. 'You know what everyone else knows: that William Cecil Broadgate is dead. I expect the intricate details of his business life are now being unravelled by the police. You have been helpful to me in that you have kept from them what you know.'

'What do you mean?' asked Elizabeth giving Gwen a sharp look.

'There is good news also,' said Harriet ignoring Elizabeth's question. 'Your quest for justice for the activities of Dungrade has come to an end. He is dead.'

'I haven't heard of Dungrade's murder, there has been nothing on the news,' insisted Elizabeth.

'William Cecil Broadgate was Dungrade,' said Harriet with disdain.

'And you have William Cecil's book.'

'What book?' asked Gwen.

'You know what book. You are in the caravan, you didn't stay there on a whim, Gwen. You were looking for it or some similar evidence of a connection between yourselves and William Cecil's murder. When I raced Lizzy back to Banksea and saw you in the caravan, you were guarded, Gwen. I knew you'd found it. I could feel it.'

'Why do you need the book?' asked Elizabeth. Gwen gave her a warning look, but it was too late. There was no point in pretending there wasn't a book. Harriet knew of its existence.

'I have worked for Dungrade, as you know, Gwen.'

Gwen looked down when Elizabeth looked at her. Harriet had clearly remembered her when she'd visited Dungrade as a uniformed police officer. The thought of their dead colleagues ran through her mind as well as the contacts Harriet must have made at her and Gwen's work.

'You should go to the police,' said Elizabeth. 'Come clean. Tell them all you know.'

'I do not wish to involve the police,' warned Harriet in a whisper.

'Ah,' said Gwen.

'And then if you go to the police, there's your ruined careers. They will not listen to you. After this you will both be totally unemployable.'

Elizabeth lunged at Harriet, but Gwen jumped up and pulled her back.

'We already are unemployable, and you were involved in our destruction,' seethed Elizabeth.

Harriet smiled. 'It doesn't take much to tip your determination for right into an unmanageable obsession. Nor does it take much to change people's view of you. A small word here, a hint there. Before long, your own responses to the subtle change of belief in your abilities and trust in your honesty and, there you are, ruining your own careers.'

'You enjoyed it,' said Elizabeth angrily.

'Perhaps you had William Cecil murdered,' said Harriet accusingly.

'We didn't murder anyone,' said Gwen, angry too.

'The notebook will tell me who is the murderer. Tell you what, we can go and collect the book and we can take it to the police together.'

'You will never go to the police,' said Gwen.

'The book is not at William Cecil's house nor at the caravan nor in the beach house. I have had them checked recently. You have it somewhere.'

'I am not carrying it on me,' said Gwen.

'Bag!' demanded Harriet.

Gwen gave up her bag to Harriet who rummaged in it. Not finding the book, she shoved the bag back at her.

'Lizzy, bag,' demanded Harriet.

Elizabeth passed Harriet her bag. Harriet pulled out handfuls of useless bits of paper, a comb and a purse from Elizabeth's bag, threw them back in and shoved it towards her.

'No phone?'

'We got rid of them,' said Elizabeth.

'So, Gwen, you'll keep an eye on the door of the café opposite the lingerie shop in Banksea at three this afternoon. Be there with the book. Do you understand?'

'Why should I?'

'Elizabeth is coming with me,' said Harriet.

'No,' said Gwen.

'It will be fine,' said Elizabeth.

'Don't do anything stupid,' said Gwen to them both.

'You don't have to worry about me. It would be bad for business to be associated with her disappearance,' said Harriet. 'But I do have a gun.'

Gwen looked at Elizabeth. Elizabeth gave her a tense nod in agreement with Harriet as she looked down at the device pointed at her stomach.

'How obscene to put everyone here in danger,' said Gwen.

'Only Lizzy,' said Harriet. 'This is just to emphasise how important it is that you do as I wish. Lizzy has already virtually disappeared. Would anyone miss her?'

'Stay calm, Gwen. We will just do as she says,' said Elizabeth.

'Get up slowly,' said Harriet.

Elizabeth went to Harriet's car, which she thought looked as if it was a hired vehicle, and Gwen returned to the railway station.

Campbell looked at the laptop computer Frank Norton had been holding. The forensic computer expert introduced himself as Alan and set about checking it for fingerprints and taking some swabs of the surfaces. Eventually he opened the laptop with care. A sheet of paper, slotted between the screen and the keyboard, lifted by the movement, slid out. Wearing gloves to prevent any contamination of the evidence Campbell picked up the sheet and read it while the expert checked the keyboard and screen for fingerprints and chemicals.

'Looks like a list of passwords,' said Campbell.

Still examining the hardware Alan said, 'This laptop seems to be mostly undamaged.'

'There was a man on top of it,' said Campbell.

Jenner entered and said, 'Good morning.'

Campbell and Alan replied briefly but without taking their concentration from the machine in front of them.

'Jenner, this is a key piece of evidence,' said Campbell.

She came over.

Alan pressed the on button and the machine started immediately. 'The power's a bit low,' he advised, and he pulled out a charger from his bag and plugged the computer in.

'Why would anyone include a list of passwords with their computer?' asked Jenner.

'Because this isn't Frank Norton's machine and whoever owns or owned it wanted someone to know what was on it,' replied Campbell.

Campbell and Jenner stepped away from Alan and the computer, so he could open some of the files with the list of passwords and back up all the files on the computer without distraction.

Campbell turned to Jenner and said, 'Someone did turn Anne Crowlie's home upside down looking for something,' said Campbell. 'Possibly she guessed that would be the case and gave her computer to Frank Norton.'

'It could be Frank Norton's computer,' Jenner pointed out. 'He was holding it.'

'We didn't find any of Anne Crowlie's computers or phones,' said Campbell.

'We had the local police check Frank Norton's address on his driving licence already. The address is in the North of England. They phoned back almost straight away to say the place is empty except for a few bits of furniture.'

Campbell thanked Parnold for the information and passed the phone that had been found on Frank Norton to Alan. Alan looked up from the lap-top and said, 'Thanks. A minute more and I can let you look at this computer.'

'That's grand,' said Campbell.

A moment later Alan said, 'I've backed up all the files, so I can let you look at it. There's one you will find interesting. It was the newest stored file. It's a video.' Alan picked up the evidence bag in which he'd placed the back-up record of the computer files and left.

Alan had left the video recording ready to run. Campbell clicked 'play'.

A smart woman in her forties with ash blonde hair and a face haggard with worry started with 'hello.' Campbell recognised Anne Crowlie from the pictures they had of her on the train more than from the sight of her face in death.

'It's dated the day she was murdered,' said Jenner.

'I have sent you this to keep it out of the hands of Watcher. Please make sure Frank, Frank Norton, is safe. He's all I care about now. I tried to remove all knowledge of him from my possessions and flat. I know Watcher would look for him.

'I don't know who Watcher is, but I'm scared I shall die.' Anne paused.

'I confess. I put the note in Elizabeth Rattagan bag. Watcher asked me to do it. It was easy enough to do. It was just a prank. I don't know what the message said. Watcher found out about a financial discrepancy at my work, he blackmailed me into it.' Anne wiped her eyes.

'I have sent you this as it was one of your officers who phoned me and said if I ever want to talk about the events on the train or anything else someone would be willing to listen.'

Jenner gave Parnold a long look. 'You are beginning to sound as understanding as Garden.'

Parnold raised his eyebrows and his neck reddened.

Jenner said, 'I want to check the train security footage again,' and left the room.

Campbell barely noticed the exchange as his left hand gripped his chin in thought.

CHAPTER EIGHTEEN

Campbell stood in front of Tarnish. He looked carefully at the wall to the left of his superior officer. He found it difficult to engage Tarnish's piercing blue eyes.

'Anne Crowlie has confessed to putting the note in Elizabeth Rattagan's bag under Watcher's instructions,' said Campbell. 'She may or may not have known that there is more than one person fitting that description. Her actions make the link between Elizabeth Rattagan's letter and Watcher.'

'Okay,' said Tarnish. 'Anne Crowlie can still be Messenger Watcher.'

'She hasn't confessed to that,' said Campbell.

'That doesn't mean she didn't do it,' said Tarnish.

'A man called Frank Norton is in hospital suffering from burns,' said Campbell.

'I heard,' said Tarnish. 'Well done for rescuing him,' he added reluctantly. 'Is he connected to this case?' he asked.

'Frank Norton had the computer which had Anne Crowlie's confession on. From what she said she was trying to protect him, it seems, from Watcher.'

'Could Watcher have got to Frank Norton by trying to set fire to him via this Jess Barratt,' asked Tarnish. 'It should be a short step to find both Murdering and Messenger Watcher now. I want to tidy all this up and wind up the investigation as soon as possible.'

'We have Jess Barratt in custody for the arson on the beach hut. She will be interviewed today,' advised Campbell.

'Good,' said Tarnish impatiently.

'I believe there is more behind these murders and I believe the death on Daneton Howe Beach of the man we know as Robert Epsy is connected.'

'Are you sure that death is relevant?'

'He may well have been murdered too. Messenger Watcher sent me to Daneton Howe Beach when the man known as Robert Epsy died.'

'That could well be coincidence,' said Tarnish.

'I think it is worth checking out.'

'Have you checked out Robert Epsy's accommodation?' asked Tarnish.

'As Harriet Epsy's uncle, Robert Epsy, died some years ago,' Campbell reminded Tarnish respectfully, 'his house was sold on a while ago after his death by his niece, Harriet, as she was the benefactor of his will.'

'And?' asked Tarnish with irritation.

'We are trying to find Harriet Epsy. We have a witness who says that the dead man was kissing Harriet in a non-uncle way and that the man was not Robert Epsy, and this was backed-up with photographs.'

'I see,' said Tarnish irritably. 'This had better be relevant, Inspector Campbell.'

'We are stuck with our investigations around Robert Epsy without proper identification of the body.'

'Get someone to jolly up his pathology photograph and put it about. We might get a taker,' said Tarnish.

'Thank you, Sir,' said Campbell amazed that he'd been allowed the wherewithal for the exercise. 'And I will have to wait to talk to Frank Norton,' explained Campbell. 'We have a police officer with him at the hospital. I will be alerted as soon as he is able to talk to us.'

'Right,' Tarnish said begrudging any approval that word represented.

'We will be interviewing Frank Norton to see how he fits in with Anne Crowlie. She used his car before her murder.'

'Indeed,' said Tarnish in a similar tone.

'I also need to speak to Elizabeth Rattagan and Gwen Blythe after Anne Crowlie's confession.'

'Why bother with those two women? Let it go,' said Tarnish. 'It just sounds like spite of some sort to me.'

'In her confession, Anne Crowlie said that she'd put the note in Elizabeth Rattagan's bag directed by Watcher, Sir,' Campbell reminded Tarnish. 'But, Elizabeth and Gwen have made themselves absent and our investigations have shown that Gwen Blythe is ex-police and Elizabeth Rattagan has worked for the prosecution service. I don't know how they are tied up in this. I am convinced their behaviour is significant. And we still don't know who murdered William Cecil on the beach. We cannot just wait for Frank Norton. He might be a dead end from an evidence point of view.'

'Is he likely to die?' asked Tarnish.

'He's got a more than fifty percent chance of survival,' said Campbell.

Tarnish nodded, the top of his head catching the light. 'You thought initially William Cecil Broadgate was a professional job?'

'That is still a possibility. Some people may well have the skills, or someone could have requested and paid for it,' said Campbell.

'The information from the antipodes has returned about Fenella Florris's children,' said Tarnish. 'William Cecil's second wife's children have remained in New Zealand. And, her mother has not budged from South Africa. She is quite frail now, apparently. The children favour the simple farming life and communicate very little with the outside world according to our colleagues in New Zealand.'

Campbell raised his eyebrows slightly at his boss's sudden animation.

'So, that is another area dealt with,' said Tarnish rubbing his hand across the top of his bronzed head. 'We will have to wait for Frank Norton, but we can wind back the investigation in the meantime. He could well be your messenger Watcher. He was in Cambridge at the right time.'

'Hopefully we'll be able to interview him on that one, Sir,' said Campbell wondering how long he could continue working on the broader lines of the enquiry without arousing Tarnish's suspicions. 'The Cambridge team have started dragging the river to see if they can find the vehicle – very possibly a bicycle – and phone used by Messenger Watcher. That should help identify the party.'

On leaving Tarnish's office Campbell's thoughtful steps took him to the team area where he went over to Lindy's desk, his mind ranging around his spider's web of thoughts.

'Lindy, see if you can find out anything about the beach hut where we found Frank Norton,' he said. 'Who it belonged to, that sort of thing.'

Lindy agreed with her usual enthusiasm and Campbell walked away knowing that the events of the Friday of the school reunion had not yet been fully unravelled.

Elizabeth Rattagan shuffled reluctantly along the main street of Banksea town centre with Harriet Epsy at her shoulder. Harriet made various threats which Elizabeth hoped were empty, but she also feared Harriet and the gun in her pocket. Her connection to Dungrade filled her with the old sinking dread she'd faced every day towards the end of her time at the Seaminster office.

Gwen saw Lizzy and Harriet enter the café opposite the lingerie shop on the corner from her vantage point outside The Gull Inn at the far end of the street. She felt in her bag. This time William Cecil Broadgate's notebook nestled there.

Barbs was examining underwear in the lingerie shop in Banksea. She liked the closeness of the shop to the Gull Inn. They always got her size in for her and she liked the chat from Louise Green and her mother.

'I've ordered this one in a lovely mauve for you,' said Louise. 'It arrived yesterday. I'll just get it from the back shop.'

'Ooh that's great,' said Barbs. 'I need two, so I might have them both.' While Louise disappeared into the back shop, Barbs went to the window and contemplated the delight of the possibility of her purchases. The café opposite was busy, but she noticed two women approach the door. One she recognised, Harriet Epsy. She reached for her phone and rang Inspector Campbell. Little madam.

Parnold and Garden sat opposite Jess Barratt in the interview room. Jess looked down. Her solicitor gazed into space.

'You were seen leaving the scene of an arson attack,' explained Garden to Jess.

Jess looked back at her with a purposefully blank expression.

There was a knock on the door and Campbell put his head around and called Parnold out. Garden paused the interview and Parnold got up.

'That's a bit rude,' complained Jess. 'I came here specially.'

'You were arrested,' said Garden flatly.

Parnold followed Campbell out and the Inspector closed the door and said in a low voice, 'We have to go, Parnold. Garden too. We've had a call about Harriet Epsy going into a café in Banksea and I think she is with Elizabeth Rattagan from the description that was given.'

'Okay,' said Parnold.

'Jenner's confirmed that Jess Barratt was caught by her boss Sarah Radley's security cameras at the tea kiosk at Daneton with a petrol-can looking very much like the one found at the scene,' added Campbell. 'Also, she could be the hoody in the swimming pool carpark breaking into Anne

Crowlie's car. Jenner's had a look, but she can't make up her mind.'

'Right,' said Parnold, as he returned to the room and resumed the interview.

'You've been caught on camera with a petrol-can, matching a can found at the scene of the fire. You were smelling of petrol. I am charging you with arson.' Parnold read Jess Barratt her rights and suspended the interview.

Barbs tucked the bag of bras under her arm and thanked Louise and left Green's Lingerie. Where was that Campbell, she wondered. These policemen were never around when you wanted one. She crossed the street to the café. She would take a relaxing tea away from the pub. It would be good for her. She slipped into the café. No-one looked up. She couldn't see Harriet Epsy. The only free table was half way down. She spotted Harriet with two women at the back of the shop but looked away quickly. She vaguely recognised the two girls she was with. She thought they might have been at the old girl's night at the Gull Inn but couldn't be sure. It had been busy.

Despite her size Barbs felt she was well hidden behind a large plant and a fish tank and her light step and ability to move discretely around chairs meant she had disturbed no-one on her entry to or transit through the café. The three women at the back were absorbed in their discussion. Barb's attention was drawn to the front door where a tall fair-haired man was entering with a neat blond woman. She recognised Sergeant Parnold, but she wasn't sure of the woman – Sergeant Jenner, perhaps? Barbs hadn't had direct dealings with her but had seen her about. She looked back at where Harriet and the two other women were sitting. But there were now only two. Harriet was gone.

Sergeant Parnold and the blond woman walked through to the table and calmly spoke to the two remaining women. Jenner spoke into a device Barbs couldn't see and Sergeant Parnold moved off immediately into the kitchen area. Jenner stopped speaking into her device and went down the corridor towards the toilets. A couple of uniformed police officers arrived through the front door and sat with the two women.

Jenner found herself in a dark narrow passageway with several doors off it. One was to the kitchen which, from the commotion inside, Parnold was thoroughly searching. Two doors were toilets which Jenner checked. A further door was locked and described as private. Jenner stuck her head in the kitchen and asked for the key. A very flustered woman stepped forward and handed her the key. She opened the door and ran up the stairs behind it. She couldn't hear anyone. She worked her way through the flat. It was large and ran along more than one of the shop fronts in the street her heart sank.

Harriet must know this place, thought Jenner. There must be another exit from it through another shop. She contacted Inspector Campbell who was waiting in the back yard of the tea shop with Garden expecting to retrieve any escapees from the tea shop. 'There's another exit,' she explained, seeing another set of steps with the door at the bottom shutting on a self-closer. She ran down and pushed open the door. 'Looks like Harriet came this way,' Jenner informed Campbell and glanced around looking for a street sign. 'She's come out in Baker's Alley. There's no sign of her and there are three exits off it. This is well away from you.'

'Aye,' said Campbell. 'Are there any security cameras on the alley?'

'I think so. I should think it belongs to the shop next door. I'll arrange collection.' She was disappointed. Any security footage would only confirm what she already knew: Harriet had slipped away. Campbell would be disappointed.

'We'll secure the area,' said Campbell, 'and check through.'

'No Harriet,' Campbell confirmed to his staff as he and Garden went in to interview Elizabeth Rattagan.

'Okay, said Jenner as she and Parnold headed down the corridor to interview Gwen Blythe.

An hour later Campbell gathered the interviewers together in a meeting room to compare notes.

'We need to act quickly here,' said Campbell. 'Elizabeth has told us that Harriet Epsy has a gun. No-one saw it in the café. No-one told us about it at the time. Now we can't take any risks,' said Campbell. 'I have put out a full search. We have an arms unit on stand-by. It would be preferable if we could pick her up alive,' said Campbell.

'We can't guarantee that,' said Parnold.

'Public safety is paramount. They may give us a shout if there is any chance of negotiation, but they have to do what is best, so we may lose her evidence. We will have to live with that possibility.' Campbell continued,

'Let's have a quick résumé of what we have learnt from Elizabeth Rattagan and Gwen Blythe.'

Jenner looked a little pale. 'I should have thought about a gun.'

'We didn't know,' said Campbell. 'This is the first time a gun has been used by anyone we have been investigating.'

'Neither Gwen Blythe nor Elizabeth Rattagan said anything when we went into the café,' said Parnold.

'Shock,' suggested Garden

Jenner moved her head slightly. 'Did she have any intention of using it? She didn't fire it. Could it have been a replica?'

'We will know when we find it,' said Parnold abruptly. 'It won't make any difference to her fate.'

'Aye,' agreed Campbell. 'Jenner, what did Gwen have to say?'

Jenner nodded. 'Gwen wanted to know if we had Harriet.'

'So did Elizabeth,' said Garden.

Campbell paused and stretched his bony shoulders. 'All that has taken place relates to someone called Dungrade according to Elizabeth Rattagan,' said Campbell. 'He sounds like some small-time crook skimming money from here and there.'

'Gwen says he's dead, or at least that's what Harriet Epsy told her,' said Jenner.

'Harriet told them William Cecil Broadgate was Dungrade,' said Campbell.

'I asked Gwen that,' said Parnold. 'She said she saw William Cecil's picture on the television and she couldn't see that he looked like the man she met calling himself Dungrade.'

'We asked Gwen whether Harriet confessed to killing the man known as Robert Epsy,' said Jenner. 'She said she didn't know anything about it.'

'No, nor did Harriet confess to Elizabeth,' said Garden.

Jenner flicked through some papers she'd brought with her. 'Dungrade's case was the one that Elizabeth Rattagan was working on when she left the Havensea Prosecution Service,' she said.

'Gwen Blythe wants us to chase up this man, Michael Pilmer,' said Parnold.

'Why?' asked Campbell.

'She says the Pilmers are connected to Dungrade and are continuing Dungrade's criminal activity.'

'What about Abigail Pilmer, Michael Pilmer's wife?' asked Campbell. 'Elizabeth didn't mention her.'

'Neither did Gwen,' said Jenner.

'So, what are the Pilmers up to?' asked Campbell. 'Elizabeth says they are stealing money.'

'It seems the Pilmers are trying to skim inheritances among other things,' replied Parnold. 'And as some sort of proof that William Cecil Broadgate was also involved Gwen produced this notebook. She thought he was laundering Dungrade's money, but the book apparently shows Dungrade to be William Cecil Broadgate. This book, Gwen says, is what Harriet was after. Harriet thought it might tell her who killed Dungrade/William Cecil Broadgate. Gwen couldn't see why.' Parnold passed a black covered book to him in an evidence bag. 'Gwen said she found it in William Cecil's caravan.'

'That caravan was just about stripped and put back together,' said Jenner. 'It couldn't have been there then.'

'Okay, let's quickly get it swabbed and fingerprinted,' said Campbell. 'We need to see inside it.'

Parnold, Jenner and Garden agreed.

'Gwen gave us an address in Cambridge,' said Jenner. 'They met Michael Pilmer there about Gwen's grandmother's will. All appeared well enough until he came out of his office after them and gave them the name of an investment professional as they were leaving.'

'What was the name?'

'Gerome Godolming,' said Parnold.

'Gwen thought Godolming's office was in the same building,' said Jenner. 'She remembered the name from the menu at the front porch. They didn't look at the card at the time as they ran into Harriet Epsy.'

'Elizabeth's story matches Gwen's. We'll need to follow up Godolming,' said Campbell. 'Wasn't Abigail Pilmer in Banksea on the Friday afternoon?'

'She was at the school,' said Jenner. 'Listening to the head mistress.'

'Let's double check that one,' said Campbell. 'You might need to speak to Jess Barratt again she might have seen her from her kiosk on the Friday of William Cecil's murder.'

'Right,' said Parnold.

'And Ralph Peterson was in full view of all the Banksea Market Place cameras painting his picture on Friday,' said Campbell.

'That leaves the offices used by Pilmer in Cambridge,' said Campbell to Parnold. 'You need to continue with that interview with Jess Barratt. I'll meet up with our Cambridge contact, Sergeant Percival, and visit

Godalming.'

As Jenner and Garden started to leave to carry out their tasks, Campbell added, 'There's one last thing that came out of Elizabeth's interview and that was that she thought her note had been torn out of the ledger they found in William Cecil's caravan. Forensics will be able to check that one against the note. We already have Anne Crowlie's confession to putting it in Elizabeth's bag, so we'll have to wait and see what connection that gives us.'

Parnold, Jenner and Garden left, and Campbell blinked at the tingling light and rubbed his eyes wanting to make everything clearer. So many different colours were trying to come into focus, as they had that morning when he'd woken up on the cupboard floor and watched the sun acting through the trees and onto the pieces of his mother's patchwork blanket. He shook his head and picked up the car keys.

CHAPTER NINETEEN

The next morning Campbell stood outside the offices where Elizabeth Rattagan and Gwen Blythe had said they'd met Michael Pilmer and he had suggested seeing the financial advisor, Gerome Godolming.

He pondered briefly that yesterday Arabella Macfine had confirmed to Jenner that Abigail Pilmer had been at the school all Friday afternoon. The baby was unmissable, she'd said.

Campbell skimmed down the tenants' list at the entrance. The borrowed office on the top floor was now listed as vacant where Gwen and Elizabeth had seen Michael Pilmer. Campbell held Godolming's name printed on a rough piece of paper up to the list and found a match on the second floor. He rang the buzzer.

Campbell was surprised to find that he was answered by a female voice he thought he recognised.

'Ah, sorry,' said Campbell as if he'd pressed the wrong buzzer. He hoped Harriet had not recognised him.

At that moment Sergeant Percival arrived from the Cofen Station. Campbell pulled him to one side and explained that Harriet Epsy was in the building and she may have a gun. Sergeant Percival immediately arranged for armed back up.

'We aren't to approach,' advised Sergeant Percival as an office worker arrived at the office porch returning from his lunch.

'I'm afraid you can't go in there, Sir,' said Sergeant Percival. He turned away to continue talking to the action desk.

'Have you got a key?' asked Campbell of the neatly suited office worker.

The man nodded and handed him an entrance card.

Campbell went inside and up the stairs.

He tried the door to the office of Gerome Godolming, found it unlocked and pushed the door open. The room was empty. He tried two more offices on that floor and was met with shocked faces. In a third, a female clerk pointed silently to a fire escape. Campbell went over to it and opened the door.

Campbell observed the dropped gun on the fire escape. He stepped out onto its metal landing but there was no sign of Harriet. Sergeant Percival appeared behind him and Campbell pointed to the gun and turned away from the fire escape to let him alert the local police to Harriet's escape and secure the site, while he returned to the office of Gerome Godolming.

Once back inside the room with its thick carpet and large heavy desk, he viewed the office and started a careful, general search wearing evidence gloves. There was nothing in the drawers, no business effects such as business cards or personal effects. Either Gerome Godolming didn't exist, or he had long gone.

As he came out of the office Sergeant Percival was coming down the stairs and said, 'Local Council security footage hasn't got anything on Harriet Epsy for you,' he said. 'She must have disappeared into another building.'

Campbell looked towards the large glass building.

'That's where Anne Crowlie used to work,' observed Sergeant Percival.

'Aye,' said Campbell looking at the name of the company. 'She did.'

At Horseton Police Station Parnold and Garden picked up the suspended interview of Jess Barratt. Parnold led on the questioning.

'What do you know of this car?' asked Parnold showing Jess a picture of Frank Norton's car in the swimming pool car park.

'That's Bradley Yorkman's sort of thing not mine.'

'But you are burning beach huts?' queried Parnold.

'Look, he has the same sweat shirt as me?'

'One with a hood?'

'Yes. They had them in at the shop on the front of the quay in Banksea a month or two back. I've seen him in it.'

'Are you sure?'

'Yes, I'm sure.'

'So, you are the one burning the beach huts?'

'Yes,' said Jess with defiance.

'Why did you blame Bradley Yorkman?' Garden asked.

'I didn't. You did.' Jess pointed at Garden. 'I think Sarah Radley, me boss, mentioned his name to you and you came and asked me.'

'I think because you had mentioned him to her,' said Garden.

Jess Barratt looked down. 'I only burn them down when the owners want to claim off their insurance. But people can't get fire insurance on them at a sensible rate any more so interest in burning them has dried up.'

'So why this one, last night?' asked Garden.

'I don't know.'

'Right now, this looks like a charge of attempted murder.'

'You've arrested me for arson.'

'Yes, but there was someone inside the beach hut.'

'I didn't know that.'

'Are you sure.'

'Yes, I asked the guy.' Jess looked as if she wished she hadn't said that.

'What guy?'

'The one who paid me to do the job.'

'Who's that?' asked Garden

'He was a chunky sort of guy. He was wearing a big black coat in the middle of summer. Wore diamond studs in his ears. He was trying to cover his bright clothes with that black coat.'

Parnold suspended the interview and left the room to find Jenner. He found her at her desk. She looked up from her computer. 'This Herbert Brandon?' He enquired surprised to find her in.

'I'm about to get out after the Pilmers and Ralph Peterson,' she said. She was clearly frustrated. 'I'm just doing a bit more investigation about them and I've been looking through the book that Harriet Epsy was in such a big fuss to get her hands on and checking it against the business of William Cecil Broadgate that we know about.'

'We could be a hair's breadth away from nailing the man who set Jess Barratt to burn down the beach hut with Frank Norton in it,' said Parnold. He described the man on the train and they peered at the poor-quality picture from the on-board security footage from the Friday morning train.

'That looks like him but also quite like a few other people. Let me have a quick look on the internet for a better image. Yes, here he is. I've got a picture of him. That one on the train wouldn't be good enough to show anyone and it isn't neutral. It shows him somewhere doing something. Here you are.' Jenner printed the picture she approved of. 'Let me see if I can find you half a dozen similar faces to show Jess Barratt.' Within a few minutes she had set the printer whirling into action again.

Parnold returned to the interview room where Garden was sitting opposite Jess Barratt. Jess quickly picked out the photograph of Herbert

Brandon from the others and Parnold closed the interview before going back to Jenner. 'Looks like Herbert Brandon ordered the burning of his own beach hut, and he could have ordered a lot else besides,' he told her. He pulled out his phone and rang Inspector Campbell in Cambridge and told him about Herbert Brandon.

Garden passed Parnold at Jenner's desk and said, 'I'll wait out in the car.'

'Bradley Yorkman?' asked Jenner.

'Yep. That's who Jess's pointing the finger at for the car at the swimming pool,' said Garden. She really didn't believe it was Bradley Yorkman who broke into Frank Norton's car in the swimming pool carpark, but she knew that Parnold would believe it.

Campbell closed the call with Parnold and Jenner and looked at the modern office next to him. He found Sergeant Percival and asked him to join him.

'I'll just contact Cofen Station and let them know,' replied Percival.

'I have to talk to Herbert Brandon again. I will have to leave other officers to look for Harriet Epsy.'

As Campbell and Percival entered the engineering company's open plan office, Herbert Brandon wobbled and sat down on the nearest chair.

'I'm going to tell you everything,' said Herbert.

Campbell pulled up an office chair and sat a couple of feet away. The rest of the office workers made themselves scarce. Sergeant Percival placed himself by the exit but close enough to take notes.

'I loved her you see?' said Herbert.

'Who?' asked Campbell. Assume nothing, he had always been told.

'Anne Crowlie. I loved her too much. I thought about her all the time. I knew she was seeing this Frank Norton, so I took to following him. It was easy, he works in that old building next door.' Campbell remembered the name pad on the door. He hadn't seen Frank Norton's name but that didn't mean that he didn't work there.

'I have a beach hut as you have probably found out. I had given Anne Crowlie a key. A couple of days ago I followed Frank Norton to it.'

'What happened after that?' asked Campbell.

'I was talking to a woman on the beach. She was really chatty. She told me that she could arrange an accident for Frank Norton. I was so angry about him, but I never asked the woman to kill him.'

'What did the woman look like?'

'She just wore a grey hoodie. I didn't see her hair. She was shortish, shorter than me and I'm not tall.' Herbert's hand hovered at just below his eyes.

'Okay,' said Campbell. 'Were you so wildly jealous of Frank Norton and Anne Crowlie that you had to kill them both?'

'No, no, no,' said Herbert. 'I didn't kill Anne, Frank Norton killed her.'

'She wasn't frightened of Frank Norton,' said Campbell. 'It seems she was frightened of someone else. Do you know who that might be?'

'No.' Herbert Brandon twitched anxiously.

'Was she frightened of you?' persisted Campbell.

'No certainly not.' Herbert Brandon's complaint was shrill.

'Did she speak of anyone else?' Campbell used his Edinburgh accent to slow the question down, to calm Herbert Brandon.

'No, not really. She didn't speak about Frank Norton. I noticed them meeting outside, through the window. They were very close.' Herbert sounded calmer.

'And that made you jealous, enraged you?' asked Campbell.

'Yes, I couldn't help myself.'

'Did you follow her to Banksea swimming pool and murder Anne Crowlie?'

'No, Frank Norton murdered her,' repeated Herbert.

'You sound very sure? Did you go there? Did you see Frank Norton at the swimming pool?'

'No.'

'Did you see Frank Norton on the day Anne Crowlie died?'

'No. But he must have done it.'

'Why?' asked Campbell, drawing the word out, enhancing its meaning.

'Because they were lovers.'

Campbell breathed deeply trying to control his frustration. If he lost his patience he would not retain Herbert Brandon's participation. 'On the Friday you all came back from the London conference you went through to Ely with Graham Aspen to work at a factory there.'

'Yes, but I didn't stop. I got off the train and took another one back to Cambridge.' Herbert looked a little more relaxed.

'Why?'

'Anne was distressed on the train and I thought it might have something to do with the fact that Frank Norton had travelled with her. She was not herself, she'd had her suit ruined by a baby's drink.' Campbell looked at Herbert and knew he had no idea of Anne Crowlie's confessing to the note being planted in Elizabeth Rattagan's bag.

'What did you think about her reaction to the drink spill?' asked Campbell. He let go the fact that Herbert had lied during his first interview with Jenner.

'I knew she was wound up because her reaction was completely over the top. I thought Frank and her must have had a falling out because it was really unlike her to behave in that way.'

'Frank Norton isn't dead, he's in hospital. He will be permanently disfigured,' explained Campbell.

'Thank goodness he isn't dead. He can now be punished for killing Anne.'

'We have no reason to believe he killed Anne,' said Campbell. 'You arranged for Frank Norton's attack,' he accused Herbert.

'I heard about the fire on the news after it had happened. I worried what that woman would do after I had spoken with her. I wanted to stop it. I didn't know how. She didn't leave me any way of contacting her. I would never have agreed to it. Why would I have wanted my beach hut torched?'

Campbell pursed his lips pondering this question for a moment. 'So, in what way did you agree to it?'

'I was telling her about him and how I thought he'd killed my lovely Anne. It was the girl in the hoody's idea that I did something about him.'

'And?'

'I agreed. She didn't say what she was going to do.'

'Did you have to pay?'

'No, I didn't, not then.'

'When?'

'She didn't say.'

'So, on that Friday when you came back from Ely did you come back to the office?'

'Yes. It was already late morning by then, about eleven-fifteen.'

'How was Anne when you arrived?'

'She wasn't in the office. I thought she might have gone home. But she came back, and she was very distracted. She said she felt unwell and came and went to and from the office several times.'

Campbell made a note of this and said, 'Anne said she attended some meetings.'

'Yes, she did. When she came in she had bought herself a new suit and she went to her afternoon meetings. Later, I noticed she'd taken her bicycle from the rack sometime during the day and it was no longer there.'

'The news said that Frank Norton was saved by a policeman.' Herbert Brandon looked at Campbell's bandaged hand.

Campbell looked down at his hand and said to him, 'We'll be asking you to say this all again formally at the police station, make a full statement. Sergeant Jenner will come down for that.'

'Yes, yes of course, Inspector,' said Herbert Brandon. 'You want my confession and you shall have it.'

Campbell beckoned to Sergeant Percival and asked him to arrest and caution Herbert Brandon for his involvement in the attempted murder of Frank Norton. He followed Sergeant Percival and Herbert Brandon out of the building. Campbell asked him how far Judy Wong's office was from here. Sergeant Percival pointed out the way and offered to arrange a lift.

'No, thank you,' said Campbell. 'I'll pick up a drink on the way.' As he set off he felt a spot of rain.

CHAPTER TWENTY

Parnold drove fiercely towards Cricklestaithe Farm. Garden looked at him mildly alarmed. She hoped he wouldn't bully Bradley Yorkman. Parnold could usually contain his temper and behave professionally, but sometimes she was aware that it was a bit of a struggle.

In front of his family's cottage, Bradley was fiddling with his motorbike. He was wearing the hoodie which Jess Barratt had mentioned were sold in the town and had been featured in both the security footages at the swimming pool car park and by the tea kiosk at Daneton's promenade.

'I checked with the shop on the harbour,' Garden said to Parnold seeing his neck redden. 'They had ordered twenty of them but forty arrived. They were going to send the extra back, but they sold well through a cold week in the spring, so they kept them. A lot of people have them.' Garden opened the passenger side door and stepped out into the sunshine.

'Mm,' grumbled Parnold as he got out of the car.

'Hello,' said Bradley sounding jaded at their presence.

'Were you at the swimming pool the night before last?' asked Parnold.

'No,' replied Bradley Yorkman.

Garden inwardly sighed at Parnold's style of questioning. He should have allowed Bradley to say where he was not where he wasn't. He had alerted him to the reason for them being there.

'Can someone vouch for you?' asked Parnold.

'My Dad already told you I was with him watching the cricket highlights.'

'We are talking later than that. During the night?'

'I went into Norwich. I go to college there.'

'It's in recess for the summer,' said Garden calmly.

'I've got mates there. I stopped with them. We went to the pub and we had a good time. Look, we took a few pictures and posted them on line if you don't believe me.' He showed Parnold his phone.

'Why didn't you say before about Norwich?'

'You wanted to know about earlier in the evening.'

The two police officers looked at him questioningly.

'Okay. We got into a bit of trouble at a club, The Four Beaks,' said Bradly quietly. 'Broke something. We got thrown out. I didn't want to get my mates into trouble.'

'We'll check it out,' said Garden.

'Please do,' said Bradley defensively.

'Do you swim?' asked Parnold.

'A bit,' Bradley stepped back and folded his arms across his chest.

'You go to Daneton Howe Beach and Banksea Beach regularly,' said Parnold.

'One or the other most days during the summer and Cricklestaithe bay too. I swim there most days.'

'Are you a good swimmer?'

'I'm ok. You have to mind the tides.' Bradley Yorkman scratched his head. 'What is this about? A lot of local people visit the beaches daily at this time of year.'

Garden gave Parnold a warning look. This was not what they came for. They had no evidence against Bradley, just other people's insinuations.

Bradley looked at his phone. 'I'm sorry I've got to go.' He started his motorbike and rode off down the lane.

Campbell sat opposite Judy Wong in her office. William Cecil's step-sister-in-law looked tired. 'Did Harriet Epsy visit you today?' he asked.

'Yes, she did,' she said raising her eyebrows questioningly.

'Any particular reason?' asked Campbell.

'Nothing important.' Judy Wong's head tilted to the side, curious. 'She came to tell me about the old girls' day as I hadn't had time to attend. I am writing up an important piece of research at the moment,' she explained.

'Did you recognise her from your time at Strath-Kind School?'

'I was teaching at the school after Harriet's time there, but she was always about after that – involved in school fêtes, that sort of thing.'

'And she knew where to find you.'

'Yes, old girl's network I expect.'

'What time did she leave?'

'About twenty minutes ago.'

'I lent her a brolly.'

'What colour?'

'Nothing special, just a plain black one.'

Campbell regretted his refusal of a lift and stopping for a drink. There was little chance of picking out Harriet from all the other black brollies out in the now steady rain.

'Did she talk about anything else?'

'She asked if I was pleased William Cecil was dead. I said his death would not bring back my sister.'

'How did she react?'

'She looked annoyed. I can't help the way I feel. I am sad, not angry, Inspector. Harriet soon left after I said this. She'll be on our security footage if that helps.'

'Thank you, Miss Wong,' said Campbell. 'Do you know where she lives?'

'Not now, her mother used to live in Daneton with her uncle until he died, and Harriet used to live with them. I think, after that, her mother moved away, and she moved into a flat behind the Gull Inn.'

Half an hour later Campbell walked with Sergeant Percival from the bike shed at Anne Crowlie's work and along the river down to where they thought the Messenger Watcher had finished transmitting from.

'Where did you say that you lost the signal for messenger watcher?' asked Campbell of Sergeant Percival as they reached an area where police divers and a dredging boat were working.

'About here,' said Sergeant Percival. They stood at a point where the river was quite narrow. Willow trees on one side brushed the water with their dangling stems. Reeds had been cut away for the benefit of boats being punted up and down the water way, but the river was closed here today.

'We've been searching it for the bicycle and the phone,' said Sergeant Percival.

'I've got an appointment in Banksea I must get to. You'll let us know when you find them?' enquired Campbell of Sergeant Percival.

'Of course,' replied Sergeant Percival.

Campbell strode through the woods on Banksea Beach and viewed the arc of beach huts on either side of him. He walked slowly down the row to his left until he came to the two burnt out beach huts that Jess Barratt had originally claimed were torched by Bradley Yorkman. Already the sand had shifted to hide any trace of the scene of crime investigators' activities. He turned away. He felt a little like those burnt out beach huts. He smiled at the thought and headed towards the kiosk. He noticed it was open and he found Sarah Radley, the owner, inside brewing tea and instant coffee for the holiday makers.

'Having to do this myself,' she said. 'I haven't had time to find out how Kara is doing down at Daneton Prom.'

Campbell remembered Kara Leonard chasing after him that Friday. The day of the two deaths on two different beaches. He leaned on the counter, 'Tell me again about Friday; the Friday William Cecil Broadgate was murdered.'

'I was only here at Banksea Beach for a short time to check up on Jess. You police know that.'

'I know. Tell me again in detail,' said Campbell.

And she did.

Campbell was back at Horseton Police Station when he received the call from Jenner, already in Cambridge, to say that a bicycle had been found and that Herbert Brandon had identified it as Anne Crowlie's. He put down the phone and Parnold said, 'All ready.' Campbell got up and went into the interview room with him.

Jess Barratt looked up defiantly, her duty solicitor looked down at his papers.

Campbell sat opposite her and Parnold ran through the procedure for the interview.

'I have remembered something about the Friday that William Cecil Broadgate was murdered,' said Jess.

'Have you?' asked Campbell with pleased surprise.

'There was a swimmer. Came around the headland from the next beach.'

Campbell felt a sigh coming on. He quelled it. 'A man or a woman?' he asked.

'A man,' said Jess.

'We'll look-into that,' said Campbell, unconvinced.

'No other witnesses on the beach had mentioned any swimmers arriving from the next beach,' observed Parnold.

'However, I do have some news for you,' said Campbell. 'We have Herbert Brandon in custody for his role in the attempted murder of Frank Norton. He confirms your story of the burning of the beach hut at Daneton beach. He says it was your idea to kill Frank Norton. Herbert Brandon had followed Frank Norton there and you approached him. Why would you do that?'

'We just got talking, that's all.'

'How did that happen?'

'I said I liked his earrings and he said he liked my hoody and then we got chatting and then he told me about his broken heart and how this man Frank Norton had killed the love of his life. He was certain of it.'

'Did he say anything about witnessing anything which made him certain of this?'

'No, he didn't. I felt he was right.'

'I think it is more than that. But I shall come back to this subject.'

Parnold looked at him sharply.

Campbell continued, 'I've been down to Banksea Beach last evening and looked at your kiosk.' Campbell readied himself to gauge her reaction. Her eyes narrowed and then widened.

'So?' she said irritably. 'It's not my kiosk, it belongs to Sarah Radley. I just work there.'

'That's true which is why I spoke to Sarah Radley. She remembered that when she called on you – as is her routine – on the Friday of William Cecil Broadgate's murder you were not in your kiosk.'

'I had gone around to the toilets,' said Jess.

'Yes, Sarah Radley walked along the beach to meet you.'

'Why didn't she walk through the woods like anybody else?' asked Jess.

'She walked to the bank that runs along the creek down to Banksea Harbour.'

'So, what?'

'So, what, indeed. Don't you think it odd that no-one saw anything unusual that day?'

'I saw swimmers.'

'Yes, you saw more than anybody.'

'I work in the kiosk.'

'Yes,' agreed Campbell. 'As you know our scene of crime team went thoroughly through the kiosk and nothing untoward was found there. Nothing was found in the toilets either. You pointed one of our officers in the direction of the burnt-out beach huts.'

Jess frowned slightly.

'I think you are actually proud of your work. That you like people to see it. I think the car in the swimming pool car park that was broken into was your work. You knew it was on security camera, and you knew you were not identifiable.'

Jess looked at him, clearly trying to look uninterested and looking insolent.

'Do You know anything about what happened at the swimming pool?' asked Campbell. Did you take a laptop from the car in the swimming pool carpark?'

'I didn't.'

Campbell leaned forward slightly. 'Jess, you have sent us running about here and there. You keep putting Bradley Yorkman in the picture for arson and you said he broke into Anne Crowlie's car. Why was that?'

'He hangs around the beach. He looks shifty.'

'That's not enough to accuse someone. I think your accusations are a diversion from yourself.'

'Why would I do that?'

'Exactly so, why would you do that?'

'Human nature,' she suggested archly. She continued flatly, 'There was nothing in the car. That was a complete waste of my time.'

'Are you admitting to breaking into the car?

'Yes, it was just a car.'

'It was a murder victim's transport.'

'I didn't know that at the time.'

'Did you know Anne Crowlie, the murder victim at the swimming pool?'

'No, I only did the car.'

'Why?'

'I was asked to do the car.'

'Who by?'

'I don't know. I just got a note and some money.'

'Now you understand the circumstances I will ask you again: did you take anything out of the car?'

'I took a phone.'

'What did you do with the phone?'

'I threw it in the sea.'

'Did you go into the swimming pool that night?'

'No, I didn't.'

'Did you see anyone leaving the swimming pool that night.'

'No, it was shut.'

'Let me come back to Banksea Beach and your kiosk. There was one difference today compared to when our officers checked the area after the murder. A fold up sign on the bank pointing towards the kiosk, saying "teas coffees cakes", was there.'

'It is always there.'

'No, not always. As I say, I have spoken to Sarah Radley. When she came looking for you on the Friday of William Cecil Broadgate's murder it wasn't there. She told you off about it when you appeared around the corner from the toilets.'

'So, what?' said Jess. 'It's just a sign.'

'No, it's not just a sign, is it? Not anymore.'

'I don't know what you mean?'

'The sign has been modified.'

Campbell produced a selection of photographs from which Parnold read out the exhibit numbers for the benefit of the interview recording.

Campbell showed her each picture in turn, indicating the modified construction which included two stainless steel rods with sharpened ends fitted into the framework in such a way that the sharpened ends were concealed in the corner mountings.

'These items are being forensically examined,' said Campbell. 'Initially they look like a match for the murder weapon used on William Cecil Broadgate. Who modified this sign?'

'I did,' said Jess. Campbell thought she looked panicked. 'I was asked to, but I didn't kill William Cecil, it was the swimmer.'

'You don't believe that. You have thought of that as another way to push the blame elsewhere like you've always done. Did you kill William Cecil Broadgate?'

Jess erupted into tears. Campbell wondered if this was another of her skills. Her forehead was supported by the heels of her hands as she looked down at the table.

'I was friends with his wife, Fenella Florris.' Jess looked him straight in the eyes. 'She was a lovely lady, but when she found out what William Cecil was really like with all his shady businesses and he was so manipulative you wouldn't believe! She wanted to hand him in to the police. I'm sure he had her poisoned.'

'Fenella Florris died from a congenital problem that she didn't get treated,' explained Campbell.

'She let herself die?' said Jess tearfully. 'Oh, no. That's worse. That man's hands are stained with her death.'

'I believe she was your friend, but that is not why you killed William Cecil Broadgate, was it? You would have done it much earlier when still in the first throws of grief for your friend.'

'I wanted to,' Jess gave a large sniff and straightened up. 'Actually, I got instructions left at the kiosk with a bundle of money and those rods.'

'But afterwards you couldn't part with the rods for some reason.'

'You can't trust the sea to hide your secrets. Sometimes it does and sometimes it doesn't. And you lot had metal detectors over the sand.'

'Where did you hide them?'

'I slid them under one of the caravans when I went to the toilet. I do a bit of cleaning in there. No-one even noticed. I knew you lot would start checking the caravans, so I got it back washed, boiled them and put them back in the sign. I'd got a metal worker in the town to do the sign. He'd made a work top for the kiosk, so I knew him. I said the sign was a bit wobbly and needed strengthening and I had just the thing.'

'You had crossed the line. You had assisted a murderer. Did you want to go one step further? Did you attempt to murder Frank Norton?' asked Campbell.

'Yes, yes I did. And you are right I am a murderer.' Jess started to rise angrily to her feet. The uniformed police officer stepped forward to restrain her and Parnold stood up.

'Please sit down, Miss Barratt. We are charging you for the breaking and entering of the car parked in the swimming pool car park overnight on the night of Anne Crowlie's murder and for your involvement with the murder of William Cecil Broadgate. Sergeant Parnold will administer the charge.'

Campbell stood up and left the interview room while Parnold wrapped up the formalities with the uniformed officer and Jess Barratt's duty solicitor in attendance. When Parnold joined him outside the interview room, Campbell said, 'We all need a break from this,' while rubbing his forehead.

'Why aren't you charging her with William Cecil Broadgate's murder?' asked Parnold.

'I don't think she murdered William Cecil. She will stew on this. She doesn't know who paid her for that job. Her crimes are spiteful in nature, I don't think she's got the skills for that one. I believe her about hiding the weapons. I believe also that she hid the weapons in the sign beforehand, ready for the murderer. The alteration had made them intrinsic to the structure. Without the rods, it would fall over. Jess panicked and decided she couldn't risk the soiled rods being found in the sign which is why she hid them and the sign in the caravan site to retrieve later. We can check when it was made with the business who altered the sign. We can get the details of the company from Sarah Radley, the kiosk owner.'

'Right,' said Parnold. 'I'll see if I can check out that sign alteration right away.'

'We haven't got to the bottom of this yet,' warned Campbell.

'But we're close,' said Parnold.

'Aye, I hope so,' replied Campbell.

Campbell returned to his desk and stretched his feet and rotated his shoulders and turned on his computer. Waiting for him was a document from forensics about the notebook found in William Cecil's holiday caravan. He picked it up.

Elizabeth Rattagan and Gwen Blythe's fingerprints were on the front cover – as expected – despite saying that they were wearing gloves. William Cecil Broadgate's fingerprints were also there. There was a remaining shred of paper by the spine of the notebook towards the back. On examination, the tear had matched the jagged edge of the note delivered to Elizabeth. No fingerprints were found around the ripped paper.

Anne Crowlie's fingerprints were not on the notebook but a match for her prints were found on the envelope of the note found in Elizabeth's bag; thus, backing up Anne's computer delivered confession that she delivered the note to Elizabeth's bag on the train.

There was now a clear connection between Elizabeth Rattagan, Anne Crowlie and the murdered man, William Cecil Broadgate. Campbell considered the histories of the people on the train on that Friday. His finger traced around the summary board to Elizabeth Rattagan. She had been working on the case of a man called Dungrade when she left her job. Perhaps this too was connected.

He stood up and shouted for Parnold. 'I need to speak to Elizabeth Rattagan,' he told his Sergeant. 'See if they can be found,' said Campbell, not holding out much hope. He stretched and rubbed the back of his long, tired neck.

CHAPTER TWENTY-ONE

Georgia sat on an old timber bench fixed to one wall of the old stone barn. Sean stood opposite her in the doorway.

'This is the last time I am going to meet with you, Sean,' she said. 'I only agreed because of what happened on the beach. We do need to straighten a few things out.'

Sean looked distraught. 'I didn't realise what you were really like. I didn't know you were twisted up in your grandfather's business.'

'And I thought you were nice,' said Georgia, 'And all the while you had a pregnant girlfriend.'

'But your grandfather was buying people's livelihoods,' complained Sean.

'Your father rented his land off him. That was all. It was no-one's fault. It was your greed, your belief in entitlement, nothing else, which made you think something underhand was going on.' Georgia looked at him steadily. 'I never knew what my grandfather did. I just found I'd inherited all this money and land and businesses after his death. I really wish he hadn't left it to me.'

'Well give it to me,' said Sean, moving into the barn, towards her.

She looked at the greed in his eyes. 'I will not.'

She watched his face. She wondered if he would snarl or weasel round her to try and get what he wanted. She continued with her intention and said, 'I will give the land to your father. I thought about giving the money to your daughter, but she doesn't need that much trouble.'

'I loved you,' said Sean with a note of desperation in his voice.

'You had no right to love me. You were not available to love me. You had given yourself to someone else.'

Sean started to cry, but he was calmer now.

Georgia walked passed Sean towards the door of the barn. She looked back at him and stepped out of the barn. As she brought her face round to the front and she nearly walked into Ralph Peterson who was standing in front of her on the narrow track.

'What do you want?' she asked.

'I was waiting for you,' he said tossing a long fringe of dark hair off his face.

'Have you been following me?' asked Georgia.

Ralph sneered. 'You're giving my land away.'

'Why would I do that?' asked Georgia as reasonably as she could.

'I heard you.' Ralph's whole face was twisted with hate.

'That's my land not yours,' said Georgia. 'I can give it to whoever I want.'

'Dungrade said it would be mine.'

'I don't know anyone called Dungrade.'

'Dungrade is dead.'

'I'm sorry for your loss. And now you must fend for yourself. That's what I feel I need to do now without Grandpa Wills.'

'Dungrade is why you are so rich. He made my family rich until now. I've worked for this. He was going to leave us that money and now I shall have nothing.'

'But I don't see how this is my problem?'

'Grandpa Wills?' exclaimed Ralph slamming his left fist against the barn wall. 'You call him Grandpa Wills like he was some sort of sweet old man! William Cecil Broadgate was a swindler and liar even to Dungrade. Your grandfather was a money launderer.'

Georgia felt something metallic and hard touch her leg. She looked down away from Ralph's face and saw a shotgun looped under his right arm. 'I don't want this money and these businesses,' she said.

'I don't believe you. You won't give it to me. You'll go running to the police about threats and menaces.' Ralph shoved her over with his left hand and pointed the gun at her.

Sean came out of the barn. 'What's going on?' he managed to ask before Ralph shoved the butt of the gun hard into his gut. Sean folded over, his legs buckled, and he tumbled onto the ground.

'Keep away from Georgia, Sean Foragehall. She's mine now,' threatened Ralph.

Gwen stepped away from the taxi that had dropped her and Lizzy off near to Gwen's car, parked in a side street in Banksea Town.

'Back to the caravan,' said Elizabeth. 'I need to recover from this.'

'No, we're not going there. The police know where we are staying now.'

'Does that matter anymore?' asked Elizabeth.

'We need to find Michael Pilmer. We don't know what he is up to with my money.'

'Yes, but isn't Dungrade dead like Harriet said?' enquired Elizabeth.

Gwen ignored the question. 'Don't you think Michael, after Cambridge, would join his family on holiday in North Norfolk?'

'Leave it to the police, Gwen,' said Lizzy getting in the car. 'They have William Cecil Broadgate's black book now.'

Gwen opened the door and slipped in behind the steering wheel. 'I've tried leaving it to the police. That didn't work for me, or you. We were the police and prosecutor. Surely you have no faith left in the system?'

'Inspector Campbell seems different.'

'Eccentric, I would say.'

'He seems respected by his colleagues,' said Lizzy.

'That doesn't make him straight.' Gwen started the car.

'Gwen, where are we going?'

'The Gull Inn. Abigail mentioned she was staying in the Barn Annex. We can wait for her there.'

'All right,' said Lizzy reluctantly.

After driving through Banksea Market Place, Gwen steered the car into a space in the Gull Inn car park.

'There's a camera and a parking restriction sign,' said Gwen. Frustrated, she grabbed the steering wheel and dug her fingernails into the palms of her hands.

'We parked in the car park by the quay when we came to the Gull Inn for the old girls' do,' said Lizzy, 'and collected it the next day.'

'We'll be chased off or fined or something here.' Gwen started to drive out when she saw in her rear-view mirror Abigail Pilmer and her baby getting in their car. 'I'll wait up the road and see where they go,' she added.

'Do we have to?' complained Lizzy.

'They will lead us to Michael Pilmer.'

'How do you know?'

'Do you remember at the school reunion how Abigail was all over Maccy?' asked Gwen

'She was a bit.'

'What does the headmistress have that the Pilmers might want?'

'The old bungalow by the coast,' suggested Lizzy.

'Exactly so.'

'And I believe Michael Pilmer and all are quite closely connected to Dungrade.'

'Not just doing the same sort of scams as Dungrade?'

'The Pilmers are the next generation of scammers, Lizzy. They were, and they may still be part of the Dungrade network, don't you agree?'

'Yes,' replied Lizzy.

Gwen felt a change in her friend and turned to her. Lizzy looked back. Her friend's eyes were sharply focused and there was agreement, satisfaction and determination in her voice. She saw inside Lizzy the flame flickering from the injustices that had been metered out to them both. 'Good,' she said. 'Here comes Abigail now.'

'She looks so much like her sister Shana,' observed Lizzy. 'We both forgot we all look older now when we saw Abigail that Friday.'

Georgia crept into Ralph Peterson's car with him pointing the shot gun at her face. Her hands were firmly tied. Her mouth was gagged with a scarf, but it was already working loose. Ralph pushed her down onto her stomach on the back seat. He tied her ankles with rope and looped it around the tie for her wrists. As Ralph Peterson drove away she found herself unable to push her way up to the window but she managed to work the gag off on the edge of the seat.

'This isn't just about money, is it Ralph?' she asked.

'Shut up,' said Ralph.

'What is it? What have I done?' pleaded Georgia.

There was a short delay before he answered her with, 'You have always ignored me.'

'When?' asked Georgia. 'When have I ignored you?'

'At my sister's birthday party.'

'I don't know what you mean? Abigail's?' Georgia paused for a reply. There was a confirmatory silence. 'You weren't there.'

'Yes, I was,' said Ralph.

'I didn't see you.' Georgia felt lost. She didn't understand why Ralph was so upset.

'You sat next to me. You must have seen me.'

'No, I honestly didn't see you.'

The car turned off the road and bumped onto rough ground. She heard Ralph open the glove compartment, shut it, open the driver's door and get out.

Georgia struggled to open the rear door and could not. Child locks she decided. She tried the window. That was similarly unmoving. The door swung open underneath, she fell forward. She craned her neck up to see Ralph holding the door.

'I had my arm around you. I've got a photo,' said Ralph. He showed her a photograph from his pocket. On it she saw herself seated next to a boy. He was probably twelve, she was fifteen. Next to him on the far side was Abigail and beyond her their elder sister, Shana.

'I'm sorry,' she said. She could see he was distraught. 'It was a group photo. You were a little boy.'

'I was only a year younger than you. I was just small. I'm fully grown now.' Ralph gagged her mouth with tape, shoved her back into the back seat and shut the door. She heard him walk away and again started looking for a means of escape.

Parnold came and stood in front of Campbell's desk wondering if his boss was ready to resume quizzing Jess Barratt.

Garden came up to them both. 'I've had a call from Bradley Yorkman. He went to meet Georgia Lomond at the barn where he leaves his motorbike and he found Sean Foragehall bound and gagged and Foragehall is saying that Ralph Peterson has taken Georgia.'

'Is Jenner still down in Cambridge interviewing Herbert Brandon?'

'No, Sir, she's back and she's gone down to the Gull Inn looking for Ralph Peterson, Michael and Abigail Pilmer.'

Campbell sent Parnold and Garden to talk to Bradley and Sean, and he phoned Jenner.

'I'm at the Gull Inn,' she said. 'Barbs has said that the Pilmers and Peterson have left, and she didn't know where they've gone, but she was fairly sure they've not gone home. She heard them say something about Strath-Kind school. I'm just setting out to the school now.'

'I will be there as soon as I can,' said Campbell. 'We might need back-up: Ralph has got a shot gun.'

'Okay, I haven't had a chance to speak to you about Herbert Brandon,' said Jenner.

'People running around with guns kidnapping people has to take priority.'

'What's happened?'

'Bradley Yorkman phoned in about an incident at that old barn by the coast down the hill from Cricklestaithe Farm. I've sent Parnold and Garden to find out what happened.'

'Right, I'll see you at the school, Sir.'

Garden and Parnold drew the car up the lane by the barn at Daneton and jumped out of the car. Parnold ran into the barn and found Bradley Yorkman using a small penknife to free Sean Foragehall from the nylon baler twine which was tied around his wrists.

Sean was saying, 'Ralph's taken Georgia Lomond. He's got a shot gun. My shotgun. I brought it down to the barn and then thought better of it and left it outside. I'm scared for Georgia.'

Bradley pulled his arm back to hit Sean and Parnold caught Bradley at the elbow

Elizabeth and Gwen hunkered down within a circle of sand dunes within sight of the timber bungalow nestling a hundred metres or so from the beach. They were sure they had not been seen by anyone as they'd hidden the car in a copse half-way down the lane.

'Hello ladies,' said Harriet from behind.

Elizabeth and Gwen turned around. They stared into the double barrel of a shot gun.

'I thought it was too easy, all the gates unlocked,' said Gwen.

'We've been expecting you. No amount of intimidation has kept you away. I told Dungrade that, but he wouldn't listen. He said murdering you two was too messy. But it is a permanent solution.'

'Until the police catch up with you.'

'Permanent for you though,' said Harriet.

'Dungrade?' queried Elizabeth.

'He's dead,' said Harriet. She clouted Elizabeth with the gun and followed through with a swipe at Gwen.

CHAPTER TWENTY-TWO

Elizabeth could feel the sore place on her cheek where the shotgun had caught her. Clearly Harriet had not intended to damage her further otherwise the bone would be broken. She noticed Gwen – just a short distance away – had a similar mark on her face. They were both tied and gagged and seated on the floor of the bungalow. Elizabeth looked around the room. The living room was familiar but had been decorated and refurnished since she and Gwen had come here with Maccy. Wooden chairs and table which were at least seventy years old and a more modern, cloth covered sofa furnished the room. A black stove stood cool and quiet in the summer heat.

'Take Gwen's car and park it by the beach road just outside Daneton,' said Michael to Abigail as she came in from the kitchen, startling Elizabeth out of her reverie.

'I've left the gates open,' said Harriet joining the conversation as she came through a door slightly behind and to Elizabeth's right.

Elizabeth knew that it led to a corridor which had two bedrooms coming off it.

'You can drive down the lane as far as the main road,' Harriet instructed Abigail. Here's the key to the gates, you can lock them behind you. I'll pick you up in a bit from Daneton. Park the car on the promenade and I'll meet you in the tea shop in about three hours' time.'

'Ok,' said Abigail evenly. She took her baby from the kitchen and banged the back door as she left.

Ralph Peterson and Michael Pilmer looked at Elizabeth and Gwen. Harriet was making sure the women did not escape by waving the same double barrelled shot gun she had when she caught them in the dunes. But, Elizabeth soon realised that there were more firearms in the room. Ralph held a second shotgun and Michael Pilmer had some sort of hand gun tucked in his belt.

Michael spoke to her and Gwen, 'I'm very lucky, Ralph is a master forger of signatures. Between us we put together a number of altered wills. I now have your signature from the other day. It is most generous of you to leave all your recently inherited wealth to Abigail. She will be pleased.'

Gwen grunted angrily behind her gag and she worked ferociously against her bindings.

Harriet pointed her gun at Gwen and told her to, 'Stop!'

Gwen stopped

'It was a shame you hadn't thought about William Cecil Broadgate making another will with that other solicitor, Godfrey. You should have made a more up to date version,' complained Harriet to Michael.

'We are putting that right now,' said Michael Pilmer. 'I'll see to the boat.' He went out and left the back door open.

Harriet turned to Ralph. 'Shut the back door,' she demanded.

Ralph looked at her hatefully but did as he was told.

'Let's get the other one from the bedroom,' she said.

Ralph went to the door of the bedroom corridor and dragged Georgia out of one of the bedrooms through to the living room.

'And the lovely Georgia, so in love with Ralph, has left him all her money,' said Harriet to Georgia. 'I managed to find a document with your signature on it in William Cecil Broadgate's house.'

Georgia's bruised face was already stained with tears and she started to gasp. Ralph looked pleased.

'There wasn't any trouble picking her up?' Harriet asked Ralph.

'No, I told you there wasn't,' he snapped back.

Elizabeth was worried for Georgia. She seemed to be very still.

'We don't want her to die here: take her gag off,' said Harriet. She observed Georgia closely until her breathing recovered. 'We've just about got a swimming team here,' said Harriet crunching up her black curls with her fingers. Her white skin seemed to develop a murderous glow. 'Let's get some swimsuits on them and take them out for a boat ride.'

Georgia stirred and wriggled up into a seating position. 'You can have…,' she started to say.

Ralph slapped her across the face with his gun.

Georgia fell back.

'Shut up,' growled Ralph.

Harriet dropped two swimming costumes in front of Elizabeth and Gwen. 'They were in your car she explained.' A third costume she dropped in front of Georgia. Georgia looked shocked. It was a school team costume.

'I got it from William Cecil's House along with your signature.' One at a time she unbound each one and made them change into them while Ralph trained his gun on the two who were not changing.

Elizabeth was the last to get changed. She was consumed by the presence of the guns the whole time. She had heard that this was a normal reaction to a gun being in the room. She forced herself to think what she could do to avoid the drowning that their captors clearly had in mind for them.

'Put the hoodies on and the tracksuit bottoms,' said Harriet, dropping them out of the plastic bags. They were similar to the ones that Harriet was wearing. 'They're not to keep you warm, they're just in case you are seen. People might think it odd to be sitting in a boat at this time of day in just light swimwear.'

Ralph was watching Georgia keenly. 'You weren't in the swimming team, were you, Harriet,' sneered Ralph.

'Shut up,' said Harriet. 'This is a great way to get rid of them. Stupid competitive swimmers swimming where they shouldn't when a rip tide is running through. Couldn't be better. The seal trips have finished for the day. It will be easy. And stop looking at Georgia, Ralph. You need to watch Gwen too.'

'What about the boat, we might not make it back?' asked Ralph.

'It's high tide now. We go now and drop them an hour or so before dark. We've got an outboard motor.'

'What are you doing, Lizzy?' shouted Harriet shoving the gun barrel into Elizabeth's chest.

'Nothing,' lied Elizabeth.

'I don't think so,' said Harriet pulling the plastic bags out of Elizabeth's tracksuit bottom pocket. 'I saw you thumb those in there. Thought you'd make some floats out of those bags? Well, you're mistaken.' Harriet threw them in the cold stove and slammed the stove hatch shut.

Michael said, 'Right let's go,' as he swung the back door open in the kitchen and came in bringing a wave of sand into the room.

The three swimmers were pulled to their feet and their bindings removed.

The shore was deserted. The sea was quiet. There was no chance of escape with Harriet and Ralph pointing their shotguns at them as they forced them into the boat down at the water's edge. Harriet gave Gwen a snide knock with her gun and shoved her, Elizabeth and Georgia in turn into the front of the boat and sat down opposite them. She pointed her shotgun at them.

Michael Pilmer and Ralph shoved the boat off from the shore, Michael's hand gun stuck in his belt and Ralph's shotgun slung across his back with a piece of string as a strap.

Ralph jumped in and sat by the outboard motor. Michael followed and sent Ralph into the centre of the boat with Harriet while he took up position by the outboard motor.

Michael said to Harriet and Ralph loudly, so Elizabeth, Gwen and Georgia could hear, 'This will be a most profitable little boat trip.'

Jenner arrived outside Strath-Kind School and was soon joined by Campbell 'Herbert Brandon gave a time-consuming confession,' she said to Inspector Campbell after the briefest of nodded greetings. Everything had seemed to have contrived against her making this visit to the school earlier and now she was here under the pressure of a nutcase with a gun. Campbell informed her that he had asked for an armed response team to be available if necessary. But there was no sign of visitor cars in the driveway. They both relaxed.

Jenner rang the doorbell of Strath-Kind school.

Arabella Macfine opened the door herself, turned and walked straight into the study. Campbell and Jenner followed.

'I hope you can help us, we're looking for Ralph Peterson,' said Jenner.

'He's not here,' said the headteacher.

Campbell moved away within the hall and advised the Horseton Station of that fact while Arabella moved towards a photograph of a timber building. 'Ralph may be with his sister,' she said to Jenner. 'She's rented the bungalow. I used to go there for days with the students; bird-watching, that sort of thing. It was absolutely brilliant. All the girls loved it. In recent years, I've allowed some of them to hire it out in the summer months.'

Jenner asked, 'Where is it?' Jenner looked at the wooden building behind a row of school girls. The bungalow had four windows along the front and a verandah. It was surrounded by spikey grass and sand dunes.

'It's between Cricklestaithe and Daneton,' said Arabella Macfine.

'Thank you,' said Jenner. 'How do I get to this place?'

Arabella Macfine gave Jenner a map. 'The gates will probably be unlocked down the lane but the one by the main road I asked them to keep it locked. There's no point in trying to phone them down there. I expect they've got ordinary phones and there's no signal down there,' she explained. Arabella reached into her desk drawer and pulled out a key. 'For the gate,' she said. She produced another set of keys. 'For the bungalow,' she added. 'Try not to break it. And Abigail has her baby with her if you are planning any rough stuff.' She gave Campbell a hard stare as he came back in the room.

'Thank you, for your help, Miss Macfine,' said Jenner as she left.

Campbell nodded in acknowledgement and followed Jenner outside onto the front drive. He said to her, 'We'll take both cars. I'll contact Lindy at the office and let her know we're going to the nature reserve between Cricklestaithe Bay and Daneton Howe Beach and get her to inform the fire arms and back-up team.'

When Jenner reached the gate at the top of the lane, it was unlocked and open and there was no sign of the response team. She contacted Lindy.

'They're on their way,' said Lindy.

Jenner had her car door window slightly open as she reached forward and started the car.

'You are to wait for their arrival,' said Campbell. His quiet voice carried with its inbuilt firmness and determination.

'Yes, sir,' she said.

CHAPTER TWENTY-THREE

Georgia, Elizabeth and Gwen huddled down almost out of view from any possible onlookers. Michael lowered the outboard motor into the water. Elizabeth noted their captors were all wearing life jackets and she, Gwen and Georgia were not. Once the motor was going, land soon started to shrink into the distance.

Out in the gently lifting waves of the North Sea Harriet continued to cover them with her gun. Elizabeth looked around for the seal watchers' boats. But there were none. Confirming Harriet's view and they had, no doubt, already returned to Cricklestaithe Quay in readiness for the change in the tide. Gwen was also alert despite coming off worse from the butt of Harriet's weapon as she entered the boat. Georgia was bruised and cowering. Ralph had taken every opportunity to spite her with a snide punch or kick. Now Elizabeth and Gwen shuffled themselves to form a shield around her. Harriet scowled but did not stop them. She leaned forward and ripped the tape from their mouths. If it wasn't for the gun Harriet would look like them dressed in her tracksuit, thought Elizabeth.

'We can't go too far,' complained Ralph. 'We'll not get back in ourselves. This boat isn't up to staying out far into the North Sea.'

'No, I want to go further,' insisted Harriet.

'Leave it,' ordered Michael Pilmer.

'These are good swimmers. I know how far they can go,' said Harriet.

'Get their tracksuits off. They want to be chilling off before they go in. They will have more chance of cramping,' said Michael.

Harriet agreed and had them take off their tracksuits. She threw them over the side of the boat. 'You won't be needing them again,' she said.

'I've been practicing by myself each day swimming right along the coast by Cricklestaithe Bay. I can swim well now,' said Ralph putting on a green and red swimming hat, a Strath-Kind hat.

'He's insane,' said Harriet.

'I know how far I can swim. I know the abilities of this boat. I'm not insane,' retorted Ralph.

'I knew I should have married your older sister, Shana, not Abigail. She never wanted anything to do with you, Ralph,' complained Michael Pilmer.

'You wouldn't have had the use of my skills,' sneered Ralph.

'I shouldn't have married Abigail just because she got pregnant,' said Michael pointedly at Ralph.

Ralph threw his shotgun into the bottom of the boat. Michael Pilmer stood up. Ralph lunged at Michael and punched him down. Pilmer's knees folded and the outboard motor died. Pilmer recovered and the two men wrestled in the back of the boat.

Ralph's shotgun slid down the length of the boat towards Elizabeth, Gwen and Georgia. Elizabeth watched it get closer to them.

'No, you don't,' said Harriet, grabbing the gun and throwing it over the side into the North Sea.

Harriet turned on Ralph. He was straddled across Michael Pilmer, his legs holding him still. His hands held Michael around his neck. 'Where did you get that gun, Ralph?' she asked. 'You said it was William Cecil's. You said you found it in the house,'

'I did,' said Ralph.

Michael pushed Ralph off. Ralph returned before Michael was fully up. They grappled with each other exchanging blows. Harriet watched them as they came close to her.

'We've got to go now,' whispered Gwen to Elizabeth, 'to have a chance.'

'What about, Georgia?' asked Elizabeth.

'We take her with us, between us we should be able to bring her to shore,' said Gwen.

'They'll come after us in the boat,' said Elizabeth looking at Harriet.

Harriet had her back to them quizzing Ralph about the gun. 'I left a gun in William Cecil's house, but it wasn't the one I just chucked out of the boat,' Elizabeth heard her say.

'They might not follow us,' said Gwen. 'But we'll tip the boat anyway. Come on, Harriet's distracted.'

Harriet wavered and half-turned towards her prisoners.

Elizabeth dropped her head and looped her arm around Georgia in an apparently comforting way.

Ralph must have loosened his grip as Michael Pilmer landed a punch on Ralph and pushed Ralph off. Ralph fell back and knocked Harriet's gun. Angrily she turned back to Ralph and Michael to shout at them.

Gwen nodded, and Elizabeth went over the side backwards with Georgia, dragging the boat over with the movement of their bodies. When she and Georgia bobbed up in the sea she saw Gwen cartwheeling off the side off the boat. Harriet was out of her view.

Swimming on her back, Elizabeth immediately started to tow Georgia towards land while Gwen went back to give the boat another shove. It was still rocking from her exit as Gwen grabbed the opposite side and pulled hard in rhythm with the rocking. Elizabeth could see Harriet crouching in the bottom of the boat. As Gwen swam away Harriet tried to stand up in the rocking boat. She turned awkwardly and fired both barrels of the shotgun at Gwen. Harriet tumbled backwards into the water from the recoil of the gun. The shot-gun pellets blasted a massive hole in the boat. The boat's hull dropped in the water. Michael and Ralph stood up in the boat still wrestling. Elizabeth saw Ralph land a punch on Michael which sent them both into the sea.

Elizabeth started to swim hard with Georgia in tow. She didn't know what had happened to Gwen but now Harriet, Michael and Ralph were in the water. She knew Harriet was a strong swimmer and Ralph had already said he was a practiced swimmer. If either of them was sound of wind and limb one of them could easily catch her.

Gwen bobbed up next to her. A moment of relief flooded through her.

'I'll help,' said Gwen.

They put Georgia between them and swam in unison through the water. There was no sign of Harriet or Michael, but Ralph's green and red Strath-Kind School swim-cap was closing the gap between them.

Elizabeth took Georgia's full weight and Gwen slipped down and away into the surrounding sea. She could see that Ralph had stopped and was treading water, trying to spot them. Elizabeth tilted her head back to try to disappear among the undulating waves. The calm sea was their saviour and their captor. She could swim readily enough but she could not hide herself and Georgia. When she looked again it was clear Ralph had seen her and was heading straight for her. She wondered briefly where Gwen was, but she trusted her. Well, she thought she did. She looked again. Of course, she trusted her.

Gwen's head appeared a short distance from Ralph's just as he grabbed at Georgia's leg. Elizabeth was pulled under with her. Georgia came back to her. Ralph's pull was gone. All she could see was foaming water as Gwen and Ralph fought. Elizabeth towed Georgia away as fast as she could for as long as she could. She stopped wondering how long it would be before the tide ripped through. And, she saw Ralph still in the water supported by his life jacket.

Gwen swam over to Elizabeth. 'He's got a life belt on. I've put him the right way up.'

'You're injured,' Elizabeth could see that Gwen could only move one arm. 'You can use him as a float as long as he stays unconscious.'

'And if he doesn't…' Gwen grinned and gestured a knock-out punch with her good arm.

Elizabeth watched as Gwen retrieved Ralph in his life-jacket.

The current started to pull them away from land. Elizabeth could barely hold Georgia. Gwen was no longer able to help. Gwen shook her head.

'We'll be alright,' said Elizabeth as she spat out sea water. 'We'll tread water.' After a couple of minutes, she heard a roar in the water. She looked for its source.

'A boat's coming,' said Gwen.

Elizabeth strained every sinew to see what sort of boat it was. Her heart leapt with hope.

'Is it Harriet?' asked Gwen.

'No, even she could not have got back that fast and found a boat so quickly,' said Elizabeth. 'She'll be hoping we're drowning.' She could see a red-orange rubber boat bouncing along the top of the water and silhouetted shapes. 'There are two armed men. Looks like an Inshore Rescue boat.'

'Armed police,' suggested Gwen. 'They must know about the guns.'

The orange boat came closer and two unarmed men and two unarmed women came forward to haul them out of the water. The armed men stood in the middle of the boat watching. The hauled-out Ralph and Georgia first, and then Gwen. And, finally, Elizabeth found the boat underneath her.

As they wrapped them in blankets, Elizabeth found she knew two of the rescuers as Sergeants Parnold and Jenner. The others said they were Inshore Rescue including a further woman holding the steering wheel in the center of the vessel.

Elizabeth told Parnold and one of the in-shore rescue team, 'There were two more from the boat that sank: a man and a woman.'

'We have another man,' said Sergeant Parnold. Nodding at a man behind her wrapped in blankets.

'Yes, that's Michael Pilmer,' she said screwing her face up as if it had been slapped. 'He's got a gun.'

'Not now,' said Parnold. 'Armed response has it.' He nodded at the two armed officers.

'Harriet Epsy was on the boat that sank too. And Abigail Pilmer is waiting for Harriet at the little tea shop on Daneton Promenade.'

'Oh right, didn't know about her. The other man didn't say,' said the lifeboat man nodding at Michael Pilmer.

'She had a life belt on,' said Gwen.

'I still can't hold out a lot of hope for her. We've not got a lot more daylight. We have a helicopter on its way. It will search the area,' said the lifeboat man.

'I'll get Garden up to the kiosk.' Elizabeth heard Sergeant Jenner say to Sergeant Parnold. She turned and spoke to the lifeboat captain, who passed her the radio. She spoke into it. Elizabeth couldn't hear what was being said.

'What do you think?' asked Gwen of Elizabeth.

'Harriet's away. The police are going to search for her along the coast as well as in the water. They are not going to catch her,' said Elizabeth. 'Do you think Georgia's going to be okay?'

'I think so,' said Gwen as Georgia stirred under the administration of the paramedic.

Ralph was still unconscious. Elizabeth sighed. There would be some explaining to do to the police. She looked at Gwen.

'I know,' said Gwen as if she read her thoughts.

'Secure your seats,' said the helmsman of the inshore rescue boat. She powered up the engine and headed the life-boat back along the shore line.

When the boat stopped up on the beach, a tractor and trailer was waiting to haul it up the sand to its shed.

The rescued, police and lifeboatmen all decanted from the boat. Ambulances and paramedics were on hand. Beyond these were probably twenty police officers. Elizabeth assumed their cars were parked out of view. She saw the willowy figure of Inspector Campbell standing on the highest part of the beach. He looked thoughtful with his left hand holding his chin. She braced herself for his inquiries.

Ralph and Michael were placed in one ambulance while Elizabeth found herself travelling with Gwen and Georgia to the hospital. Police officers joined each ambulance and when they arrived at the hospital Elizabeth found that more uniformed police officers were on duty watching them.

CHAPTER TWENTY-FOUR

Tarnish looked up from Campbell's interim report. Campbell stood with his hands behind his back and looked steadily at the nearside edge of Tarnish's desk. He felt the pressure of these update meetings with his senior officer. But he was livid at the delay of the armed response team. The delay had led to a near catastrophe out on the Wash. He expressed his misgivings to Tarnish.

'You've done well, Campbell,' said Tarnish as if he had not heard a word Campbell had told him. 'That last operation has cleared up all the side issues. Michael Pilmer seems to be giving us all the scams Dungrade was up to and Ralph Peterson is recovering in hospital.'

'Georgia Lomond is also recovering well,' said Campbell.

'Yes,' said Tarnish without interest. 'I'm sure that the charge sheet is already quite long for Michael Pilmer and Ralph Peterson,' he continued with enthusiasm.

'Abigail Pilmer is also keen to tell all she knows,' said Campbell. 'She was where Elizabeth Rattagan said she would be: at the little tea shop kiosk at Daneton Promenade. She is hoping to avoid being seen as part of the crimes, but Michael is telling a different story.'

'All good news, Campbell,' said Tarnish with a flourish.

'We haven't got Harriet,' said Campbell. 'The search crews haven't found her, and they are already believing she has been swept out to sea.'

'This case is as good as closed,' said Tarnish frowning. 'Concentrate on the paperwork now and let's put really good cases forward for the prosecutions.'

'We don't have Dungrade,' said Campbell, 'or Messenger Watcher.'

'Anne Crowlie was Messenger Watcher. You have her bicycle that she used,' complained Tarnish. 'William Cecil Broadgate was Dungrade.'

'Anne Crowlie didn't confess to that. Why would she confess to the note but not the phone messages? Nor could she have been William Cecil

Broadgate's killer, she wasn't there. And why was she then killed?'

'Because she was Messenger Watcher,' said Tarnish with frustration. 'Jess Barratt has confessed to the murder of William Cecil Broadgate.'

'Jess Barratt didn't murder William Cecil Broadgate. She is too scared. We are interviewing Ralph and Michael, but Ralph was definitely in Banksea Town Centre all day and Michael was still in Seachester.'

'Ask Jess Barratt,' said Tarnish. 'She seems to know everything.'

'Parnold and Jenner are carrying out a further interview with her as we speak,' said Campbell trying not to sigh by stretching his fingers which were still folded behind his back. He was unconvinced by Tarnish's advice but would following some of it. Too many questions remained unanswered to call the case closed and shouting at Jess Barratt would not get the answers.

'Good,' said Tarnish dismissively.

Parnold and Jenner sat opposite Jess Barratt and her studious note taking solicitor, waiting for the answer to Jenner's question.

Jess Barratt fiddled with her fingers for a while, curled her top lip and said, 'I don't know who employed me to kill William Cecil Broadgate.'

'What do you mean?' asked Jenner.

'It was just a message left on the counter of the kiosk. I never saw who left it.'

'Just a message? Was there any money?' Jenner sat still resting her hands on the table.

'Not at first,' said Jess.

'Where did you leave your replies?' asked Jenner.

'Pinned to one of the beach huts on Banksea beach.'

'How did you do that? Explain how you did that, Jess.'

'I used just an ordinary plastic topped pin for notice boards.'

'Where did you pin it on the hut?'

'At the back, underneath the hut, like attached to under the floor, by one of the legs that hold the beach hut out of the sand.'

'Which beach hut did you use?'

'I used both of the beach huts that are now burnt down.'

'Did you burn them down?' asked Jenner unable to keep the surprise from her voice.

'Of course, I did. I had to remove any evidence of my DNA. I watch telly. I know these things.'

'And the weapons for killing William Cecil Broadgate. How did you come by those?' asked Jenner.

'They were left with the money underneath the beach hut.'

'Which one?'

'I don't know. One of the burnt-out beach huts.'

'Do you have any of the notes?'

'Who to?' asked Jess.

'You.'

'Burnt them.'

And how was the money paid?'

'By?

'The person whom you said wanted William Cecil Broadgate dead.'

'Some cash before and some after.'

'Which days was it delivered?'

'The Thursday before the murder and the Monday after, but the Monday money never came.'

'Who do you think paid you to murder William Cecil Broadgate?'

'I really don't know. Perhaps you'd like to tell me,' said Jess Barratt.

Campbell arrived at the door and Parnold addressed the recording machine suspending the interview.

Parnold, Jenner, Garden and Lindy gathered around the incident board and Campbell asked Parnold for his résumé. Sergeant Parnold drew his verbal report prompted from Jenner's neatly written notes.

On completion Campbell said, 'We can get the scene of crime team to double check DNA on any pins they have already found on the site which might have been used to secure notes on the burnt-out beach huts at Banksea Beach.'

'Jess pointed us in the direction of the huts days ago,' complained Garden. 'Why would she do that?'

'Because she thinks we won't find anything,' replied Parnold, 'and it made her sound like an outraged law-abiding citizen as well as sending us after Bradley Yorkman.'

'Scene of Crime Investigators have checked but with the shifting sands it might be worth searching again for a pin or some other remains,' said Campbell.

The team nodded in agreement.

'Jess was and is confident she's destroyed any evidence, and so she might have. We'll just have to wait on that one,' added Campbell.

'It's just another one of her lies,' grumbled Parnold. He felt that the murder investigation had ground to a halt, but Campbell still looked doggedly determined despite his bandaged hand and heavy dark rings forming around his eyes.

'We are nearly there with this, but we need to stick at it. We still have to check out what Jess Barratt says,' Campbell reminded him, promptly moving on with, 'Herbert Brandon and Anne Crowlie and all those from Cambridge were at the seminar in London on Thursday. Let's get that confirmed with security camera checks at their hotel for Thursday. Lindy and Garden, can you look into that? Jess Barratt is our link to the murderer.'

'Yes, Sir,' said Garden.

'Do you really think she didn't kill William Cecil?' asked Parnold.

'I do,' said Campbell.

Parnold looked at Campbell. The Scotsman had an uncanny ability to read people, so he nodded and said, 'Ok,' in reply.

Lindy continued with making notes until her phone rang. After listening for a couple of minutes, she said to Campbell, 'They've got Bradley Yorkman's dad on the phone complaining about the way his son has been treated by the police.'

Campbell nodded. 'I'll go up and see him.'

On reaching the Yorkmans' cottage, Bradley Yorkman's father strode out of the front door of the cottage. After introducing himself and Campbell explaining his role, Mr. Yorkman senior said to Campbell, 'We can talk out here.'

'It's a grand day. You can see right across to Cricklestaithe Bay and the North Sea from here,' said Campbell in a friendly way.

Mr. Yorkman frowned. 'Bradley's at the hospital with Georgia Lomond this morning. She is being discharged and he is going with her to Scotland, so she can be with her family.'

Campbell absorbed that information with a slight stretch of his shoulders. He said, 'I understand you are concerned about the treatment that your son has received.'

'My son, Inspector, has been accused of just about every crime that has occurred locally in the last month,' said Mr. Yorkman. Campbell could see he was bristling with anger and frustration. 'From what he's told me, all he's done wrong as far as I can see,' continued Mr. Yorkman, 'was to wear a hoodie which he bought in the area and ride his motorcycle around the lanes – oh, and like Georgia Lomond.'

'Regrettably, Mr. Yorkman, all those things you mention have put your son with an ability to be at the scene of a number of these crimes. His association with Georgia could have connected these actions to these crimes, and his hoodie put him into a collection of people who had the same hoodie that was used in a crime,' explained Campbell.

'And what about Bradley's swimming? He was asked about his swimming.' Mr. Yorkman shook his head with confusion.

'Sometimes during investigations, we have to ask what appear to be odd questions without giving any reason for it. It is the nature of the work. We cannot tell people how our minds are working. Your son has been cleared of any involvement in all the crimes and no charges will be brought for the brawl he had on the beach with Sean Foragehall.'

Mr. Yorkman looked startled at the name. 'Bradley never caused the fire he was accused of when he was young. It was Sean Foragehall. I never would say anything because I believed his father owned the cottage we rented. I never read the rental agreement my wife handled it. I was away working at the time. I did sign it though. She passed away quite a few years ago. I should have sorted it out, but there was so much to do bringing up my son on my own. Now I know Foragehall senior never did own the cottage, I can tell the truth.'

Campbell looked at him, surprised.

'Sean confessed to Bradley just afterwards,' said Mr. Yorkman. 'Bradley said he'd seen him do it and Sean Foragehall knew it.'

How much harm had Mr. Yorkman's lack of support for his son's innocence affected the present situation, Campbell wondered. A veil of suspicion had fallen on Bradley and Bradley Yorkman had not been able to brush it off.

'I believe no action was taken against your son at the time, Mr. Yorkman,' said Campbell, recalling the research that had been carried out on Bradley. 'If you or Bradley have evidence to put forward then action can still be considered.'

Mr. Yorkman turned away. 'Too late now,' he mumbled.

'If you wish to take the complaint about your son's treatment by the police further then you will need to contact the complaints people,' said Campbell in understanding tones. 'I brought a leaflet.'

'I don't want your leaflet. I've had my say,' said Mr. Yorkman going indoors.

Campbell started to walk down to the bottom of the lane by the coast road where he'd left the car. He was trying to settle the elements of the case in his mind as he walked up to the Yorkman's cottage. Now he returned to his thoughts as his strides took him back down the track. He stopped to admire again the view of the North Sea stretching out into the distance beyond Cricklestaithe Bay. Between the coast road and the bay, a white walled farmhouse with blue painted windows was almost blinking in the sharp sunlight.

Jenner phoned. Her usual smooth tones had an edge of controlled panic. 'I'm at the hospital. Frank Norton has gone missing,' she said. 'I came down to talk to him because the hospital had said he was conscious.'

'Surely, he wasn't well enough to leave hospital on his own?' Campbell asked with his Edinburgh brogue.

'No, he wasn't; nor was he well enough to be discharged into someone's care,' explained Jenner flatly. 'It looks like he's been taken. Someone's also tried to take wound dressings with them.'

'What about pain killers?'

'All locked up,' replied Jenner.

'Obtainable elsewhere though,' Campbell heard Parnold say from somewhere near to Jenner.

'Did you hear that?' asked Jenner.

'Aye,' said Campbell.

'The team are up here digging around for clues, checking security camera footage and all that,' explained Jenner sounding calmer. 'Garden has just said a woman who might be a match for Harriet Epsy is on some recent footage from the cameras. Any suggestions for finding Harriet?'

'Try Strath-Kind School. Arabella Macfine, the head mistress,' suggested Campbell. 'Harriet, Ralph and the Pilmers found their way to one of the school premises – the bungalow – perhaps Harriet has found her way to another one.'

'Okay,' said Jenner. 'I'll get down there.'

Campbell put away his phone and continued down the hill towards the coast road and his car. Before he reached it, he noticed large "sale for redevelopment" signs. He crossed the road and headed down the access lane to the farmhouse. Hadn't Arabella Macfine said she used to live in the school's farmhouse?

By the entrance to the front of the farmhouse stood a sign, "School Farm". There was a blue car he vaguely remembered from Daneton's promenade the Friday of William Cecil Broadgate's murder. Could it be Harriet Epsy's?

He wasn't going to wait for back-up this time. The guns had been accounted for by the armed response teams search of the bungalow and Elizabeth Rattagan's and Gwen Blythe's statements. He rolled over the top of the stone wall and skirted around the back using a couple of timber sheds to keep out of the view from the windows at the front and from those at the back of the house.

Behind the house he found an extension built on the back. Beside the door were two taps and a boot washing trough. The door was ajar. He slid through not risking moving the hinges. The first area was a lobby with numerous coat hooks. He moved across the room which had several sinks and a hand-washing trough and into the next room, again the door was slightly open.

He hoped this room would lead into the house. Old charts lined the walls explaining the anatomy of cattle and sheep and another listed the diseases that could be passed on to humans. The wall at the end adjoining the farmhouse was solid, no doors into the house. On the floor, he found a new wound dressing still in its wrapper. He picked it up. Hospital issue.

He phoned Jenner. 'No need to go to the school,' he said softly not daring to wait for her acknowledgement. 'I'm at the farm that's up for sale just up from Cricklestaithe Bay. On the seaward side of the coast road, just opposite the Foragehalls' place and the Yorkman's cottage.'

He closed the call. He wasn't going to wait for Jenner's inevitable warning to wait until the response team arrived. He left the teaching rooms with their remains of long gone veterinary activity and back into the yard. He could see a lean-to extension which he now guessed would be over the kitchen. Stooping low to avoid being seen from ground floor windows, he crossed the yard to the lean-to door. It was old, but the timber failed to creek as he opened it. He was expert at lifting latches without making a "click" from living in an old cottage himself.

Once in the kitchen he could hear voices. Concentrating on them he was aware that he could hear a woman's voice. He had heard it only twice before, Harriet Epsy. The kitchen door was slightly open as if Harriet had been in too much of a hurry to close it, so he could look through the gap afforded by the old, large hinges. He hunkered down by the living room door.

He saw Harriet's black curls wrapped in a broad head band. She was kneeling next to a mattress. Her pale hand touched a blanket laid on the bed. He presumed she must have dragged it down from upstairs. The bed was occupied, and he could hear a man groaning from there.

'It's all right, Frank,' said Harriet.

So, Harriet, thought Campbell, had hurried through the house looking for items that might help her with Frank Norton's injuries. She clearly dared not leave him for long. Perhaps she hoped there were dressings here that had been kept for the animals, even painkillers. That would explain the open drawers in the teaching room.

'Why did you take me out of the hospital?' growled Frank Norton at Harriet.

Campbell leaned closer to the door.

'I didn't know what to do,' said Harriet.

'I always expected to be in hospital,' wheezed Frank Norton.

'But not for long,' pleaded Harriet. 'Just a disfigured face. That was all we planned. But that Inspector Campbell was there, at the beach, so I couldn't let you out quick enough.'

'Now I'm going to die,' said Frank Norton through gritted teeth. Campbell could see him with his left eye bandaged and his blood-shot right eye staring at Harriet. Frank closed his eye and became quiet and limp.

Campbell wondered if he was dead.

Harriet pulled at Frank Norton. He groaned.

'Frank, we planned all of this together, so Dungrade would be dead,' pleaded Harriet. 'So, you could live again free of prosecution.'

Frank opened his eye and wheezed, 'Yes, but I was misinformed about William Cecil Broadgate's status. When he died all the money was meant to come to me. That solicitor of yours had written Broadgate's will. William Cecil's money was mine. The money was meant to come to me.'

'We were not to know he went and wrote another will,' said Harriet.

'You should have. You should have updated the will anyway.'

Harriet turned from Frank Norton, towards Campbell's hiding place. He dodged away from the gap by the door.

Harriet turned back to Norton, her body stiff. 'Why did you let Anne Crowlie get involved?' she asked. She sounded insulted. 'You couldn't resist charming her into believing that you were some sort of victim.'

Campbell returned to the gap by the door-hinge.

'What's this about Harriet?' asked Frank Norton. 'Are you jealous? She was just convenient. If they'd caught her, she'd have said that Frank Norton was in danger, not Frank Norton was the danger. She believed everything I told her. How I was in danger from a swindler and murderer. She believed it all.'

'Leave that stupid note in Elizabeth Rattagan's bag was not in the plan,' retorted Harriet.

'It may not have been in your plan, but it was always in mine,' spluttered Norton. 'Anne Crowlie never saw through me. She didn't see that I was the same person who was blackmailing her into leaving that message for Elizabeth Rattagan. I wanted to make Rattagan's life a misery, so people would know not to mess with me. Anne Crowlie left the note for me and took the blame. It was easy.' Norton broke into a fit of coughing.

Campbell recalled the lap-top computer tucked so carefully under him, protecting Anne Crowlie's statement that Frank Norton was a victim as well as her confession. Frank Norton knew what it said and had been protecting it from the flames for the authorities.

Campbell felt he had waited long enough to see what Harriet and Frank would say to each other, and he wondered how much longer the back-up team would be. This thought was interrupted by Harriet. She sounded angry.

'She could have got us all arrested. I killed for you. Anne Crowlie didn't kill for you.'

'Only some old tramp.' Frank Norton closed his unbandaged eye briefly. 'Harriet, I need pain killers.'

She means the dead man on Daneton Beach, thought Campbell. He heard a car stopping on the gravel at the front of the house. He wondered if it was his back-up team.

'You and Anne Crowlie were lovers,' Harriet accused Frank Norton. She dragged a pillow from under Frank's head and put it over his face.

Campbell was not going to risk Frank Norton's death. He pounced out from behind the door. He wrapped one of his long arms around Harriet and used the other to grab the pillow. He dragged Harriet off Frank Norton and out of reach of him. Norton wheezed.

Campbell heard the crunch of gravel on the front drive of the farmhouse. 'Looks like you get to live,' he said to Frank Norton. 'The back-up team is here.'

Campbell held Harriet Epsy down, issued the caution and fixed handcuffs around her wrists. 'Where did you get your Uncle Richard from?' he asked her.

She swore at him and everything went black for Campbell.

CHAPTER TWENTY-FIVE

The armed response team entered the living room. The Team Leader of the response team looked around the room. 'One down,' he said.

Another member of his team checked the person on the ground. 'Female, serious head wound, cuffed,' he reported.

The team moved through securing the building.

'No sign of Inspector Campbell,' the Team Leader reported to Parnold and Jenner who were looking at the injured person on the floor. A female paramedic was already in attendance. Her dark blond pony-tail waggled as she tilted her head examining her patient.

'We think it's Harriet Epsy,' said Jenner. 'We've got a picture of her from the tea shop in Daneton and security footage from the café in Banksea.'

'That's a really bad head injury,' advised the paramedic as she and the ambulance driver set about securing her ready for removal from the farmhouse. 'We've called out the air ambulance to take her to Cambridge,' she said. 'We will drive her to meet it.'

Parnold followed them out saying anxiously, 'I'll arrange the scene of crime experts to attend to the farmhouse.'

Jenner remained inside the farmhouse and wondered if Campbell had left any clue to his whereabouts. She crouched down beside the blood stains next to the mattress on the floor. Already her heart rate was dropping back. Campbell was gone.

'Search the immediate area,' she heard Parnold, outside, instruct the uniformed Sergeant in attendance. 'He might be concussed.'

What would Campbell do, Jenner asked herself. She shut her eyes tight and opened them again. Like switching off the events from just a short time ago as if they were a film. She looked afresh at the room. Most of it had been cleared for the sale of the property, but a photograph had been pulled down presumably in some sort of struggle. She moved over to look at it – it was like a family photograph. She lifted the picture and took it back to her car.

'We won't be able to question her for some time,' complained Parnold watching the ambulance leave. 'I'll put together searches further afield for Campbell as well as the local search. There's churned gravel in the front. Harriet's car's here, so if he has been taken we don't know what vehicle they're travelling in.'

'Did we pass them on the way here? They can't have got far,' said Jenner. 'I still have some questions I want to ask Arabella Macfine.'

'Okay,' said Parnold. 'The officers are already looking at dash-cam footage.' He walked towards his car with his head down.

'I've got a couple of matters I need to discuss with you,' said Jenner to the headmistress standing in the doorway of Strath-Kind School.

'Come through to my office,' said Arabella Macfine in her clear English. 'I hear you've made some arrests,' The head teacher said over her shoulder as she marched across the hallway and into her office.

As Jenner followed she recalled that onlookers had already gathered about the farm shop driveway. Gossip spreads like wild-fire, she thought.

She asked the headmistress about the photograph of the old girls taken together on the afternoon of their reunion day. Before sitting down, she pulled out a copy of the photograph and placed it in front of her.

'Can you confirm that this was taken during the afternoon on the Friday of the old girls' reunion. And, can you confirm the time?' asked Jenner.

'I have given you this information before,' replied Arabella.

'Yes, but I would like you to look at it again,' insisted Jenner.

'The picture was taken about five pm,' said the headmistress. 'As you can see everyone was there that was on the list. I took the photograph.'

Jenner said, 'Yes I have the list of attendees of the old girl's day you gave us.' She took the list out of her pocket and placed it in front of Arabella Macfine. She pointed out, 'Harriet Epsy is not on the list.'

Arabella Macfine pulled her own copy from a file kept in a cabinet behind her desk, and she examined it closely. 'I'm not sure how that happened,' she agreed. 'And you are quite right, she is not on the photograph. I think someone mentioned she'd gone to Daneton Howe Beach in the afternoon, Sergeant. I'm so sorry we get so tied up with lists. It was a busy day.'

'Was Harriet Epsy a pupil at your school?'

'Yes, she was, but before my time as head mistress. As I told you before my father was headmaster here and I lived in the farmhouse. I interacted with the school and the pupils for many years.'

'Yes, I believe you were the swimming coach for a time?'

'That's correct but I did other things too,' said Arabella Macfine. 'Now look at this photo,' she said taking Jenner over to a wall and pointing at a picture.

Jenner went over and looked. There were a group of girls in swimming costumes.

'This is Harriet Epsy,' explained Arabella Macfine. 'I have taken all the photographs on this wall.'

'But she's blond in this picture,' complained Jenner. 'Are you sure this is the same person who came to the open day.'

'Quite sure,' said Arabella. 'I knew these girls well. I know their faces, personalities. Harriet was always changing her hair. I wasn't surprised to see it black and curly this time.' Arabella moved on to another picture. 'Look,' she said pointing at another photograph. 'I took this one and here she is again. She was about sixteen in this picture. She left shortly after this.'

Jenner noted the red hair. 'Was there any reason she left the school?'

'Not from a behavioral point of view. She was never asked to leave. I think her family were on reduced circumstances and she went to the local college to complete her education.' Arabella chuckled to herself and said with affection, 'But no-one would have thought that she wasn't on the list on Friday! She probably managed to wangle a free lunch at the old girl's day. Typical of her. It would be just her way to say to the cook that she was someone else. She could never resist a freebie.'

More seriously she said, 'She was here with everyone else in the morning. Abigail Pilmer was making a huge fuss about her baby and I was busy with the camera, so that was my overwhelming memory. I forgot all about Harriet. They all dispersed after the photograph was taken.' Arabella shook her head sadly, 'About quarter past five. I think you knew all that already.'

'Thank you,' said Jenner, noting that Harriet had left the school with enough time to kill the man on Daneton Beach and William Cecil Broadgate.

'Clearly Harriet must have done something wrong for you to seek her like this,' said Arabella. 'She was a naughty, cheeky girl but I didn't see any badness in her when she was here. Do you think that I have said something to the girls that may have made them greedy? "Be bold and try for your ambitions they won't happen on their own," I told them. But of course, they need to be the right ambitions.'

'Every word we say is interpreted by the listener. They apply their personality and their personal history to it,' said Jenner.

'Yes, you're right,' said Arabella.

'This picture,' said Jenner producing the one she'd found in the farmhouse, 'can you tell me about it?'

'That's Gwendolyn Blythe and Elizabeth Rattagan and Shana Peterson. Abigail is so much like her big sister and that's Hye Woang, known to all as

Judy Wong.'

'I thought she only worked here briefly.'

'Yes, she did, but she used to come over the summer months for several years while she was at university.'

Jenner shook her head as she took in this information. 'Thank you, Miss Macfine, for all your help.'

Jenner and Garden arrived at the caravan at Banksea Beach, not long ago rented by Georgia Lomond and her grandfather. On checking her phone she'd found Campbell had sent an email sometime before his visit to the farmhouse explaining his theory for the resolution of the case.

'It's as if he knew something was going to happen,' said Garden.

'Elizabeth Rattagan and Gwen Blythe,' said Jenner firmly. 'One of them knows some key fact about these events. That's what Campbell thinks. The note saying Elizabeth was the cause of a death had already been planted in Elizabeth's bag before William Cecil's murder.'

Gwen Blythe was heaving a suitcase outside and Elizabeth Rattagan was tidying up. 'We're leaving today,' said Gwen.

'I see,' said Jenner flatly.

'We're going home. Elizabeth's going to stay at mine for a while. Come in.'

Garden showed them the picture in its protective plastic bag which Jenner had found in the farmhouse and shown their former headmistress.

'How funny, said Elizabeth. 'I remember this don't you, Gwen?'

'Yes, I remember that day and many like them. But that was the day you rescued me from the water. Maccy was very proud of you,' said Gwen.

'And that's Judy. Judy Wong,' said Elizabeth. 'Her real name is Hye Woang. She got a great job in Cambridge.'

'Hye Woang's sister was married to William Cecil Broadgate,' said Jenner.

'Oh, I didn't know that,' said Elizabeth. 'That must have been after our time at Strath-Kind, I think. Did you know, Gwen?'

'No, I didn't,' said Gwen. She was studying the photograph as she spoke. 'And that's Shana Peterson. That's funny because I thought Abigail was Shana when we first saw her at the old girl's day. But, of course, Abigail is ten years younger.'

'Did you ever meet Michael Pilmer at that time because he's more Shana's age than Abigail's?'

'No, I didn't,' said Elizabeth.

'No. The first time I met him was at the offices in Cambridge about my grandmother's will,' confirmed Gwen.

Garden produced the photographs Jenner had arranged to show

Gwen and Elizabeth and handed them to Jenner. Jenner stayed outside with Gwen and Garden went in the kitchen area of the caravan with Elizabeth, so Jenner could show the women the pictures separately.

Gwen looked. Jenner could tell before she answered that she did not know any of the men.

Jenner was disappointed. One of the pictures was Frank Norton taken from his driving document. Campbell had said in his email that he was sure they would know Frank Norton. Yet Gwen hadn't recollected him, neither had she known the dead man from Daneton Howe Beach, known as Robert Epsy.

'Are you sure?' Jenner asked.

'I'm sure,' said Gwen. She sounded disappointed too.

Jenner was still awaiting any DNA match on Frank Norton from police records, but Campbell wasn't holding out much hope. Dungrade's DNA was unlikely to be on record as he had no record of any convictions.

'You believe you saw Dungrade once,' said Jenner.

'Yes,' said Gwen. 'I went to visit him with an investigating officer when I was in the police. He didn't look like any of the men you have shown me today. He was older.'

Inside the caravan Jenner showed the pictures to Elizabeth. She went through them several times. She paused.

'I know this man,' said Elizabeth pointing to Frank Norton. 'But not like this. He was my first boyfriend years ago. I know the eyes. I would always know the eyes. A lot else is different.' Elizabeth opened her bag, took out her purse and pulled out a photograph.

The caravan door opened. 'Can I come in?' asked Gwen.

'Yes,' said Jenner.

Elizabeth looked up at Gwen.

'Do you remember Gerald Tyne?'

'No. I didn't see him. That was the last summer after school finished. You spent time up here. I was already away with my mother sorting out with her about my father's death. I didn't even have time to say my goodbyes.' Gwen looked away briefly and then at the photograph Elizabeth had taken from her wallet. 'You wrote to me just the once before we moved away, and you told me about him. Was he not too old for you?' asked Gwen.

'You didn't give me a forwarding address,' complained Elizabeth. 'I thought, in my naivety that he was sophisticated. He said he was a solicitor.'

'Why did you keep his photograph?' asked Gwen

'To remind me not to be taken in by charmers,' said Elizabeth.

Jenner asked, 'Do you remember anything about him?'

'Gerald Tyne,' said Elizabeth thoughtfully. 'He was Maccy's cousin, but she wouldn't have anything to do with him, which, of course, made him more attractive.'

'Which solicitor's office did he work at?' asked Gwen.

Elizabeth thought for a moment, 'Styde and Rayn.'

'That was my father's solicitors,' said Gwen. 'But I never heard of Gerald Tyne.'

Jenner said, 'Thank you,' to the two women. 'Just one more question, when you were prosecuting Dungrade did you ever meet him?

'He declined to come and talk to us,' said Elizabeth. 'He's a man in his seventies.'

Jenner intended to leave with Garden and return directly to Strath-Kind School and speak to the headmistress about her cousin, Gerald Tyne. She started to walk towards the car with Garden. 'Strath-Kind,' she said.

'Have we got time for that just now?' asked Garden. 'We can confirm Gerald Tyne's identity later with the Headmistress.'

'You are right. Judy Wong has some knowledge we need to get from her,' agreed Jenner. 'Campbell thought so. His email included the incident of Harriet turning up at Judy Wong's office on the day he and Sergeant Percival visited the temporary office of Michael Pilmer in Cambridge.'

CHAPTER TWENTY-SIX

The hall cupboard was black except for a chink of light under the door and a small grill at the top.

'Harry!' shouted the six-year-old Raymond Campbell. 'Harry, let me out.'

'I don't like you watching me all the time,' said Harry Burnett with threatening undertones from the other side of the door. 'I'm going to the fair. Everyone's gone except you and your family.'

'Harry, I'm sorry,' said Raymond. 'I won't do it again. I just don't like…' he was going to finish the sentence with, 'sitting in the flat with my mother,' but he could hear Harry Burnett running down to the street, a place Ray was not allowed to go.

He would have to wait for his mother to rescue him or wait until someone friendlier happened by. Raymond sat down in the empty cupboard and kicked the door with his foot from time to time in the hope of attracting attention.

A while later he heard steps running up the communal stairs. They were a man's heavy tread and he was striding up two steps at a time. Raymond stopped kicking the door and he didn't shout out. There was something urgent, angry in those foot falls. He shrunk back and squirmed his way to the back of the cupboard. The floor was cold; the stone walls were cold; he shivered.

He heard screams. His mother. Raymond leapt to the door and shouted to be let out. She screamed again and again, but the building was empty. The only sound was the male strides returning down the stairs. He wanted to sob his heart out for his mother, but he found he couldn't.

A while later the cupboard door opened, and Mrs. Burnett smiled at him from the doorway. 'I've sorted Harry out,' she said. 'You'll have no more trouble from him.'

'My mother?' Raymond asked.

'You'll be coming to ours for your tea,' said Mrs. Burnett kindly but firmly.

Campbell started to regain consciousness. His vision of the past retreated but his sight remained blurred. For a moment he thought he was back in the tenement in Edinburgh sitting in his room. He very carefully waggled his very sore head then he viewed his surroundings from the chair he was tied to. He was in a timber-built bedroom. It was not like the log cabin at the bird sanctuary where he had first met Elizabeth Rattagan and Gwen Blythe. It was old, and the walls were lined with vertical wood slats painted the palest blue. He could make out that there was an adult-sized lump in the bed across the room, he supposed it to be Frank Norton.

The lump moved with a groan. 'You're awake then,' said Frank Norton, in his fire-damaged, rasping voice.

Campbell pulled together his thoughts by recalling his desk. He mentally pulled a file towards him and opened it. 'Hello, Frank Norton, or should I call you Mr. Charles Wilfred Dungrade?' asked Campbell.

The man in the bed looked at him with his one unbandaged eye. 'Frank Norton,' he replied. 'Whatever you call me, I have the call of life and death over you now.'

'Are you going to get Harriet to murder me?' asked Campbell. 'I think she is more likely to kill you.'

'She's not here.'

'I think you would do well to give yourself up to the police,' said Campbell.

'Why should I do that?'

'We have security footage of you purchasing a ticket for London to Banksea Halt for cash at a ticket office in Seachester, Sussex,' said Campbell. He noted more carefully the dye of the man's hair. It was a light brown, very similar to Sean Foragehall's hair tone.

Although there was little to see of Frank Norton's face through his bandages, his demeanor from the night at Daneton when Campbell had rescued him from the burning beach hut was of a man older than Sean Foragehall, probably by fifteen years. But he did not give the impression of being as old as the bodies of William Cecil Broadgate or Robert Epsy. He had not seemed like a man in his seventies as Elizabeth Rattagan had said he would be.

'We have evidence that you changed train carriages on the Banksea Halt train at Cambridge. You got out of the train, slipped into the toilet and changed into a grey hooded sweat-shirt, and you put the hood up to hide your face. You got back on the train – all while the rear carriages were being unhitched.'

'Anyone can wear a hoody,' said Norton.

'How did you know what shade to die your hair to cause confusion with the next passenger in that seat?'

'Partly luck. I asked Harriet if she knew anyone who would be travelling on that train that might look a little like me. A few days later she came back with the name, Sean Foragehall. Harriet told me she had gossiped with the waitress she knew in a café opposite her mother's old shop. Louise Green from the shop takes her baby to a London hospital regularly because she has a genetic disorder. Louise had told the waitress that they'd planned to meet up on the train. And, even more useful to me, it was to be done in secrecy. I just followed Louise Green onto the train. I saw the seat opposite hers was reserved from Cambridge, so I sat in that.'

'We have images of you sitting on the third carriage of that Friday's train. Once we knew who we were looking for it was easier to find you,' said Campbell.

Norton grunted.

'And you were picked up on cameras at Banksea Halt with your hood up.'

'That could have been anyone,' complained Norton again.

'The shifting sands gave us a finger print on a piece of charred wood where you left your messages for Jess Barratt at Banksea beach,' said Campbell. 'I expect it will be yours. We found one on Anne Crowlie's laptop which you were clutching when you came out of the burning beach hut. You thought her confession would prove your innocence.'

'Harriet murdered Dungrade,' said Frank Norton lazily.

'I am not talking about Harriet. I am talking about you and William Cecil Broadgate's murder. Dungrade isn't William Cecil Broadgate despite what the black book says. We had the hand writing checked. You thought you could murder William Cecil Broadgate and get the money back he had laundered through his businesses and, with the help of this book, you could have had him identified as the hard-to-find criminal Dungrade.'

Frank Norton grunted.

'But the book never belonged to Broadgate,' continued Campbell. 'It was a forgery. We found a small amount of William Cecil Broadgate's writing in a bank box.' Or rather Garden did, thought Campbell.

Frank Norton swore and muttered, 'Ralph.'

'You put your black book in the caravan, but you were too late,' explained Campbell. 'Perhaps you were disturbed on the day of the murder, perhaps even by your own helper, Jess Barratt hiding the murder weapons – too close for comfort. You had to go back later but what you didn't know was that you went back after the police had carried out their search. By this time, you'd told Harriet that you'd killed William Cecil Broadgate, so she started watching the police for you. She soon found out that your efforts to point the blame at Broadgate as Dungrade would miss-fire if the book was found in the caravan after it had been searched. So, she attempted to get the book back, so it could fall into the hands of the police in the way you wanted. But it didn't quite work out. We turned up too soon.'

Frank Norton twitched.

'You hoped we would believe William Cecil Broadgate was Dungrade,' continued Campbell. 'And that would be the end of investigations into Dungrade.'

'Dungrade,' growled Norton, 'is dead.'

'Before that fateful Friday, you sent Harriet to fetch all the paperwork out of William Cecil Broadgate's house and she took one of the two shotguns that were there. Harriet couldn't retrieve the book from the caravan because of the police activity and Georgia staying there but she sent Ralph to keep an eye on Georgia and Broadgate's house. Ralph was also meant to get the other shotgun from Broadgate's house too, but police officers had already removed it.'

'Harriet's a fool and now she's a dead fool,' said Norton.

Campbell absorbed this information. It explained his attack from behind in the farmhouse and the sound of a vehicle drawing up on the gravel on the front drive.

He continued with the open file of information in his head, turning the pages. 'You have had facial surgery to change your looks. It was noted by the doctors at the hospital,' said Campbell. 'And, on occasions you have made yourself appear to be a much older man to tie up with Dungrade's identity. You dressed up when needed.'

'I am Frank Norton, not this Dungrade person,' complained Norton.

Campbell ignored Norton and continued, 'Harriet was in North Norfolk all morning at her old girl's day waiting to take someone, who would not be missed, onto the beach and kill him as Dungrade.'

'I had nothing to do with the death of either of the old men you keep on about,' said Frank Norton stubbornly. 'Nothing you say matters.'

'If I remember rightly,' continued Campbell. 'When we were at the farmhouse, Harriet said she murdered the man on Daneton Beach, so you could be free of Dungrade. Perhaps, you didn't work out that I had heard.'

'I am not Dungrade, Harriet was mistaken.'

'We will find witnesses to your identity, to all of your identities,' said Campbell. It was a gamble. A hope that the weakened man may feel paranoia tapping incessantly on the door of his mental control.

Norton spat with fury. 'I should never have come back to this area,' growled Norton. 'I watched and waited, watched and waited. William Cecil Broadgate was tying my money in knots. He knew I couldn't risk coming back here in case I was spotted. But, it was the only way I was ever going to see my money again. And then William Cecil Broadgate had a second will made.' Norton gripped the sheets with his good hand.

'And Harriet told you to lie low while she redirected the transfer of funds from Georgia Lomond to yourself.'

Frank Norton nodded slowly.

Campbell felt a twinge of satisfaction among the complaints from his bound hands and feet. 'You stayed on the train to make sure Anne Crowlie left the note for Elizabeth Rattagan. What was all that about?'

'Power,' replied Norton. 'And I enjoyed killing her too.'

'You killed Anne Crowlie?' asked Campbell.

'Yes, I did. But none of that matters now.'

'She had your car.'

'I hired one to get to Banksea.'

'Who was Messaging Watcher?' asked Campbell ignoring Frank Norton tapping his bed covers with temper.

'Anne Crowlie,' said Norton.

'She never confessed to that,' said Campbell.

'You found her bicycle in the river.'

Campbell looked at him. 'That information was not released.'

'It was there. It was obvious that you would find it.' Frank Norton sighed.

Campbell asked, 'Why did you turn over Anne's flat and have your car broken into in the car park?'

Frank Norton didn't answer.

'I think you were looking for Anne Crowlie's computer. You knew she'd put something on there, perhaps you had come in on the end of her recording and you didn't know what it was about. You got Jess Barratt to break into the car and get it. When you looked at it you saw that she had sent a message to the police just as you'd asked her to do as Watcher, but her message was different. She wasn't getting you into trouble she was saying that she was scared for her Frank Norton. She was scared Watcher would harm you. You who are Watcher.

'None of that matters, because you are as good as dead already.'

Campbell looked around the room. The curtains were drawn. Who would have brought him and Frank Norton here if Harriet was dead? This could not be the coastal hut where the Pilmers and Ralph Peterson had been staying. He could not hear the sea and it would have been the first place the police would look.

A woman opened the bedroom door. Campbell watched her come into the room.

'Shana,' said Frank Norton with affection.

'Jeremy,' she said, 'I've brought you food.'

'Why did you bring Campbell here?' asked Frank Norton making no comment about being called Jeremy.

'I didn't know what to do with him,' said Shana.

'You should have just left him,' complained Frank Norton.

'I did what I thought was best. I couldn't ask you. You'd passed out.'

'Do you know Harriet Epsy?' Campbell asked Shana.

'Yes, my sister, Abigail, knows her. Harriet stays at mine sometimes.'

'Does Harriet know you know Jeremy?'

'No, why should she?'

Campbell ignored the question and asked, 'Are you Messenger Watcher? Were you sending messages for Jeremy here?'

'Don't say anything,' growled Frank Norton.

'His name is not Jeremy,' said Campbell. 'The last name he's been known by round here is Frank Norton.'

Shana looked from Campbell to Frank Norton and back again. She spoke in a rush, her eyes wide: 'He had me forward on these messages he sent to this phone he gave me, and he gave me a key to a bicycle lock he asked me to use. It was a bit of an adrenalin buzz really. He said it was some hoax he was doing. Just an elaborate joke. He knew I was a good cyclist. It was a challenge. He said pedal as fast as you can along the path and at this point chuck in the bicycle. Which I did. He said I wouldn't get caught, the bike shed didn't have any security cameras and he said he'd seen to the ones along the river path.'

Campbell asked. 'What did you do with the phone?'

'I broke it and threw it in the river when I got close to my home.'

'I wouldn't waste time giving him a load of lies about how innocent you are. You killed Harriet, now kill him. The money will automatically be transferred later today to our account. We don't need your sister or anyone else. We have an exit route,' said Frank Norton. 'We can get rid of Campbell.'

'Harriet might not be dead,' suggested Campbell to Shana. 'You sent messages later on Friday to the emergency services as Watcher.'

'Yes, I did. He'd already put the message on the phone. It was a different phone. I just sent it.' Shana squinted at Frank Norton. 'I destroyed that one too as instructed by Jeremy,' she said.

Jenner arranged for Sergeant Percival to stay in reception while DC Garden stood by the door and DS Jenner sat down opposite Judy and said, 'I understand from Inspector Campbell that you know Harriet Epsy. Have you seen her recently?'

'She came in randomly on the same day Campbell came to see me. I told him that she asked me why I hadn't gone to the old girl's day.'

'Have you met anyone else from the school recently?'

'Oddly enough I met Shana Peterson the same day Harriet came into the office followed by your Inspector Campbell. We had supper in a restaurant near here. She was at Strath-Kind School. We're friends. She came to pick her sister Abigail up from school one day and we got chatting. We've kept in contact ever since. She lives in Cambridge.'

'Have you ever met any of her friends?'

'Except for Harriet, only once, a man came to collect her when we were having a meal in a pub nearby. She seemed totally besotted with him.'

Jenner showed her the selection of identity photographs which included Frank Norton. 'Do you see him among these photographs?' She slid them towards her.

'This is him,' she said. 'Without a shadow of doubt.'

Frank Norton's picture, observed Jenner. 'Do you know his name?' she asked.

'Jeremy,' said Judy. 'She said he was called Jeremy.'

'Do you have an address for Shana?'

'Yes.' She wrote it down on a card. 'She's local to the office here. I think Harriet's been staying with her off and on. I believe she's off on her holidays just now.'

'Where's she going?'

'Somewhere in the Caribbean.'

'Thank you, Hye Woang,' said Jenner.

'Only my mother calls me that,' said Judy with a wry smile.

With Sergeant Percival and Garden back at the cars, Jenner said, 'That day Harriet escaped from the office in Cambridge you, Sergeant Percival, went across to Herbert Brandon's office with Campbell, Shana Peterson met up with Judy Wong,' explained Jenner. 'Campbell suspected that there was another person working for Frank Norton and that the picture in the farmhouse with Shana in it was the clue.' Jenner handed Shana Peterson's address to Sergeant Percival and said, 'We'll follow you.'

216

CHAPTER TWENTY-SEVEN

At Horseton Police Station Parnold put down finished the phone call he'd just received from Sergeant Jenner and went through to the interview room. He sat down opposite Abigail Pilmer and next to his co-interviewer.

Superintendent Tarnish had informed the team that the initial search for Campbell around the area of his disappearance had not come up with any sign of him. Further questions had to be asked, so Parnold decided to try a Campbell-style sideways push for information. 'Why did you tell the story about Harriet stealing the pudding at the Gull Inn? You knew Harriet. Was it to draw attention to her? You don't like Harriet, do you?'

Abigail stared at him clearly trying to look blank, but a twitch of her shoulder gave away that she did not like Harriet.

'We've removed all the computers and records at all of Michael's offices,' explained Parnold.

Good,' said Abigail. 'I want rid of that man. You can lock Michael up and throw away the key for all I care.'

'You have told us everything about Michael and Ralph. You have not told us anything about Frank Norton.'

'I don't know a Frank Norton.'

Parnold felt his patience thin but he was determined to stick to his narrative. 'Your sister Shana does. She calls him Jeremy. We now also have Shana's computer. There was to be a timed transfer of funds into her account from yours. Michael was going to put all his monies he's been skimming off Frank Norton's funds and some from his own fraudulent activities into an account in your name.'

Abigail folded her hands in her lap.

'He thought he, as well as Frank Norton, was going to get a big payday following the death of William Cecil Broadgate,' continued Parnold. 'He knew Broadgate was the money launderer. But it was not to be. All William Cecil Broadgate's money went to Georgia Lomond, so the plan was to kill her to get it back. Ralph had forged her will. And you know the funny thing is Georgia would have handed over all the money, she didn't want it. Ralph was so angry that she didn't love him he wanted to see her die, so he stopped her talking.'

'Ralph's an idiot,' said Abigail. 'We only kept him with us because of his skills.'

Parnold was confident that she was opening-up. He was going to go for the direct approach. 'Is Shana going to get rid of Frank Norton? With them out of the way you thought you and she could share the cash. You had Michael's money and she had Frank Norton's – or Jeremy's, as she called him. Shana was going to the West Indies. She might have gone already. She's not at home. We have stopped the funds transfer.'

Abigail Pilmer stared back.

'Where might she go?'

Abigail looked at Parnold her whole demeanor full of loathing and said, 'No comment.'

Shana trembled as she put a phone down on the dressing table. Campbell noted that Shana's tall muscular body was full of tension and she moved with swift, jerky movements. He also observed that Frank Norton was watching her too.

'Jeremy,' she said. 'What is this?'

'A phone,' replied Frank Norton anger filling his fire damaged voice.

'I found it in the car. Who's is it?'

'It's mine.'

'My phone has a different number for you.'

Campbell wanted to join in the conversation, but he also wanted to preserve his health. This was not the time to enlighten Shana about her Jeremy's other relationships with women in his pseudonym of Frank Norton.

'I have several phones for business purposes,' explained Frank Norton reluctantly. 'I leant that one to Harriet.'

'I can hear her voice on it,' said Shana with tears in her eyes. She turned on the phone and showed the screen to Campbell. The picture showed Banksea Beach at nine am on the day of the murder of William Cecil Broadgate. The sun was shining, children playing on the beach. Harriet was giving a commentary pointing out a close-up of Georgia Lomond and then one of William Cecil Broadgate supping tea in his deckchair.

'Harriet did murder him,' accused Shana.

'Harriet had no idea why she was filming that scene for me,' Frank Norton replied. 'Did you bring some food?'

'You can starve for all I care.' Shana turned her back on the man in the bed.

'You watched and assessed what you were going to do while you stood at the station in London waiting to get on the Banksea Halt train.'

'You may have your ticket to the Caribbean, but you won't get the money without me,' Frank Norton warned Shana ignoring Campbell.

He considers me already dead, thought Campbell.

Shana turned back. Campbell could see from her face that her moral outrage had simply been an excuse to ditch Jeremy and collect the money for herself.

Jenner closed the call from Parnold.

'Try Elizabeth Rattagan,' suggested Garden. 'She is in this picture with Shana.'

'Yes,' agreed Jenner. 'She is.' She was already dialing Elizabeth's number. She put the call on speakerphone.

'Hello, it's Sergeant Jenner here.'

'Hello, Sergeant Jenner. I wanted to thank you and Inspector Campbell for all your help,' said Elizabeth.

'That is our job,' said Jenner more abruptly than she intended. 'Inspector Campbell is missing,' said Jenner feeling she had to break with procedure and explain the enormity of the situation they were in.

'Oh,' was all Elizabeth managed.

'You and Shana Peterson were close at school. Have you kept in touch since?' asked Jenner.

'No, I haven't. I'll ask Gwen.' Jenner heard a muffled repeat of her question and a muffled reply before Elizabeth came back with, 'No, Gwen hasn't either. It's been over twelve years since we were at school together.'

Jenner felt hope slipping away.

Garden touched Jenner's arm to ask her if she could ask a question. Jenner nodded. 'There must be somewhere else the swimming team used to swim from time to time, you and Shana?' asked Garden.

'We used to swim in the quay when it was set aside for competitions.'

'What about further afield. Perhaps competitions you entered.'

'There's a place about half way between Banksea and Cambridge – an old sand quarry. They made an artificial beach on part of it and it was used for sailing when we weren't using it for swimming competitions.'

'Do you remember the name of it?' asked Jenner.

'I know how to get there,' said Elizabeth.

Garden took down the directions while Jenner started the car. Garden phoned Parnold with the news as they set off.

'So what money is it?' Campbell asked Shana. 'Georgia Lomond's money is not coming your way. She's still alive.'

Shana looked at Frank Norton with alarm and anger rising in her face.

'I've got other money,' declared Norton to Shana. 'I'm cleaning out my accounts and going. Like house moving,' explained Frank Norton. 'I'm going to set up shop elsewhere where the rules and the policing are slacker, once I've collected my money.'

'This policeman is annoying me, Jeremy,' said Shana moving closer to Frank Norton.

'We've got time to get rid of him,' replied Norton.

'He won't go jogging with me on a lonely road,' said Shana with a smirk, 'to be caught by you on a bend like the others.'

'He won't be having an affair with you, like the others, either,' replied Frank Norton. 'No one will mistake his death for an accident.'

'Your mechanic friend won't be able to critically interfere with the car either,' said Shana.

Campbell thought Frank Norton was trying to smile under his bandages. This conversation seemed flirtatious between them. Shana opened her large brown eyes wide and visually weighed up Campbell. In turn, he assessed her strength. She looked strong and he wondered if she carried a weapon.

How would she attempt to murder him? He'd been trying his bonds for some-time. They were cable ties and they were tight. There was no-way he could lever his hands free.

'I can't kill him,' she said suddenly. 'You'll have to do it.'

'I'm in no condition to kill him.'

'He's tied up,' said Shana in frustration.

'Get me a gun,' said Norton

'I haven't got a gun and there's no time to get one.'

'Get me a knife,' demanded Frank Norton.

Shana went through to another room and after a few minutes returned. 'There's nothing here.'

'You got me into this bed, now you get me out of it and into the car.' Frank Norton shuffled himself up to a sitting position wincing, moaning and angry. 'And you can do the seat belt up. I'm worth more to you alive than dead.'

Shana moved across to him.

'And, you can hurry up our transport will soon be arriving.'

'What shall I do with him?'

'Drag him outside on the chair and I'll run him over with the car.'

Campbell watched Shana struggle out of the bedroom with Norton. When they were gone he rolled the chair over attempting to break it. The old chair remained intact with Campbell still secured to it. He wrestled the chair, so his feet stood on the floor with his body bent into the chair. He tried crashing it against the stout dressing table. The chair scraped along its front edge and fell causing Campbell to knock his head on the floor putting his vision in shock.

As his eyesight cleared he saw Shana coming back in. She grasped the back of the chair and dragged it over the wooden floor to the door. 'I got you in here, so I'll be able to get you out. And, by the way, I destroyed your phone. Your colleagues have no chance of finding you until you are dead. And, you have no chance of sending them any information about us.'

'You don't know everything,' said Campbell. 'Your Jeremy, isn't Jeremy. I knew him as Frank Norton. Some people know him as Dungrade, an older gentleman, others know him as Gerald Tyne.'

'I don't care how many names he has,' replied Shana.

'And he has had a liaison recently with an Anne Crowlie.'

The chair stopped briefly but soon continued being dragged across the floor.

Campbell rocked it until he felt his head being hit by a large metal object and became senseless.

When he awoke from his unconsciousness, he blinked and waggled his head to clear it. Before him was the front grill of a large black car. Through the windscreen he could see Frank Norton in the driving seat and Shana next to him. He could hear the roar of the engine as Norton pedaled the throttle impatiently.

Shana watched Jeremy. She loved him. She knew he'd betrayed her, but their relationship was different. She had never expected sexual loyalty. And, she didn't care that he had pseudonyms. She always knew their way of life required duplicity. She had followed his plans for securing the funds. Nothing and nobody would stand in the way of it.

She looked at the policeman in front of her. Chief Inspector Campbell was in her way. 'Get him,' she shouted to Jeremy.

The car lurched forward.

The black car hurtled towards him. Campbell rocked the chair he was tied to as hard as he could and tipped it over. The chair's wood-frame broke, and he and its remains of the chair continued to roll. Suddenly he felt himself falling. Plants stung and ripped at his skin as he fell. Immediately the black car, hurtled above him. He could not move. The car crunched to a stop, the front wheels close to his face. His arms, back and legs felt dampness. He had landed in soft mud. He had been saved by a ditch, but he was stuck. The car above him creaked and started to move down towards him.

Parnold pulled up at the same time as the local police by the lake. The caretaker's cabin sat on the corner of a field marked by a perimeter hedge. The cabin's back door stood open. A large black car stood tilted down into what must be a ditch, though he couldn't see it for the lush growth growing out of it. The car's passenger door was wide open. A movement caught the corner of his field of vision at the edge of a woodland area. A woman with auburn hair was running towards the trees. He turned and ran across the grass in pursuit. He pumped breath into his lungs and power into his legs. He was gaining ground. The runner entered the woods over a style. Parnold vaulted over the obstacle and gained ground on her. 'Police,' he called when he thought he was within a distance that the runner could hear him. 'Stop.'

The runner continued. Parnold was getting closer with every stride. He caught the woman around the legs and she fell.

'Get off,' said the runner sitting herself up.

'What is your name and why are you running away from an accident?'

'Shana Peterson. And I had nothing to do with it.'

'With what?'

'Killing the policeman, that Inspector Campbell.'

Parnold looked at her and rage filled every part of his body. He could feel his hands flexing, wanting to strangle her. Her whole attitude told him she was lying. 'What do you mean?' he spat out through clenched teeth.

'Jeremy ran him over,' replied Shana Peterson. 'I can tell you everything,' she promised.

Before Parnold's resolve not to kill her weakened a couple of uniformed police officers arrived, and Parnold handed her over to them.

When he returned to the black car he saw that Jenner and Garden had also arrived as well as a team of police cars responding to the incident call-out. As he walked towards Jenner and Garden, who were standing at the front of the vehicle by the hedge, an ambulance arrived, he strode forward carefully. He instinctively avoided several pieces of wood – not pieces of tree or hedge as he would expect from the location but furniture wood, shaped, sanded and varnished.

Garden disappeared.

'Don't touch the car,' Jenner warned him. 'We can't wait for the tow-truck.'

Parnold could see the driver's seat was occupied and the occupant was still. He nodded acceptance to Jenner and slowed. Now he could see Garden was lying on her stomach just behind the front wheel of the car on the passenger side. Her feet were just visible under the open passenger door.

Parnold trembled with the certainty that they had found Campbell's body. He slowly moved around the open passenger door to find the grass changed to nettles and hog weed. He could see the front of the car was wedged in the ditch. Garden's body was bent down from the waist into the nettles. The rest of the ditch was so full of greenery it had become hidden, just the car's angle indicated its existence. He could hear Chief Inspector Campbell answering Garden's questions about his ability to move.

A moment later Campbell's head appeared, and Garden was reaching under an armpit to pull him up. Parnold dropped down onto his stomach to assist. He placed his hand under Campbell's other armpit and gave a tug. His boss was secured to bits of wood furniture wood like the pieces he had passed on his way to the car, clearly the remains of Campbell's chair.

Parnold swore with relief.

'Don't touch the chair bits or bindings until forensics have been here,' said Campbell. 'I rolled into the ditch,' he explained. 'I didn't even know it was there. Neither did they. Fortunately, they went so fast at me the car went over the top of the ditch and partly wedged itself into the hedge on the other side.'

A tow-truck arrived, and its driver fixed its hook onto the car and steadied it while paramedics removed Frank Norton from the driver's seat and took him back to hospital.

'Thanks for the email,' said Jenner.

'Did Elizabeth Rattagan know Frank Norton?' asked Campbell.

'Yes, she did. She knew him as Gerald Tyne,' said Garden.

'Shana Peterson called him Jeremy.' Campbell said. 'Is Harriet dead?' he asked.

'No, brain injuries though,' said Parnold.

Still secured to the remains of the chair, Campbell stretched his neck and dropped his shoulders while Parnold watched a paramedic approach with a scene of crime expert.

A helicopter buzzed overhead and quickly disappeared over the lake and woods. Parnold ran back to the car to find out who it belonged to.

CHAPTER TWENTY-EIGHT

Campbell and Jenner stood outside Strath-Kind School.

When Arabella Macfine answered the door, she looked tired, but her hair was neat, and her clothing was smartly arranged. 'Come in,' she said. She walked through to her office. 'This whole business has brought shame upon the school. How could Harriet and Abigail use the school buildings in this way? I'm totally devastated.'

'Did you know Harriet was using the farmhouse?' asked Campbell.

'No, not at all. She had no permission to be there at all,' replied the headmistress. 'All I know is that the police and armed officers have been all over both the bungalow and the farmhouse. Whatever they were doing it was clearly criminal.' She turned away and pulled a tissue from a box and blew her nose. 'Excuse me,' she said tucking the tissue back in to her hand.

'Miss Macfine, I understand you have a relative, Gerald Tyne.'

'I do,' said Arabella, 'I haven't seen him for many years, thank goodness.' She looked up at the police officers. 'Is he involved in this?'

'Why do you say that?'

'He's a cousin of mine, regrettably. He used to work at a local solicitors' office. He left the area. My father was horrified at his unethical activities.'

'Do you know, or did you know a man called Dungrade?' asked Jenner.

'My father knew a man called, Dungrace,' replied Arabella looking at the tissue in her hands. 'He was a lovely man. If he'd lived, he would be in his seventies now. Gerald Dungrace was his solicitor and executor.'

Campbell nodded to Jenner and she produced the photographs that she had used for identifying Dungrade.

Arabella pulled out the photograph of Frank Norton from the rest and went to an elderly bureau on the far wall of her office. She brought down the desk-lid and rummaged for a moment.

'I had a break-in years ago and the only items taken were a few papers and photographs of Gerald Tyne. I was pleased that they were gone. At the time I didn't even think about it. I hadn't long been headmistress. Now it seems that Gerald was covering his tracks?' She turned questioningly to Campbell. He gave her no reply. 'Ah well,' she continued. 'Later, I found this in the attic. I only kept it because my father is on it.' She took two envelopes out of the bureau. The first envelope she opened and passed two photos across to him. 'My cousin, Gerald Tyne, is on the left of my father.'

Campbell looked at the picture of the distinguished headmaster and Gerald Tyne. Jenner looked up at Campbell. She confirmed in her face what he also knew: this was the same man that Elizabeth Rattagan knew as Gerald Tyne. The eyes were the same as Frank Norton, or Jeremy, but the nose and chin were different in ways only surgery could achieve.

As Campbell reached the front door of the school he looked up at Jenner already at the car. Arabella Macfine placed her hand gently on his arm.

'I have this,' she said. 'I found it in my father's things. I believe it appertains to your family. You should have it. You need to deal with your past. You are carrying the weight of it with you.'

Campbell took the second envelope that the headmistress had taken from the bureau with just a slight gesture of the head. He could see sincerity and sadness in her eyes. He went over to the car.

Campbell walked into the hospital with Jenner and went to the room where Harriet was now able, after several weeks, to communicate.

A formal interview under caution had been arranged. Jenner and Campbell took up positions to one side of Harriet's bed.

Harriet Epsy glared at them. 'I want to tell you everything. I expect another one of his women gave me this hole in my head,' she blurted out. 'And because of that I am going to tell you everything I know about that double dealing…' Harriet's voice tailed off. 'There's no point in not,' she continued. 'I could pretend I had lost my memory, but I think you heard everything in the farmhouse anyway.'

Campbell accepted this with a nod and opened with, 'We've been wanting to talk to you about the death of the man you described as Robert Epsy to our control room and to me. Your uncle, Robert Epsy, has been dead some time. The dead man on Daneton Howe Beach was not Robert Epsy. We need to know who this dead man is.'

'I picked him up in Birmingham. He said his name was George. That's all I know about him,' said Harriet.

'Did you murder him?' asked Campbell.

'Yes, I did,' replied Harriet.

'How did you murder him?'

'I injected him with a narcotic drug between his toes. And I wouldn't have had to kill him if Frank Norton had told me he was planning to kill

William Cecil Broadgate. I was setting up George to be the dead Dungrade while Frank was setting up William Cecil Broadgate for the same role. No-one has a good picture of Dungrade.'

'Why didn't you call the dead man on Daneton Howe Beach Dungrade, when you made the call to emergency services then?'

'I thought if I gave the name to the call centre someone might look it up, so I wanted you to find out later. But then, Frank phoned me about William Cecil Broadgate and I had to go and sort out Frank's mess. As a decoy for himself he had even sent the police down to Daneton Howe Beach. I was very nearly caught.'

'You hadn't told him about your plans for George becoming the dead Dungrade,' asked Campbell.

'It was meant to be a nice surprise,' replied Harriet. 'And, I didn't want him to stop me.'

Campbell frowned at what she thought would be a nice surprise for the man she loved.

'I wasn't expecting George's apparent heart attack to be attended by a Detective Chief Inspector,' complained Harriet, following this with a stream of swearing about Frank Norton.

Once Harriet had settled again Campbell said, 'The black book which Elizabeth Rattagan and Gwen Blythe had discovered in the caravan was found to be a forgery. It clearly had very little to do with William Cecil Broadgate except some fingerprints.'

'I stole the book out of William Cecil's house. Frank over-rated Ralph's abilities at forgery.' Harriet paused, took a deep breath and continued, 'I stood on that Banksea Beach at nine o'clock in the morning filming the scene for Frank. He watched it while waiting for his train in London. He never told me why he wanted me to do that – so he could visualise William Cecil's murder, that's why. He thought he was being clever. Well, this time he was too clever. Too many of his women involved. He should have just left it to me.'

Campbell played the recording of the beach scene dated for the Friday of William Cecil Broadgate's murder. Harriet watched. Her hands started to screw up over each other. 'Does Frank Norton have any weapons training, has he been in the army, SAS, anything like that?'

Harriet laughed. 'He could find out anything he wanted in that line from his criminal connections. He wasn't just a petty criminal or a lawyer for criminals he ran a network of criminals. But he couldn't resist getting involved himself. He loved the buzz it gave him to get one up on people.'

'Ordinary bereaved families?' asked Campbell.

'I bet you can tie him into his recent activities, but I bet the identity and paper trail you have doesn't link you right in to Dungrade's older crimes. I am that link.' She considered how that sounded. 'I don't expect any special considerations,' she added.

'Continue,' said Campbell. Harriet was right: with the Havensea Dungrade papers missing and records erased, he needed Harriet's evidence to complete the case against Dungrade. Only then would Elizabeth Rattagan and Gwen Blythe be exonerated and be able to go back to their old lives. Other arrests would be inevitable once computers had been examined.

Sometime later Jenner closed the interview and charged Harriet Epsy for the murder of the man known as George and she informed Harriet that she would be facing other charges including charges relating to the murder of William Cecil Broadgate.

Harriet stood with her head down as she listened to Jenner's business-like delivery.

As Campbell left the hospital Parnold phoned to say he the helicopter was a charter. The company had it booked for a wedding flight.

Campbell sighed and drove himself down to Daneton Promenade Café and drank three mugs of tea slowly, served by Kara Leonard.

The motivation for the crime had been plain greed, but each element had been crossed by thwarted love. Sean Foragehall and Georgia Lomond, Sean and Louise Green, Ralph and Georgia Lomond, even Michael Pilmer and Shana Peterson, and the complications Frank Norton made for himself. He thought he could control love and greed. Each dangerous but a lethal combination, thought Campbell looking out of the window.

He watched a tug of wind lift the drying sand and Campbell's thoughts returned to his home and family. Perhaps no-one's story travels in a straight line.

Margaret, Victoria and Edmund were due back today. He decided he wouldn't tell his wife he'd been to Scotland. She might not understand, and he was trying to forget about it himself. He had returned to the dream of Harry Binding when he had been knocked out by Shana and dragged out to be run over by her and Frank Norton.

In the landing cupboard his mother's screams had torn at him until they had stopped. He heard many steps from many feet on the stairs, silence. Harry Binding's crying was followed by the light steps of a woman on the concrete steps. A key turned in the lock of the cupboard door and Harry Binding's mother stood there.

'Come out, pet,' she said, wiping his face with a handkerchief. 'You'll be having your tea with us,' she said glancing up the stairs towards his flat where police were gathering.

Six-year-old Raymond put out his arms to her.

Campbell blinked and looked at the envelope the headmistress had given him.

He wondered about his bright beautiful teenage children. The envelope promised darkness he did not want to deal with. He screwed it up and put it in his pocket.

The End

.

ABOUT THE AUTHOR

Pamela St Abbs is the author of the Inspector Campbell Mysteries. She also writes as Mary Bale for her Norman Britain Mystery, Threads of Treason. She lives in Scotland with her husband.
Other Inspector Campbell Mysteries:
Smoke Shadows
Water Weal
Twisting Tide